Tony Walker

Further Ghost Stories

CONTENTS

CHAPTER I

THE COTEHILL HIGHWAYMAN

This is the true story of John Whitefield, a highwayman who terrorised The Great North Road in the latter years of the 18th century.

Whitefield lived in Cotehill, just south of Carlisle.

The Great North Road around Barrock Fell and High Hesket was so dangerous to travel in his day that only the bravest or the most foolish would venture out on those highways after darkness fell.

With that grave warning in mind, we return to one September night in 1777, when a merchant from Armathwaite named Isaac Dodd was supping with friends in the city of Carlisle. He had intended to leave earlier in the afternoon, but the company was good and the wine flowed and he dilly-dallied until the day was fading and night was on its way.

The clock in his hosts' house on Fisher Street chimed out the hour.

"Already four o'clock!" Dodd said, finishing the port wine with a swig.

"How time flies when you're enjoying yourself," said the wife of his host and, "You'll have another, of course?"

Isaac shook his head. "Look at the hour! I need to be on my way. You distracted me with your convivial hospitality and I neglected to attend to the time."

His host pointed to the failing light on that dreary September afternoon. "Isaac, look at it! It'll be dark before you're halfway to Armathwaite. Stay the night with us."

And his host's wife chimed in. "Not halfway to Armathwaite, indeed, before you're at Durranhill, you won't see your hand in front of your face."

Isaac Dodd laughed and shook his head. "No, no. You are most kind, and your port is very good, but I have a wife and daughter at home in Armathwaite, and I have dallied over long. The lass will be in bed by the time I get home, but I will at least look in and see her sleeping face."

His host frowned. "Its not safe to be venturing on that road after dark."

But Isaac raised a hand. "I have enjoyed every moment of my time with you, but before God, I love my wife, I love my daughter, I love my dog, and most of all, I love my own big feather bed, and so," he stood, bowed, turned, walked to the door and hesitated, because he did not want to be rude.

"If you're sure you must go, be aware that it is against my advice," said his host, who was a Justice of the Peace and knew well what lawlessness abounded on the King's Highway in those days, after dark.

But Isaac was resolute and his host called the servant who brought Isaac his coat and boots and hat and alerted the stable boy, who brought Isaac his horse at their front door.

And so, despite their protestations, he mounted his big bay stallion on the sandstone block outside their house in Fisher Street.

As he sat astride the horse and gave a last farewell salute, they begged him one more time to stay, and for the first time, mentioned the name of the highwayman, John Whitefield.

Isaac laughed. "I fear not John Whitefield, for it is unlikely he will venture out in this drizzle, and I have my pistol and my sword to put him to flight should he show his ugly face."

And so Isaac Dodd waved away their loving concerns and reined his horse, turned its head away from them and they watched him head down to English Street, and out of sight

The stallion clip-clopped through the city, then out of the city gates, down Botchergate and onto the Great High Road that would lead, if a man stuck with it long enough, to London.

A persistent drizzle set in, making the evening darker, and by the time he got to the Carleton, even though it was only half after five of the clock, night had distinctly (or indistinctly) fallen.

As they went along, Isaac took off his tricorn hat and tipped out the rain that ran with a sputter to the ground, then he stroked the neck of his horse and said, "Sorry, for bringing you out in this, lad, and you in a dry stable on Fisher Street with tasty oats to eat."

But the horse did not toss its head, nor neigh disagreement nor complaint, but instead plodded on, head down.

The horse, Ulysses, was a good-natured beast and there was a great fondness between the two of them, and so we can presume he was, if not content with the dark journey home, at least settled.

Isaac himself was as drenched as his horse and, whether the beast regretted leaving the dry stable at Fisher Street, or no, it could not be said that Isaac regretted not accepting the offer of the dry bed at the same.

They rode southeast, and the rain fell, and the dark gathered and the wind blew across the Great North Road from west to east until they were between Carleton and Cotehill, while Isaac's thoughts were firmly lodged on home, though his attention wandered and he even began to doze as a man will on a long journey on horseback, mesmerised by the regular beats of the hooves on the turnpike, and never falling completely to sleep.

It was true he loved his feather bed, and true that he loved his dog, and truer still that he loved his wife and daughter, and to sleep under the same roof as they that night one more time was gift enough and worth this journey, however wet and wearisome, and so his heart lifted as the road lifted towards home.

Now, you will remember my saying that only the bravest or the most foolish ventured out onto the Great High Road after dark where it snakes through the Forest of Inglewood — that great wooded waste that stretches from Carlisle to Penrith — and especially so where the corners are dark, and the trees, dripping rain, hug the roadway and there is no other traffic to be seen.

So it would be a fair question to ask whether Isaac Dodd was one of the bravest of men or the most foolish?

The truth is that young men, and he at that time was only in his early 30s, never believe that the terrible outcomes that befall strangers, or even friends, will ever befall them. A young man feels he will live forever, no matter how clearly mistaken that belief is.

But for Isaac, there was indeed some evidence that he had been blessed by Providence. He had made money in shipping and in textiles—and like all of those whom the good Lord favours, Isaac thought the good luck was his own doing, rather than God's, or as freethinkers prefer it, the outcome of the rolling of Fate's dice.

So, as you see, Isaac Dodd imagined no ill-fortune would come near him. But in that, he was wrong.

By the time he reached the Cotehill turn, he could see nothing but the drifting banks of rain and shadows behind them. But, the truth to tell, his attention was not directed to danger, nor the road, and indeed his mind ran on schemes of business and profit and his wife's cooking and the smile of his beloved red-headed daughter, Janet.

Lulled by the wine and good food and the slow clip clop of his horse's hooves, Isaac did not see the shadow that awaited him. It was a shadow's shadow, the form of someone who has dressed so that he should not be seen even by the sharpest eye.

Isaac was half past that darkest of nooks where the trees stand gathered as if for prayer, just as the road starts to descend, when a man emerged from the trees.

At first Isaac Dodd did not see him, and the man was careful to be quiet and then this scoundrel brandished his pistol in what light there was, and called, "Stand and deliver. Give me all of your money and all of your gold!"

Noticing at last, though too late, Isaac Dodd was startled from his reverie. He was not the kind of man to turn and flee from danger, so he turned in his saddle and stared, pulling up short, half full of disbelief, and half of righteous anger that such a devil should pull a pistol on him.

In full defiance, Isaac Dodd roared, "And who art thou to accost an honest traveler on such a dreary night in such a dismal spot as this?"

But that man, not abashed by Isaac's defiant tone, spoke, full-confident and he said, "I, sir, am one you should know by reputation if not by name. I, sir, am one for whose sake you should have avoided this turnpike after dark. And, I, sir, am one who shall shoot you dead should you not comply with my polite and reasonable request to hand me all your money."

Isaac Dodd snorted and sat back in his saddle, the rain running from his hands and face. He said, "I'll give it to thee that thou hast been polite, but I would not concede that thou wast reasonable to demand money from me at pistol point."

The other replied, haughty-like, "I think you will find that the offer of your life in exchange for a gold watch, a handful of guineas, and what other geegaws you carry in your bags is a supremely reasonable offer. "

Isaac Dodd laughed at the man's self-possession and knew him, despite his educated words, for a rogue, and aid, "Thou wilt not find me so easily turned, thou devil. Have at thee!"

And Isaac Dodd unsheathed his rapier which pulled up smooth from its greased scabbard, and dragged out his pistol from its greased holster, but despite his actions, John Whitefield was the quicker man and he fired his gun.

The flash lit up the desolate scene for a second and the sound of the shot echoed from the trees and rolled out to the distant hills, and the pistol ball flew in darkness and struck young Isaac Dodd in the left side of his chest.

Isaac Dodd was knocked back in the saddle, but he did not fall from it, though he was sorely wounded and he felt the lead pistol shot in his lung and hot blood course through his linen shirt and seep into his woollen coat.

Isaac knew the seriousness of his condition, but he was not a man to give in to injustice and, with his knees, he urged his stallion towards the highwayman, intending to skewer him with the point of his rapier.

John Whitefield was on foot and stepped neatly aside and caught at the coat of Isaac Dodd and heaved him from the horse's back.

Isaac Dodd thudded to the ground, bleeding, and his horse, standing at bay, stamped and snorted.

Whitefield stood over Dodd, who struggled to rise, and said, "You've had enough, man. Lie still and give me your money and I will be gone from here and leave you to bleed."

But, in answer, Dodd reached up and snatched at the highwayman's coat, ripping a silver button from it. And as Whitefield stepped back, not realising his button was gone, Dodd clenched his fists tight around the metal thing.

Whitfield shook his head. "You're done man. Your life is running away in the rain. So will you give me your gold and your watch now, or will I take it from you?"

"Take it, if you can."

"Take it I will, you damnèd fool."

Bleeding and weakened, Isaac Dodd could not prevent John Whitefield from stripping him of his expensive coat and taking from him his gold watch and looting from his pockets, his pocketbook full of bank notes.

And Dodd lay on the pine needle floor among the mossy cobbles of the turnpike, and his blood pooled around him.

Whitfield said, "And now mount your horse, get in the saddle and let the beast take you home, for you have not long left to live if I'm any judge of the wound in your chest. But do not think I am a vicious man, nor without feeling. You brought this on yourself by resisting, and though your end is close, I would wish that you had time to say farewell to your loved ones before you breathe your last."

And Isaac Dodd, knowing the truth of what his attacker said, tried to rise, and John Whitefield helped him up, bloodying himself with Dodd's blood as he did so. And together they got Dodd on the back of his bay stallion, and John Whitefield slapped the horse's rump and set it on its way to Armathwaite.

Isaac Dodd was bent over the pommel of his saddle, wheezing and bleeding, but the horse knew its way and took him faithfully home.

His dog, Jasper, was the first to know that his master had come back, and in the way that dogs will, the creature realised something was amiss because he barked and he howled in a way he never had before, nor did ever after.

And that roused the faithful servant, Michael Simpson, who ran to the door and stood in the rain, shielding his eyes, lifting the lantern and peering out.

Simpson heard the horse's hooves and knew it was his master returned, but the dog howled, then darted into the dark and the Simpson saw something was terribly wrong. He ran after the hound and there, at the gate, slumped on the stallion, he saw the crouched figure of his master.

"Master? Mr Dodd, sir?" Simpson called and went and put out his hand onto the soaked leg of Isaac Dodd who had no coat and whose white shirt was reddened by blood and that blood run pink by the rain.

"Oh no, master!" he called and led the horse to the door, where he helped poor Isaac down.

Isaac fell from the saddle into Michael Simpson's arms and the servant too, was blooded but he did not mind for it was his beloved master's blood, a man who had given him home and shelter when he had none.

The horse, Ulysses, stood at the door and would not leave, and the dog, Jasper stood by it.

Simpson had to take Isaac's weight on himself and limping together; he helped Isaac into the house and took him to the kitchen where the cook screamed and wailed and the dog ran round their legs whimpering.

And at that commotion, Isaac Dodd's wife Mary ran through and at her heels their daughter Janet, who had waited up for her father's return. Though this return she had never foreseen.

In a low voice, with his final breaths in response to their questions, and tears and wails, Isaac Dodd told them he had met his end at the hand of the highwayman and he told them he loved them and he told them he was sorry to leave this life so soon before his daughter was grown or his wife was grey.

But he also told them that the Good Lord mends everything and that one day they would be all again together in Heaven.

And as he gazed, he thought his flame-haired daughter so young and his worried wife so beautiful, and then Isaac Dodd breathed his last, but as he died, his fist opened and a silver button fell from his grasp and clattered on the stone floor.

Now, it was true that the authorities of the county of Cumberland had long wanted to put a stop to the predations of John Whitefield. And with Dodd's dying testimony to his wife and, because of the road and the place it happened, they suspected it was indeed Whitefield who had done this heinous murder, and they resolved that Whitefield would die for it.

They began their investigations and though Whitefield's brothers, each as wicked as he, and his father, who was worse, said he had been with them and how could they prove otherwise? the constables took Whitefield to Carlisle Castle where he was thrown in gaol and he stood, angry and yelling: "How can you prove my guilt when I have such an alibi?"

But his gaolers laughed because they knew the family and that the word of one Whitefield of Cotehill was as worthless as that of any other.

And then when he stood before the magistrate, the magistrate said, quiet and dignified, "By the button that fell from dead Isaac Dodd's hand, and from the fact that your coat lacks the same. That is evidence enough to put an end to you."

John Whitefield shook his head and spat and said, "If he had been a coward and given me what I asked without such a display of foolery and defiance, he would live still and his wife would not be a widow and his daughter would have her father yet."

The magistrate fixed him with a cold eye and said, "Your crime is all the worse for that."

Whitefield looked him straight and said, "I truly am not to blame for this man's death. Some would argue he killed himself with his stupid courage. Better to be a coward and enjoy your warm bed, than a hero and lie dead on the road."

At the next Assizes at Carlisle in February of 1778, John Whitefield was found guilty of the murder of Isaac Dodd, and the judge, the Honourable Sir William Cresswell, ordered that he be taken to the gibbet by the Great High Road under the shadow of Barrock Fell, just after the turn to Cotehill and before the village of Low Hesket, and that he should be locked in that gibbet, and left to die, as he had left Isaac Dodd to die.

And so it was done.

That should be the end of it, but it is not.

They say that John Whitefield took a full week to die and that for a long seven days, the traffic on foot and on horse that went past the iron gibbet had to endure nerve-wracking shrieks that alternated with desperate whimpers that in turn escalated to screams when a raven alighted on the iron gibbet to pick at Whitefield's still living body.

They said that John Whitefield was possessed of a demonic power that would not let him die. And the days went by and his noise was terrible, and it was worse for those who had custom to pass that place every day on their business, such that many avoided it and chose longer routes so they would not hear him.

But one such that had no choice was the driver of the mail coach that went daily between Carlisle and Penrith. This poor man was subjected to the screams of John Whitefield every time his coach passed the gibbet at Barrock Fell.

And every morning he prayed Whitefield would be dead by the next time he passed, and every noon he was not. Despite his entreaty to the Most High, the Most High did not choose to take him.

And you could argue that the coach driver was a cruel man for what he eventually did, or you could argue that he was the kindest man of all, and that his hand was guided by mercy and his heart overflowed with sympathy for the terrible plight of John Whitefield, because terrible it was, terrible beyond memory of those who heard him.

The driver of the mail coach took out the loaded musket he kept beside him for protection against such highwaymen as John Whitefield, and he shot John Whitefield in his metal cage, and after the rolling report of the musket echoed and repeated across the countryside and the land descended into silence again, John Whitefield was dead.

But even that was not the end of this story.

For it is said, that travellers along The Great High Road, even in recent times, would report hearing the screaming of a man where the road passes in the shadow of Barrock Fell, just after Low Hesket, and before the turn to Cotehill, and that sometimes they would see a shadowy form standing by the road's edge, pistol in hand, mask over his face.

Of course, it's true that those reports are becoming less common now the traffic on that road is less and most people go by the motor-way. But people still see him.

So, be careful because should you find yourself on that lonely road, especially on a dark night in November, especially on the very day that is the anniversary of that crime we have told of, because John Whitefield is not dead, for the Devil has freed him from the gibbet to let him wander the world again — looking for wayfaring strangers like you.

CHAPTER 2

THE ROMAN

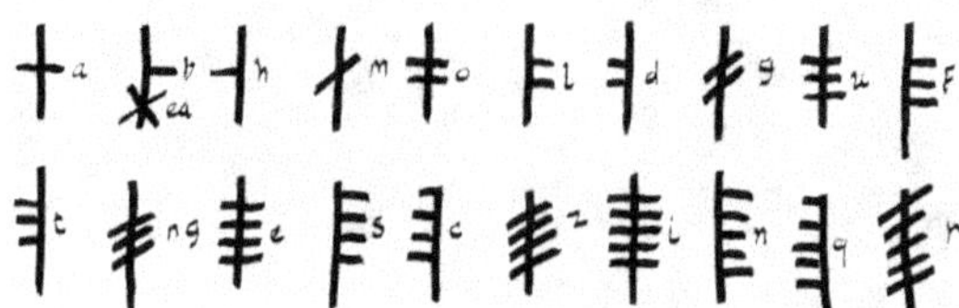

It is 1948, high summer, almost harvest, and the train chugs its way into the small coastal town of Maryport. The train windows are open for ventilation for the summer day is hot.

Gerald Reilly, an unsuccessful archaeologist, and his lovely daughter Eleanor peer at the wooded valley of the River Ellen, a rural paradise as they pass it, where tree roots reach deep in riverside pools. Then the train leaves the river behind, passes the grounds of Netherhall, and pulls into smoky Maryport.

The grand station looms ahead, all red brick walls and blue slate roofs, and the train slows as the driver releases steam, and the brakes are applied so skilfully that the train stops as if on a puff of air.

And they arrive, Gerald Reilly and his daughter smile at each other, though they do not know the place and whatever they imagine awaits them there is not how it will be.

This great Victorian station that stood there that day will not last — demolished within fifty years — but it remains in memory and in story, which is also memory of a different kind.

There is a pause on the platform; the train stands while steam hisses, then doors are opened, and people get on and people get off, stepping up, shutting doors.

Gerald Reilly still sits, seeming dazed, preoccupied with who knows what.

Eleanor touches his elbow. 'Father? We're here.'

She knows how much he's wanted to come to Maryport, how much importance he seemed to give this trip, though she has no idea why.

Gerald comes to himself, a greying man in a brown suit. He seems as if he doesn't belong, as he is a visitor to his own life. 'Yes, of course, my dear,' he says, and shaking off whatever preoccupation held him, reaches up to the luggage rack for his case and hers.

Gerald stretches up, shirt straightening over his thin belly, and hands down Eleanor's valise, then gets his own. Two small cases — not much in them for a month's stay.

Then his hand touches on the train door handle. The gap down to the platform is greater than he thought. He hesitates, arranges bags to free a hand, then together, they step, she first, smiling, he forming his lips in an approximation of a smile, almost to reassure her he is well, and then with a settling of weight to grip the bags, they walk, bags in hand towards the bridge over the track.

She is faster than him and she waits after every other step, mindful of his poor limp.

They climb up over the cast-iron bridge to the exit, and then leave through the station waiting area and the grand front doors, to emerge in the courtyard in front, where they see Guy Pocklington-Senhouse's chauffeur standing by the Rolls-Royce Phantom.

'Dr Reilly?' the chauffeur says, removing his cap.

As if finally rid of the dream, Reilly nods and gives the man his bag. Eleanor thanks the chauffeur while her father studies the car.

'This all, sir?'

'We travel light,' Eleanor says. The chauffeur nods and they get into the car. It is only a short way to Netherhall.

'What's the primary industry here?' Eleanor asks by way of

conversation as they drive along the high-walled road that leads north. Trees stand dark and thick behind it, their tops full of noisy rooks.

'Coal, miss. We dig out the coal and ship it to Ireland.'

'They have no coal of their own in Ireland,' her father mutters, as if it is some dark family secret. 'They must buy it from the English.'

"Grandmother always seemed to have coal," Eleanor says, smiling. "Her house in Drogheda was lovely and warm. Who knows? Perhaps she got it from Maryport."

Reilly frowns. He doesn't like to talk of his mother. "Perhaps."

The driver brakes the Rolls-Royce and turn right by the lodge into the Netherhall estate.

'Parrots on the gate post — how quaint!' Eleanor says.

'It's the Senhouse bird, miss — on the coat of arms. The Colonel keeps some in the orangery.'

'He's not married, is he?' Reilly says.

'No, sir.'

'Like his brother, is he?'

The man clears his throat. 'I don't know what you mean, sir.'

Reilly snorts.

And then the car pulls up in front of the long, elegant house.

'It looks old,' Eleanor says.

The chauffeur is pleased. 'It is, miss. Part of it is Roman.'

'Perhaps,' Reilly says. 'The pele tower is medieval, but the dressed stones are Roman, I think." He gets out of the car and walks over, hardly limping at all to examine the sandstone tower draped in ivy. "Robbed from somewhere near," he mutters.

'I heard it was Roman, anyway," the chauffeur says.

A man and a woman stand at the mansion's front door between the tall Doric columns. They are there to greet the Reillys. The man is dark-haired though greying, perhaps in his late forties. He sports a moustache and the clothes of the English country gentleman, tweed jacket, trousers and waistcoat with shiny brown brogues. The woman next to him is stern-faced, dressed in black.

They do not look like a couple. She stands half a pace behind her employer.

The driver steps back into the car while Reilly and his daughter approach the door.

The tweed-clad man steps forward, hand extended, the smile on his face unexpectedly shy. 'Pocklington-Senhouse'

He indicates. 'This is Mrs Latter, my housekeeper.'

Reilly says, 'Gerald Reilly and my daughter, Eleanor.'

'Nice to meet you, Dr Reilly. And of course you, my dear. I'm sure you would like to refresh yourself before dinner. Then we can have a chat. Mrs Latter will show you to your rooms.'

With a brisk nod and gesture of her hand, the housekeeper sweeps them past Colonel Pocklington-Senhouse and they follow her into the cool dark of the hall. The Colonel himself comes in with them, but excuses himself and steps left into a room where he bends to greet a waiting gun dog.

The Reillys walk through the dark house. Pictures of Cumberland scenes and oil paintings of brigs and barks on rough seas adorn the sombrely papered walls. The place feels old. It smells old — of damp, and stones and centuries.

'How long have the Senhouses been here?' Eleanor asks.

'Since the fifteen-hundreds, miss.'

'A long time.'

'A long, long time, miss. But Colonel Pocklington-Senhouse will be the last. His sisters are married away and his brother Oscar was killed in the War in France. Of course Mr Roger lives in London but he doesn't have an interest in the old house up here far away in the unfashionable north.'

They climb up flight of stairs after flight of stairs. Their bedrooms aren't on the top floor as they see stairs at the end of the corridor going even higher, and Eleanor wonders how many floors are above them and what those floors are filled with. They can hardly be in use with so few people living here.

Eleanor looks around at her accommodation and smiles. It isn't as bad as she'd feared. The rooms are fresh and cleaned but have the air of being infrequently used.

Eleanor emerges from her room to find her father fussing with his clothes and hanging them in the wardrobe. 'I suppose most of his guests have their own servants.'

'Oh, stop it, father. You are an old curmudgeon sometimes. They seem perfectly nice."

Her father snorts. 'The housekeeper was loose-lipped, giving us her views of the other members of the family. Colonel Guy's brother, Roger, is a homosexual. Did you know that? One of them! A friend of Lytton-Stachey and Virgina Woolf and the so-called smart set. Of all the Senhouses, it seems that Colonel Guy drew the short straw and stayed here in this backwater to look after the house and coal mines. But perhaps he is a timid mouse and this small life suits him.'

'At least he wasn't killed in the war like his brother Oscar.'

'No. And neither was I. We have something in common in that, at least.'

Eleanor strays to the window. 'What a lovely view of the river! There's a little weir. How sweet! Someone at some time made this a very perfect little scene, though it's rather gone a bit now.'

'I'm going to have a nap, Eleanor. You can amuse yourself, I'm sure.'

'Of course. I have my novel." She grins. "It's a Virginia Woolf.'

'Hmm.'

Eleanor laughs. 'One of the so-called smart set, but I like her writing.'

He shrugs. 'It's not for me to approve of what you do,' and sucks in his bottom lip, looking like the ten-year-old must have been once. And then he shakes his head and sighs. 'I'm not looking forward to dinner. What shall we talk about?'

'Archaeology, I'm sure.'

He arches an eyebrow, half-annoyed at first, but attempting self-mockery, which he must have read somewhere, is endearing. 'Implying that's all I ever talk about?'

Eleanor is pleased that he doesn't always take himself so seriously. Such seriousness must be bad for one's heart.

She says, 'Implying that he must have an interest in it to have invited you here.'

He says, 'Perhaps. Though he looked more the gun dogs and village fête sort of man.' Then a hesitation. 'Do you think he knows of my work?'

She says, 'Of course.'

He laughs sardonically. '"Of course!", you say, but in any depth?'

'Perhaps not in depth.'

He shrugs again. 'Of course. Why would he? I'm not famous.'

Eleanor blushes while her father continues, his long fingers reaching for his pointed chin. He's thoughtful as he says, 'He may know of my St Albans work. That is probably how he heard of me.'

'Probably'

Then they part. He naps. Eleanor reads. Time is measured by the quarter hours of a carriage clock outside their room.

We can never say how time disappears, but still the minutes slip away from us all.

The Colonel did his best to make dinner cheerful. Three of them sat around the table: Eleanor, Dr Reilly and Colonel Pocklington-Senhouse. Mrs Latter was in evidence, flitting around, fussing, browbeating the footman, Carswell, who stood waiting in the room's corner in a tired set of tails.

Once the soup was out, and Carswell gone, and probably glad to be gone, Eleanor thought, Colonel Senhouse beamed a good-natured smile, lifting a spoon and said, 'Tuck in!'.

She thought the Colonel had an otherworldly air. He seemed bemused and amused at the same time, as if in missing the detail of what went round him, but treating everything with a fuzzy geniality, nevertheless.

Soup done, he said, "So, Reilly? Planning on publishing a best-seller?"

"Sorry, Colonel?"

"Guy, please."

"And Gerald, of course"

"I mean, about your famous discoveries at Maryport."

"I haven't made any famous discoveries."

"Not yet, old man. Not yet. But I'm sure you will. Do you know my family discovered some of the most important Roman artefacts here — altars and suchlike? You know that, of course?"

"I am aware of that, of course."

"I had just thought a good find would be a tremendous help." Colonel Senhouse laughed. "This old place takes a lot to run. This old pile. You know the Government took our coal mines off us after the War? Then the bloody death duties after it. Ruined us. I don't know if we'll ever recover."

Eleanor foresaw the place in ruins. A shame, she thought, for all those years to be broken up into stones and ivy.

Reilly dabbed his lips with his serviette. "Death duties. Scandalous. Little more than theft."

The Colonel nodded. "I take it you are a Conservative like myself, then. Things were much better managed in private hands. This National Coal Board makes a mess of everything it touches, and now all the strikes. And now, of course, with our greatest source of income has gone, we have only the farms left."

"My great-great-grandfather Humphrey Senhouse built Maryport to take advantage of the coal trade to Ireland and now the council-built new port at Workington has taken our shipping and the coal mines are being run down by the Labourites. Not that they're ours now, so I suppose I shouldn't bother so about it. But it's a historical connection, you know? A sentimental one. You feel that, don't you, Reilly? Sentiment? I would have thought that essential for someone so preoccupied with the past."

Eleanor studied the tablecloth, which was plain white linen and featureless. She smiled at no one in particular. She hoped this wouldn't start her father off.

As the Colonel finished, her father began, "No, you are right, Guy." The use of his first name made Eleanor wince.

Her father continued, "The Labour Party is a dreadful shower of the unwashed and ignorant, motivated by greed and envy of those who have done better than they, worked harder than they, striven to become more educated than they."

Eleanor coughed. "Father, I wonder whether Colonel Senhouse was talking about the forthcoming dig? Perhaps he was asking about your feeling for the history of that?"

The Colonel nodded. "I suppose I was, my dear. I find I forget what I say quite often." He grinned. "Most of it's probably worth forgetting, anyway."

He nodded, wan and affable, "but I thank you for returning us to the point, young lady. My digression was merely to note that a significant find would help our finances should the British Museum become interested."

"Of course, another stone altar would be wonderful, but a gold hoard would be splendid! A gold hoard! Imagine!" Colonel Senhouse reached for his wine, a smile on his face, as if wishes were facts and beggars could ride.

Reilly said, "I should think a gold hoard would be unlikely, Colonel. Besides, serious archaeology is more interested in uncovering items to help us reconstruct the past, rather than scrabbling for baubles."

"Joking, dear boy, joking." He tapped his Patrician nose, "Old stones are all right, and damned interesting, I'm sure, to chaps like you. Just saying a gold cup wouldn't go amiss, or even a coin or two."

They went to bed early. Eleanor read Virginia Woolf. Her father busied himself in his own room.

The next morning, they ate breakfast at nine and, seated at the table, Eleanor studied her father. She thought he looked pale. She had heard him groaning in the night and muttering to himself. He always slept poorly. Perhaps it was the wound in his leg. And then, this place was so damp — between the river and the nearby seashore. That would make the old wound ache.

He admitted the physical wound, but the emotional one troubled him as much.

Eleanor missed her mother, too. But she had slept well. She was younger than he. She still felt hope with each new day, but she wondered whether her father felt any hope at all, not for living, but perhaps he had hope for his discoveries, of getting his name on a seminal paper, and being finally someone.

Last night had been very quiet, other than for his tossing and turning. The old hall was solid with thick sandstone walls. She heard the owls hoot in the trees outside, and the quiet burbling of the river over the stones from the fallen bridge, and then she slept until the morning light sparkled through the gap between the dark satin curtains.

Eleanor sat at breakfast, ready for the day, dressed as a smart young woman from London. The only concession to her surroundings and the circumstances of her visit being the sturdy boots she had bought in Beckenham High Street for the trip.

Mrs. Latter came in to see whether they were content with their food.

They both said they were — Eleanor with brimming good-manners and a smile, her father perfectly civil but less enthusiastic.

"I hope you both slept well?" Mrs Latter said.

"Excellently," Eleanor said. "Very restful." She grinned. "I did half expect to see a ghost."

Mrs Latter shook her head. "It's only me that sees the ghosts in this house. Me and the dogs. The Colonel walks straight past them, unless I point them out to him."

Eleanor tilted her head. "You're being serious?"

"Very serious, miss. My mother saw them too. She used to read tea leaves, and they'd all come, even good chapel folk as they were."

"So there are ghosts here at Netherhall?"

"None that'll bother you. Just the old spirits of an old place. Those that used to live here. They mean no harm. They've just become a habit of the house."

Mindful of her father beside her and his relentless scepticism, "I don't know whether I believe in ghosts, Mrs Latter," Eleanor said.

"They don't mind whether or not you believe in them, no more than the stones or the river do: they are. But I have other duties to attend to. I think the Colonel said ten o'clock at the front door?"

Reilly said, "He did. We shall be there."

Breakfast eaten, they climbed the many flights of stairs back to their rooms. 'I think I'm learning the way,' Eleanor said, after they'd hesitated a few times at passage ends and backtracked once.

They collected their things, made ready for the walk, and descended, emerging from the gloom into blinding sunlight.

The day was hot, and Eleanor regretted her tweed jacket.

They stood, the Colonel, with Eleanor and her father outside Netherhall's solid, ancient front door. Eleanor reached to touch the old wood, warm from the sun, that seemed to have a personality, just like the building, just like the Colonel, she thought on reflection. As if the lives of all the Senhouses over all the centuries had seeped into the stones of the house. Or perhaps the house's life had seeped into them, colouring them, making them grow like a particular tree in a particular garden.

Above, she heard the jackdaws cawing from the roof and gutters, and over in the elms and oaks, lots of toing and froing from the rooks in their colony amid the green leaves.

The Colonel stood on the gravel before the Hall, fresh-faced and fit looking — despite his age —and announced they were to walk. "It's not far, just steep, but a little exercise in sea air will do you Londoners good. My brother Roger, when he comes up, insists on taking the car round to the Sea Brows, if he ever goes at all. A walk up the steps leaves him gasping. I hope you are fitter than he!"

"We walk in Kent — on the Downs," Eleanor said.

"Ah, Kent! A beautiful county. I remember it from my youth. Of course, I rarely leave Cumberland now." He looked wistful. "No need, really. We have everything here. I was always the home bird, my mother said. Seems she was right."

And so they left Netherhall and walked down the drive, through the gate with its stone parrots, crossed the Carlisle road and found the entrance to a narrow lane. The lane rose steeply up the hill directly in front and the Colonel strode up the stone steps in front.

"Pigeon Well Lonning, they call this, or more colloquially, Thin Lonning — as opposed to Fat Lonning that runs to the sea over yonder."

"Not Parrot Lonning?' Eleanor said with a grin.

'Aha! Very good. No, it's definitely pigeons, I'm afraid. The only parrots around here are Georgie and Porgie in my orangery.'

Eleanor was slightly out of breath when they reached the top and her father's seamed forehead was moist with sweat, which he dabbed with his handkerchief and stood, gasping though manfully trying to hide his discomfort. On the way up, he'd taken off his hat and paused to catch his breath every ten steps, but the Colonel had managed the climb easily as if it were something he did every day. Perhaps he did.

"Got to keep yourself fit, Reilly, eh? Irish are you? Just asking. Just the name, that's all. Not one of these Republicans?"

"I'm English, Colonel. My parents are Irish. I was born in London."

"Sorry. Didn't mean to offend. I have nothing against the Irish. We were alongside some Irish regiments in the War — damn fine soldiers. They were good comrades to us."

"I'm not Irish."

"No, you said. Sorry to offend. Still, it's the next place over the horizon — Ireland. There have always been comings and goings betwixt here and there, and most of them friendly, some of them not, of course on both sides, but right back to Roman times, if not before. You know they say the Irish slavers took St Patrick from Maryport?"

"I've heard that, but I doubt it."

"Do you? Well, you would know. You're the archaeologist. I'm only a soldier."

There they stood on the top of the Sea Brows. "That's the Battery there." The Colonel indicated a Victorian building with his stick. "Built by the Old Queen to defend us against a sea assault. Though who might land here, I've never been sure. Perhaps the Irish!" The Colonel guffawed.

Reilly frowned more deeply.

"Sorry, old man. Again, didn't realise it was a touchy subject."

The Colonel turned to his right, indicated again with his stick. "And those bumps in the field where the sheep are, that's the Roman Fort where we Senhouses found all those altars and walls. That's where you'll be digging."

Reilly shook his head. "No, it's been dug. By amateurs, but nevertheless, it has been dug. I want fresh ground. I think we will go outside the fort. From my reading there was a *vicus* — a civilian settlement — on the landward side of the hill. That is the most promising site for my research."

"Your research, eh? Sounds grand. Capital. What research is that? What are you after?"

"I'm looking for an early Christian presence here. Such as we found at St Albans, but this is so much further north."

"No gold in that, though?"

"No."

"Take my word for it. The fort's where you'll find all the good stuff! Surely? They wouldn't let the civilians keep all the standards and ingots and things, would they? Of course not!"

"My plan is to dig over in the *vicus* area, Colonel," Reilly said, then with strained politeness, he added, "With your permission."

"Well, I should say you know best, Reilly. You're the archaeologist; I'm just the landowner."

Reilly said, "Indeed, sir. With your permission, that's where I'd like to start."

Colonel Senhouse huffed. "Very good. I have some men round here somewhere, standing ready. They'll be loitering in the battery. I'll just go and roust them out."

Eleanor gazed at the view. They were at the top of a low cliff and beyond where the land fell away, the blue sea sparkled and the Scottish hills stood round and green over the arm of glittering sea and as her eyes scanned right, she saw the Scottish hills join with the English hills, vague and blue at the head of the Solway estuary, where the Eden joined the Esk, the Sark and the Annan to merge the flow of England and Scotland as one.

Turning her head left, looking southwest, Eleanor saw the coast of England continued, a line that was lower and industrial, with chimneys and smoke and factories on the land, and the sea off it scattered with dirty steamers plying their way to and from the ports of Workington and Whitehaven.

Eleanor discerned the metal cage towers and winding-heads of a host of coal mines and the ashy slag heaps that scarred the plain — heaps of grey among the green fields. And shifting her gaze to the sea once more, further west, sat the peaked and boat-like shape of the Isle of Man.

"Where's Ireland, Colonel, did you say?" she said.

"Over the horizon. Can't see it."

"Can you ever see it from here?"

"Not from Maryport, no. From the tops of the Western Fells on a good day. And they say that from Black Combe down the coast by Millom, you can see England, Scotland, Ireland, Wales and the Isle of Man. Never been up there myself to check. You'd need a fine day, of course."

"Like today."

"Like today, young lady." He smiled at her. "There is something very optimistic about you, Miss Reilly. I like that in a person."

Gerald Reilly said, "The workmen you mentioned?"

"Oh yes, I forgot. In the Battery. Probably. Can't think where else they'd convene with tea and cakes going there for free. Come with me, both of you, and I'll introduce you."

The workmen were in the Battery. With hearty cajoling mixed with a hereditary authority, the Colonel made the men put down their tin mugs and parade outside as if they were a detachment of his Yeomanry.

Colonel Pocklington-Senhouse put his hand to his mouth conspiratorially and whispered to Reilly, "Fine lads. And the older chaps too. Good eggs, but I'd put the greybeards on the light work. Put the youngsters on the picks and shovels. The old 'uns can do the trowelling. You do do trowelling, I believe?'

"Yes. Ultimately." Reilly appraised the men with cold eyes. "What kind of experience of archaeology do these men have?"

"Oh, I should say, they've done all sorts of digging: trenches, coal mines, iron mines, allotments even."

Eleanor glanced at the Colonel, but she couldn't tell if he was joking.

Reilly said, "May I ask them directly?"

"Of course."

Reilly cleared his throat. "Excuse me — you. What's your name?"

"Glover, sir." He was a man in his forties.

"Have you taken part in an archaeological dig before?"

"I've dug before." They all laughed. "I was a miner, sir. Had an injury."

"Ah, I see. And you, that man there?"

"Gourlay, sir. I've done bits and bobs."

"Not working now?"

"No, unemployed."

Eleanor saw her father's frown deepen.

"Splendid chaps, eh? What do you think?" The Colonel said.

Reilly pursed his lips.

The Colonel persevered. "They'll do for your work, though, eh?"

Reilly grunted. "I should imagine."

"I'll leave you and they together then. See you at dinner. Pip, pip!"

After the Colonel was gone, Reilly and Eleanor walked the field that contained the heaps and mound of the old Roman fort with the surrounding ditch. The sheep looked up from their grazing. Crows ambled around, only moving at the last minute when someone came close. The workmen watched her father and her as if they were another species, which they might well have been. Eleanor felt so alien to them, but her father seemed oblivious to their gaze.

"You can easily see the shape of the fort, father," Eleanor said.

"Yes."

"But you don't propose to dig here?"

"No. I want... I need something, Eleanor." He faltered, then began again. "I'm no longer a young man beginning his career. I need to make a success."

"But you have had successes, father! At St Albans, that was a brilliant study and your paper was well-received."

"It was Richards who took the credit. I was barely mentioned — a footnote. It wasn't enough to make my name."

"Your name *is* well-respected."

"Well-respected is not enough; it's a consolation prize. I am getting older. Soon my chances will be gone."

"But the evidence of Christian presence you and Richards discovered at St Albans was so early, far earlier than was suspected."

"Mid Fourth Century, yes."

She paused. "It would be splendid to find evidence of a Christian presence here at Maryport, much further from the centres of the Empire."

He smiled. "It would, Eleanor. It would."

The rest of the day was spent walking the field to the north of the main fort with Reilly stroking his chin and frowning and the men following him at first then standing around joking with each other about things Eleanor could hardly understand because of their dialect, and even when she succeeded in deciphering the words, could make no sense of why such things should be the cause of great mirth.

As always, her father was a man apart. She watched him sadly as he stood at the edge of the work, coming closer to give instructions to the workmen or telling them to stop what they were doing and wait. They seemed happy to wait. From their mood, this was like a holiday to them — a paid holiday.

Eleanor hoped that when she was older, she would not be possessed of the great hunger that filled her father — the need to achieve and be congratulated for achieving. She hoped she would be settled, content.

She had never met her grandfather. He had been Protestant Archbishop of Armagh.

Gerald had been born when the family were living in London when her grandfather worked for the Bishop of Lambeth.

Her grandfather had wanted her father to go into the Church, but Gerald had his mind set on being an archaeologist. When the family returned to Ireland, her father had stayed in England.

Both her uncles, her father's brothers were successes, one was also a bishop, and the other Dean of the Faculty of Medicine at Trinity College, Dublin. They were jolly men, amusing and personable.

Her father walked the ground, preoccupied. He was so empty still, so wanting, but he was her father, and he was a good man at heart, and she loved him.

The day wore on, getting hotter. A workman, the one called Gourlay brought her a camp chair.

"Here you are, miss. Make sure you don't get too much sun. I can get you some sun cream if you want?"

"No, I'm fine, Mr Gourlay."

"Sam."

"Sam. Thank you for being so kind."

"No bother, miss."

By the end of the first day, after much tutting, and prodding and going down on his knee to look level at the grass, her father decided where to dig and the first turf was cut and eventually the first trench was sunk.

They found nothing.

His brow creased. "Nothing, no masonry, no rubble — nothing!"

"It's early days, father."

"Yes, of course," he said. "You're right. But perhaps we've missed the *vicus*. I thought..." He gazed to the field boundary with its ragged line of hawthorns and blackthorns and a solitary oak standing higher. A field gate of rusty iron piping tied on with twine, hung between two red sandstone gateposts.

Gerald Reilly pointed. "We'll go through there tomorrow."

At dinner, they ate with the Colonel. Three of his dogs sat by his feet and he fed them scraps furtively. "Don't let Latter know I'm feeding the dogs from the table," he whispered.

Eleanor grinned.

Her father took no notice, laboriously cutting his meat, wearily chewing, lifting potatoes to his mouth with the antique silver fork.

"Good day?" The Colonel said.

"For what?" Reilly said.

The Colonel shrugged. "Don't know, really. Digging?"

"We dug."

"Find much?"

"Some Samian ware. Not much."

"No gold yet?" Colonel Senhouse winked at Eleanor. She smiled back and felt disloyal. It was hard not to like the old duffer.

Reilly didn't look up. "As I said, I think it most unlikely that we would gold."

Senhouse said, "Never mind. Keep digging. You'll find something. Said to be set fair all week." He turned to Eleanor. "You keep your hat on when you're out, my dear. Don't want your pretty brains boiling."

Dr Reilly said, "I don't imagine brains are pretty."

"No." The Colonel said. "Now you mention it the ones I saw weren't. Anyway, my girl, keep your hat on and don't boil your brains!"

Reilly seemed about to speak, when the Colonel tossed a scrap of meat to the dog. "No, I know her brains won't really boil. It's just a saying. There, Lucifer, bet you enjoyed that, eh?"

The black dog licked its lips, then offered its long pink tongue to lick its master's hand.

As they were climbing the stairs, Reilly said, "What did he mean about us not telling Mrs. Latter that he was feeding the dog from the table? I wasn't sure if it was a joke. Was it a joke?"

"Yes, it was a joke, father."

"So, it doesn't matter if we do tell her?"

"No, we shouldn't tell her."

"So, he was serious?"

"He was both being serious and making a joke."

"What?"

"It was a joke, but he meant is seriously at the same time."

Reilly frowned. "I don't understand."

She touched his arm. "Never mind. It was a silly thing to say. Good night."

He went to his bedroom door. At the threshold of her room, she stopped. "I hope you sleep better tonight, father."

But he didn't.

The next day they began cutting trenches in the cow field to the north of the Roman fort. The men didn't seem to mind where they dug. One field was as good as another to them. The day wasn't quite as hot, which was a relief, and a woman called Mrs Turner, engaged by the Colonel, turned up at the Battery and supplied them with lemonade and tea and scones with butter and jam at three p.m.

It was about four when Gourlay shouted. "I've found summat."

Everyone strolled over. The men trying to appear nonchalant, as if this toffs' game of archaeology was beneath their interest, but they hurried all the same. Reilly stood by the trench edge.

"Bones," Gourlay pointed. "Old uns too."

"Goodness me, they are bones," Eleanor said. "Father, are they Roman?"

Reilly stepped down. "They could be."

Gourlay stood back to give the archaeologist prime position.

"Give me a minute," Reilly said. His hand shook as he put aside his trowel and took a brush and began to dab at the bones with it.

The trowel sat idle in his hand for a few minutes until he gently used its nose to turn up a flat stone to reveal more bones. All the bones were brown and looked as inhuman as the sandstone pebbles around them. Reilly suddenly snapped, "For Heaven's sake, get back so I can see what I'm doing."

His outburst hardly ruffled the men, who looked at each other and rolled their eyes. One or two tutted and Eleanor said, "Let's see if Mrs Turner can make us all another cup of tea and we'll leave Dr Reilly to it."

Glover shrugged. "I get paid by Senhouse whether I dig or not, so I'm not fussed what I do."

Gourlay said, "I'd rather drink tea than dig, any road."

Eleanor led them to the Battery where Mrs Turner was not happy at being asked to make fifteen unscheduled cups of tea. But she made them, and even found cakes.

Eleanor sipped her steaming tea at the Battery door and looked over to the field where her father crouched — a lonely figure in his trench.

The men were in no hurry to get back to digging and Eleanor didn't know whether he'd want them back yet, so she strolled over to where her father knelt. He turned his head when he saw her and then stood. He was grinning.

"Good news, father?"

He was jubilant. "I found something. Something momentous."

Eleanor's heart overflowed for her father. "Really?"

"Yes, Eleanor. Come and look."

As she stared, he opened his fist. Lying on his palm was a disk about the size of a two-shilling piece. It glinted gold in the sun and there were embossed marks on it.

"What is it?" she said.

His fingers traced the marks. "You see these Greek letters: that is a chi-rho symbol."

"Oh, yes. I see it. It's a Christian symbol, isn't it?"

Reilly nodded rapidly. His face couldn't contain his smiles.

"From what period?" she asked.

"I can't be sure, but I'd say early to mid fourth century."

"That's early!"

"As early as St Albans. Even all the way up here! Richards will eat his hat. He'll eat his ruddy hat! He'll be so jealous at what I've found this far north.."

Eleanor saw the greedy fire in her father's eyes. Her father had got nothing from the St Albans dig, while Richards went on to manage the British Museum and a Fellowship.

He grasped the golden disk. "I'll show him. I'll show them all, Eleanor. But, of course, first it has to be verified. We'll get Collingwood down from Carlisle and get it photographed and all. And we need guards. We don't want the local riff-raff turning up once they sniff out that we've found gold."

Eleanor turned and saw the men ambling back from the Battery. Her father called, "You there, you two. Come here. Quick. Run."

They didn't actually run, but they walked a little faster.

When they were gathered around, curious and talking between themselves, Reilly said, "Work out a schedule among yourselves. We need someone to guard this grave night and day."

Gourlay said, "Grave?"

"Yes, a Christian grave."

"Will we get paid for watching this hole?" Glover said.

"Yes, I will ensure it."

A man called Messenger said, "Then you're on." A cheer went up from the men. Eleanor saw their threadbare clothes and their thin-soled, scuffed boots. They would benefit from the money.

When word got around that gold had been found, families and children appeared from the town, but the guards took their job seriously and enjoyed their authority. Some were bossy and others jovial, but they didn't let anyone near the grave and Eleanor noted as she thought it, that for her too this trench was now a grave: the earliest Christian grave in the north.

As she walked with her father down the steps to Netherhall to tell Colonel Pocklington-Senhouse the news, Eleanor said, "It's amazing you've found a Christian artefact. I'd assumed that they would still be pagan at that time, this far up in the wilds. I thought they'd still be led by their druids."

"Everyone did."

"But they weren't."

He laughed out loud. "No. It would appear not."

. . .

At dinner, Colonel Pocklington-Senhouse announced, "Tomorrow is Saturday. We always have a little thing on a Saturday night here. We don't make any noise, so don't worry."

Reilly looked bewildered. Eleanor nodded with a half smile, not understanding.

Senhouse said, "Don't suppose you have much interest in spiritualism?"

Eleanor hesitated, thinking how to reply.

Reilly snapped, "No. It's tosh."

"Tosh? You're familiar with what it is, I take it?" The Colonel said.

"Yes," Reilly said.

Eleanor tilted her head. "I'm not very familiar with it, Colonel."

"Ah, well, let me explain. It's quite interesting. You know Conan Doyle was a believer? And Yeats, your fellow countryman, Reilly — ancestrally, anyway."

Reilly said, "Conan Doyle was a writer, not a scientist. And as for what Yeats was, who can say — a poet, a rebel, a madman? I'm certainly not his countryman."

"Just so, just so. But I see you're not impressed by those names, eh? All I can say is that spiritualism has brought me great comfort."

"Who attends, Colonel?" Eleanor said.

Her father sighed loudly.

"Hmm. Myself and Mrs Latter. Sometimes Mrs McCarron and her husband — pleasant couple. Lost their son in the last war."

Eleanor paid polite interest. "Ah, very interesting. I have heard, on reflection, that many get great comfort from hearing from family members who have passed away. Is that how it works?"

"Indeed, my dear. You're a sharp one! Sensitive as well as clever. But it's very comforting to know that we continue. That they are only separated from us by a veil and not truly gone."

"It sounds fascinating," Eleanor said.

Encouraged by her polite response, he said, "You could come along if you have an interest."

"Well..." She looked at her father.

"If you have lost someone, perhaps Mrs. Latter could contact them for you? She cannot guarantee, of course, because it is at *their* will, not hers, that they come."

Her father's cheeks grew red.

Eleanor went silent. Perhaps she had over-encouraged the Colonel.

She hoped she hadn't upset her father, but from deep within she felt an upswell of longing as if the Colonel's words were a key that had unlocked a door she had turned away from. Tears welled up in her eyes.

The Colonel exclaimed, "Oh! My dear, you are weeping. I am so sorry if I have caused you sadness. It was never my intention." The Colonel's voice quavered with emotion and his eyes also moistened.

Eleanor reached her hand across the table and touched the old man's wrist. "I know you didn't mean to upset me."

Her father was looking at her, wonderingly, his previous air of superior scepticism evaporated at her distress. She knew he wouldn't know how to react to her tears.

Eleanor drew her hand back, and the Colonel let it go, but was smiling at her. "You are a fine and sensitive young woman. You have lost someone, I see. I am sure Mrs. Latter can help you. She will help us both, and you too, Dr Reilly, should you wish to join us."

Reilly stared at the ceiling. He looked bewildered. He broke her heart in his emotional blindness. Not that he didn't feel. He just didn't understand his feelings; they were storm winds to him, and rather than face them, he turned away."No, thank you, Colonel. It is getting late. I will retire to bed. Come, Eleanor."

Reilly rose abruptly and went to leave the room. He stood at the door until Eleanor joined him. Eleanor nodded and said goodnight to Colonel Pocklington-Senhouse. She met his kind blue eyes, and he smiled.

As father and daughter walked in silence along the long corridor to the bottom of the stairs through the cold, dark house, that was but barely lit by eccentrically sited electric light bulbs under fringed lampshades of dyed cotton and brass wire.

Her father didn't speak, and she felt her stomach turn over. She felt the chill of the air, heard his echoing, footsteps, thought she smelled the river.

On their landing, before they went their separate ways, her father turned. "You shouldn't encourage him — such nonsense. Spiritualism! What balderdash! What nincompoopery!"

"He's just lost, father. He's a kind man."

"Weak minded. What wit he was given has worn away in this god-forsaken backwater. I swear it is more backward than Zanzibar."

Some wickedness rose in her. "Or Ireland?"

Reilly's eyes narrowed. "No, they are much the same."

She sighed. Why had she said that? Then, "Good night, father."

"Good night, Eleanor." He paused, head down. "You humoured the old fool when I couldn't. You are kind like your mother. I am not. I take after my parents."

She said, "I think you are kind," but he had already closed the door.

The next day, Samuel Collingwood of the Cumberland and Westmorland Archaeological and Antiquarian Society arrived at the dig. Colonel Pocklington-Senhouse brought him up to the field where the men were excavating another trench and where nearby Glover guarded the burial pit with its bones and its gold disk.

The Colonel grinned at Glover. "Very good, Corporal Glover. I'll leave this learned gentleman, and the other learned gentleman, and of course, the lovely young lady in your capable hands. I have a meeting with the scoutmaster in ten minutes in Christchurch hall."

"Very good, Colonel." Glover saluted. "I'll keep an eye on things for you."

"I'm sure you will, Glover. You always did. Pip pip! I'll see you gentlemen later, perhaps?" And he left.

Standing in the field, Samuel Collingwood attempted to kindle his briar pipe, cupping it, but it would not light even though the breeze was minimal. In the end, he gave up and merely sucked at the stem.

The Colonel went striding across the field, and Reilly nodded at Collingwood. Eleanor gathered they had met at Oxford.

Collingwood cleared his throat. "Interesting find, Reilly."

"I think so."

"Mind if I take a look?"

Reilly nodded and, at his command, Glover removed the tarpaulin to reveal the clay pit with its brown bones and gleaming gold disk.

Collingwood stooped and picked the golden thing up. "Roman, all right."

"Yes, of course."

"And of the right period, stylistically."

"I know."

Then Collingwood was silent. He took a jeweller's eye glass from his waistcoat pocket and pushed into his eye then squinted through it at the gold medallion. "And definitely Christian."

Reilly snorted.

"Trouble is..." Collingwood said.

"What?" Reilly snapped. "Trouble is what?"

Collingwood sucked the stem of his unlit pipe and hesitated as if trying to find a way to say something unpleasant with the greatest possible delicacy. Finally, he spoke: "Thing is. It just doesn't ring true."

Reilly's face stiffened. "I found it. Here." He pointed.

"Of course, and please don't misunderstand me. I am not suggesting you didn't find it here. But it is perplexing all the same."

Reilly jabbed a finger downwards. "I found it here. In this grave."

Collingwood took the pipe from his mouth. He wiped his forehead with the back of his left hand. "Blessed hot day, what? And that's another thing."

"What's another thing?"

Eleanor saw Glover watching the two other men as he would watch swallows chittering on a wire, mildly curious as their voices became raised, but in the end, their chattering being of little consequence to himself.

"What's another thing?" Reilly repeated.

"This burial. The way the skeleton has its knees drawn up, and the bowed chin tucked into the chest. It's reminiscent of the burials at Armagh and at Dunpatrick."

"Ireland?" He laughed. "You're suggesting this is an Irish burial?"

"I'm not suggesting anything, old man. But this does look very like those over in Ireland. There was a common culture around the Irish Sea. That was Emyr Evans's view and he should know."

"But Irish burials here. Absurd!"

"Not really. There was much toing and froing until very recently between the Cumberland coast and the north of Ireland."

"So you're suggesting an Irish Christian came here — before St Patrick's mission in the Fifth Century. Impossible. The chronology won't work."

"Well, old man, what I'm suggesting is that it isn't Christian at all and, in fact, I'm tentatively proposing that this grave here looks very much like the resting place of an Irish druid. See those bones, that little fetish buried with him? How he got here, we can't know, and how that Christian disk got in the grave with him, we can't know that either."

As he said the last words, Collingwood stared directly and studiedly at Reilly, but Reilly didn't meet his eye.

Collingwood didn't go back to Netherhall for Colonel Pocklington-Senhouse's offer of tea. He said he had business in Cockermouth and was from there returning to Carlisle.

Gerald Reilly absented himself from dinner, claiming a headache, and that left the Colonel and Eleanor with the shrieks of Georgie and Porgie the parrots in the Orangery as accompaniment.

"Your father not well, eh?"

"He has a headache."

"Hmm. I believe there was a to-do between the two learned chaps up there on the field."

Eleanor frowned.

"Don't mean to set the cat among the pigeons. Funny chaps, boffins."

She didn't reply.

The Colonel said, " Still keen on the get together tonight?"

"I don't know. I should probably look after my father."

"Oh, he's only sulking. He'll be quite well enough on his own. Come on, my girl. Keep an old man company. It gets very lonely here."

The seance was held in the so-called Red Drawing Room. It had perhaps once been red though now it was papered in a rather over-done wallpaper embellished with a garish parrot pattern.

After dinner, Eleanor had knocked on her father's door, but he hadn't opened it. He shouted through that he was having a lie down but that he'd be fine, and not to worry. She did worry, but Eleanor didn't remind him about the seance. That would make him worse.

When she came downstairs, she found the curtains drawn in the red drawing room and the illumination coming from a softly hissing oil lamp with a glass shade in the centre of a round table that was covered in a starched white linen tablecloth. Mrs Latter sat at the table. It seemed that she was to be the medium.

The Colonel stood as she came in. "Eleanor, I'm so glad you're here. Such a treat to have your company." He winked. "Your father didn't recover in time to come, I think?"

He wasn't as innocent and vague as he made out. He showed her where to sit. Mrs Latter wore a floral dress, not her customary housekeeper's uniform. A maid brought them tea, and when she had withdrawn, Mrs Latter leaned forward and turned down the lamp.

Eleanor feared they would have to hold hands, but there was none of that.

Instead there was a pause. Mrs Latter closed her eyes. The silence gathered, and Eleanor waited politely for what was to come. She heard the river outside. She heard the hiss of the burning lamp. But something else was happening.

It stole her breath. There was an electricity in the air.

Quietly, the Colonel said, "Is he here?"

Mrs Latter nodded almost imperceptibly and said, "He is."

The Colonel sat forward, hands spread on the tablecloth. "Does he have a message for me?"

"He does. The same one he always has: Be strong. You must carry your duty to the end."

"Like he did," he whispered.

Mrs Latter reached over and squeezed the Colonel's hand.

Soft tears ran down the old man's cheeks. "Like he did."

They became quiet and Eleanor had the strangest feeling that they were not alone in the room even though there was no one to be seen. She felt a presence as if someone were with them, watching them, listening to their thoughts, almost

Then the atmosphere lifted as if someone had left.

Colonel Pocklington-Senhouse turned his head. "It was my brother, Oscar. He was killed at Pas de Calais in 1915. He was a Second Lieutenant with the Coldstream Guards, you know. Father was so proud. I was only Yeomanry — Artillery, the local regiment. I've always been very local. I did my duty, I have no shame in that. But I wasn't Guards. I still miss him. He was a better man than me. Sometimes I get mother, sometimes father, but most often, Oscar."

Mrs Latter said, "Is there anyone you would like to contact, Miss Reilly?"

Eleanor said there was no one, but she knew there was. The first thought had been a resistance to the whole idea of this, but then, with a great effort, in a hesitant voice, she whispered, "My mother."

Mrs Latter nodded and frowned. "She died with a problem with her lungs? I feel a sharp pain here. And blood on coughing."

"She died of consumption."

"I'm so sorry, my dear," The Colonel said.

Mrs. Latter said, "She wants you to know she is without pain. She wants you to know she's happy. She watches over you, you know. I am sure you feel her sometimes."

"I do. I do."

"Your father doesn't believe."

Eleanor felt herself crying again. Why did she cry so much here in this old house? She said, "No, I wish he could. As much as one can tell about the relationship between one's mother and father, I think she loved him despite his unhappiness. She saw him struggling to be the person he thought he should be, but she didn't mind. She loved the man he was."

"And what about his feelings for her?" The Colonel asked with great tenderness.

Eleanor sighed. "He loved her immensely and he believes she is destroyed, gone forever."

"But you don't."

"No, I don't. I feel her. She's still here, I know."

Mrs. Latter said, "And she will be until she comes to you when it's your time. Then she will be free to go to the land of the blessed. Until then, she remains to watch over you."

"I hope you are comforted, Eleanor," the Colonel said.

"I am. Thank you. Thank you, Mrs Latter."

And whether she believed or whether she just wanted to believe, Eleanor's heart grew quiet and her eyes dried.

The lamp on the table flickered.

"Wind's got up," The Colonel said.

Mrs. Latter hissed. "It's not that."

A noise, a great clattering came from outside the closed door.

"What on earth is that row?" Colonel Senhouse said. "Sounds like a picture's fallen off the wall."

"The men will attend to it," Mrs. Latter said. "Sit still, Guy. Don't break our sacred circle."

As they sat and listened, the wind moved around the house like a beast. Windows rattled and doors shook.

Mrs. Latter gasped. Her composure vanished. She said, "Someone is here," Mrs Latter said. "Someone is here."

The Colonel was still listening to the wind. "That's a hell of a blast. How sudden. I've never heard the weather change so quickly."

Mrs Latter muttered, "Someone is here, Guy. They bring the wind with them. Someone new."

The Colonel frowned. "What? Who?"

Eleanor was frightened. She gripped the table and stared at Mrs Latter. "Who's here?" she said.

The older woman shook her head, her eyes still closed. "Something old. Someone old. Someone who thinks like an animal."

The Colonel looked, wondering, at her. "An animal? What do you mean? If it's a man, does he have a message for us?"

Mrs Latter did not answer. The furniture rattled in the room and outside the door came the sound of ornaments breaking. Eleanor heard the servants shout out in alarm, deep in the house. She glanced at Mrs Latter and then at the ceiling as the chandelier shook.

"I should go and see if my father is all right," she said.

Mrs Latter's voice changed. Her posture slumped. She had one hand on the tablecloth and the other slack in her lap and her eyelids were now open, but she was looking nowhere. Her eyes blinked, seeing something in nothing yet her gaze tracked something about the room — a figure that could not be seen.

She gasped, and then said, half whispering, half intoning in a barbarous tongue, "Roudokauros. Roudokauros sēm. Re dede esmi. Omma sēm."

"What? I don't understand." Eleanor said.

The Colonel stood, his face white. "I've never seen her like this. I should try to snap her out of it."

"It might be dangerous," Eleanor said. "That's what I've read. You shouldn't wake them."

Like a diver coming to the surface, Mrs Latter spluttered. She said, "He wants it taken away. It is not his. It burns him."

"Who?"

The flame of the lamp on the table fluttered and the wind moaned outside. Eleanor still heard the shouts of the servants as they ran around the house.

"The Red Deer. That is what he calls himself. He is so old. He has slept so long, but is now awake."

Eleanor went to the door. "I must go to my father."

"I'll come with you," The Colonel said.

"No, you must stay with Mrs. Latter to make sure she is well. I will find one of the men and go with him."

The Colonel frowned, his glance switching between Eleanor and Mrs Latter, who sat back in her seat, hands draped, dazed and bewildered.

He hesitated, unsure of which one he should protect. Then he said, "Go, find Carswell or Davey and take them with you. Something deuced unnatural is happening."

Eleanor swept out of the room. She did not take the Colonel's advice. She did not search for any of the servants to accompany her but instead ran along the gloomy corridor with its portraits of Senhouses long dead until she came to the bottom of the first staircase. She hurried up that, then across the landing to the second staircase and halted before stepping on the landing that led to their rooms.

It was there.

She felt it.

Searching the shadows, she saw it.

A shadowy thing moved in the gloom. The electric lights still shone, but as if through a dark mist. For a second she feared that something had been set alight, but this was cold smoke — black and boiling with a smell like an animal, and damp and redolent of earth and bones and graves.

As Eleanor watched, the mist coalesced into a column and then flowing downwards as if pulled by a vacuum, it slipped under the door of her father's room.

From behind the door, Gerald Reilly shrieked out and his daughter ran to the door and shoved her weight against it and burst through. The room was full of the smoking, greasy fog that boiled and took shape. The shape it took was almost a man, but almost an animal too — a stag. She saw its horns fashioned from the dark vapour. She felt its presence. She felt its rage.

Gerald Reilly stood against the wall with both hands up as fending off an attacker. "No!" he screamed. "No! I will not do as you will. I will do as I want. I will do what I need to."

"Father!" Eleanor screamed and for her father saw her at the door. "Eleanor, go, leave me. It's not safe."

It was *not* safe. Her father was not safe. Eleanor looked round for a weapon, something that would save her father from this hungry ghost.

Then she heard someone running upon the stairs behind her and the man she recognised as Davey, the chauffeur, arrived at the landing, and behind him, Colonel Pocklington-Senhouse. They came into the room to stand beside her, but then, as if its time were done for now at least, the smoke shape dissipated and escaped through the open door into the house.

"What on earth was that?" The Colonel said. "There's been nothing like that in this house before." He eyed Reilly, but did not voice any accusation. "What in Heaven's name did it want?"

The chauffeur looked pale. "Well, I've never seen the like of that, Colonel," the driver said. "What on earth it was, or what on earth it wanted, I've no idea, and that's for sure."

"But I know what it wants," Eleanor whispered.

Her father stood dazed and unhearing, staring at them as if

coming round, bewildered from an anaesthetic. He did not hear what Eleanor said. And if the Colonel heard her, he buried his curiosity as if such questions were best unasked.

Later, when the others had gone, Eleanor sat by her father. "What do you make of that thing, father?"

"What thing?"

"The ghost. The creature that appeared in this room that you told you wouldn't do what it wanted."

"Oh, that? It was a mere hallucination. I am overwrought. I haven't eaten. Perhaps I should ring down for some soup."

"It wasn't a hallucination. We all saw it." She repeated. 'What was it? What did it want?'

"It..." he stopped. "It was nothing."

A long silence fell between them. The wind had died down, and they heard the owls calling in the trees outside Netherhall. Eleanor finally said, "It's the gold disk."

"The Christian medallion?"

"Yes."

"What of it?"

"I understand Mr Collingwood was puzzled as to how it got into the grave."

He snapped. "Mr Collingwood was never quite as clever as he imagined."

She persevered. "He seemed to think it was out of place, from what I've picked up. Is that correct?"

Reilly clasped his daughter's hand. "Out of place? How could it be out of place? Eleanor, please don't worry about Mr Collingwood. The last thing I want is for you to be upset by the wrong-headed beliefs of a pompous old stick-in-the-mud like him."

"No, of course. I'm not upset. I'm just worried about you."

The moon was now up and shone from outside and its sickly light spilled onto her father's face and his skin was pale and shiny.

She saw how thin his hair had become and the many lines around his eyes. "This is so important for me, Eleanor. It's my last chance to make my name. I will finally get the recognition that I should have had from the excavation at St Albans — the recognition that Richards stole from me."

She said in measured tones, "I know how important it is to you, but..."

He didn't respond.

She looked away around the room - another strange lodging in the string of temporary places he'd gone from dig to dig and missed each time what it was he so desperately sought. Then she said, "Do you think he was a druid — the man in the grave?"

Her father shook his head. "No, of course not. He was a Christian — one of the first here. That's the whole point."

"But Mr Collingwood said—"

"—forget that babbling fool. The burial is of a Christian. The disk proves it. That is the end of the matter, and it is my footnote in history."

She spoke as if she were changing the subject. "We had a sort of séance, downstairs."

He wasn't paying her his full attention. "Silly stuff and nonsense."

"I had a message from mother."

He looked at her. "No, you didn't."

"It was very comforting. I don't know if I believe it, but it would be nice to think it were true, and she was happy."

Reilly cleared his throat. "Nothing survives the grave, Eleanor. Nothing. It is blackness, and that is the end."

Eleanor left her father. She heard him moving around the room at night. She was half afraid the ghost of smoke and antlers would return, but it did not, and she slept and did not dream.

•   •   •

The next day was cloudy. The workmen still stood their twenty-hour vigil around the trench where the brown bones lay with the gold medallion under the black tarpaulin.

Eleanor said, "Are you going to remove the gold disk for safe-keeping? Take it out of the grave?"

Reilly shook his head as he stood gazing down at the brown bones and red soil. "No, I need the official photographer. I thought he was coming down with Collingwood yesterday, but apparently he won't be here until tomorrow." He laughed. "What's the matter? Don't you trust these fine Maryport lads?"

Reilly gave a forced grin at the man standing guard, who smiled back. Eleanor guessed the man would do his duty as long as he was being paid by the Colonel.

She said, "No, of course I trust them. It's just I would feel easier if the disk was taken from the grave and put indoors under lock and key."

Reilly said, "No, it must stay until it is photographed *in situ* — just where I found it. Then I'll have evidence to put in my article. No one will be able to refute it then."

Later, despite the strange events of the previous night, dinner passed relatively comfortably. The Colonel had been presenting awards to the local Royal National Lifeboat Institution, and he entertained Eleanor with his tales of the doings of the volunteers and their antics off the coast, saving lives and sometimes larking about.

After the main course, Mrs Latter showed her face and asked how Eleanor was. Eleanor said she was fine, then Mrs Latter, rather hesitant, said, "How are you, Dr Reilly?"

"I'm well, Mrs Latter. Thank you for asking."

"Good. Had enough to eat?"

"An elegant sufficiency, thank you."

Senhouse said, "Cigar and port, Reilly?"

"No, thank you, Colonel. I shall retire to my room to read. I have several journals to catch up on."

"Pity. The Colonel turned to Eleanor. " I hope you will not retire to bed too, Eleanor. It's rather early."

"No, I hadn't thought to."

"But being a girl, no port or cigars for you. Unless you want them?"

Eleanor laughed and shook her head. "You don't mind if I do want them?"

"Not at all. We're not stuffy in this house."

"Glad to hear it."

"And I wondered if you'd care for a game of draughts in the red drawing room? Just to keep me safe from ghosts." He laughed at his own wit.

Gerald Reilly went to bed while Eleanor and the Colonel moved to the red drawing room. The parrot design wallpaper seemed even more garish.

The room felt different from the previous night — cheerier with the ceiling chandelier lit and a cosy fire laid ready for burning in the hearth. The Colonel set fire to it with his lighter and the newly laid newspaper spills caught and fed the kindling wood which in turn gave light to the coal heaped on top.

Eleanor won the first game of draughts.

"You're rather good at this," The Colonel said. "I wish I'd known, before I asked you to play."

"I'm not very good, really."

"Then it must be me who's terrible at it. I normally play the servants and I always suspected they let me win. Now, I know."

Just then, they heard the wind rise. They both fell silent. The fire burned furiously all at once, the wind outside drawing at the chimney and creating a bellows effect.

"Oh, that again," The Colonel said.

"I hope not."

"I meant just the same old bad weather."

But she knew he hadn't.

Eleanor felt it come into the house. She knew it from the same atmosphere, the same ancient brooding anger. She swallowed, hand going to throat.

"Are you all right?" He pretended, but he knew it was there, too. She saw it in his eyes.

She said, "It's nothing. Just imagination."

"Of course. Though I've never been accused of having much of an imagination."

"I think you're rather hard on yourself, Colonel."

"Do you? You are such a sweet girl."

The Colonel drew on his cigar. The odour was pleasant. It helped combat the unease that seeped into Eleanor's bones. He made small talk. She laughed at his old man jokes.

But it was here, in the house.

He said, "Do you want to check on your father? If you do, I'll come with you."

"No, it's just the wind. It's just that it reminds me of last night's incident. But it's not the same. Mrs Latter isn't here."

But she knew: it's here — in the house.

Senhouse said, "No, Mrs Latter's off tonight. Gone to see her friends in Netherton."

"Who's in the house?"

"Just you and me. Your father, of course, Carswell the footman and Davey the chauffeur. Though Davey's probably dozing by the kitchen fire and Carswell's drinking my ale in the pantry."

They heard the parrots. They were upset at something.

The Colonel said, "Damn birds, carrying on. I only keep them because of the Senhouse crest. I don't really like parrots, you know. Also, they were my mother's. She didn't like them either, but she was always one for tradition. She was a formidable woman, my mother, but the parrots outlived her. Parrots live a long time, did you know?"

He was trying to make her laugh.

"I didn't know."

"Another game?"

The fretting breeze invaded the house, the drafts coming under the doors and pressing at the windowpanes, rattling them in their frames.

She started. "Do you smell that?"

"What?"

"An old smell."

"The damp?" He shrugged. "It's an old house. These stones have been here a long time and we're right by the River Ellen."

"Yes, it's damp, but it's something more: something that has been buried a long time."

"I only smell the damp. But I'm not a very sensitive sort of chap."

The door came open by itself.

She jumped in her seat. He reached his hand out to her shoulder.

"Nobody there, Eleanor. I think the wind and last night's goings on have unsettled us."

"Someone has come into the house."

"I don't think so. I didn't hear anyone. Carswell would have answered the door, then come to announce them. He's not so far gone in beer that he wouldn't hear the doorbell!"

She hesitated, then said, "Would you come up and check on my father with me, after all?"

"Of course I will. Would you like to go now?"

"Please."

The lights went out.

Eleanor gasped. Colonel Pocklington-Senhouse took her hand in the darkness and squeezed it. "Don't worry. This often happens here. I don't think that the men that mother got to wire the place were really up to the job. I'll ring for Davey and get candles."

"We need to check on my father — to make sure he's all right."

"Of course, let me just ring and then when we light the candles, we'll be able to see what we're about."

"He'll be up there alone in the dark."

"I imagine there are candles in his room, probably in the drawer, and matches, too. Let me get some candles for us."

Eleanor stood. "Please hurry."

The room was still illuminated by the leaping flames of the fire, fanned by the wind that blew down the chimney and came under the doors. The flames fluttered orange and yellow, casting shadows on the parrot papered wall — shadows that danced and jumped like marionettes.

"It won't take long." The Colonel rang the bell, and Davey brought the candles and some matches. He lit the candles and the room was brighter. They were set in an ornate and heavy silver candelabra.

"Davey, can you bring me a couple of the brass single candle holders? That's too big to carry about."

"Of course, Colonel."

Eleanor was at the door. "I can't wait. I need to see he's all right."

Darkness had seeped in from the river and the woods and filled the hall. Orange light from the dancing candles spilled into the hall outside, but the dark dried it up and drank the light.

"He'll be back with different candlesticks in a jiffy."

"Could we not take the candelabra?"

The Colonel looked at it and cocked his head at her. "It's a bit heavy, dear girl. Cumbersome. Davey will only be a minute, truly. I'm sure your father is all right, even if he can't find the candles. He might even have dropped off to sleep."

"Please call again for Davey and ask him to hurry."

"I will, of course." He went to the wall and yanked the bell-pull. The bell clattered somewhere in the depths of the house.

"There really is something here," Eleanor said.

"Well, I don't see how. Mrs Latter is the medium. These things come through her and she's not in the house tonight. We've never had anything come here without her bringing it."

Davey came with the single candlesticks. The Colonel thanked him and Davey asked whether he wanted him to go and check on their visitor — Dr Reilly.

"Very kind, Davey, but no, we'll go. Miss Reilly is concerned about her father. We need to put her mind at rest."

Eleanor was already in the corridor, standing at the edge of the light, as far into the gloom as she dared go. She was trembling.

The Colonel said, "It'll be fine, Eleanor. All shall be well and all that. Just a matter of climbing the stairs and seeing how your papa is, then we can get back to draughts. And I shall have another port too. Come on."

He handed her the second lit candle in its brass candle holder and, holding his own aloft, set off. The candles flickered in the draft that came in through the gaps around the windows and under the void beneath the slates.

The Colonel cupped the candle flame with his left hand. "We don't want it to blow out."

Eleanor did the same, but her hand was shaking so much she burned her fingers. She fixed her gaze on the darkness ahead and quickened her pace.

The thing had got ahead of them.

They reached the bottom of the first staircase. "I think someone must have left a window open," the Colonel said. "Or one's blown open. Can't explain otherwise why it's so ruddy cold."

Eleanor stopped. "Can you hear that noise?"

"Noise?"

"Listen."

He tilted his head. "No, I hear nothing. Just the wind." Then he said, "Oh, yes. How odd."

The moaning they heard was not the wind's moaning. The sound they heard was not the sound of the river. The muttering words were not the language any living person now spoke.

The dead had been disturbed. They had returned from the vast darkness beyond life that no living man may look into.

Eleanor started up the steps. She ran, right hand holding up the candle though its light was feeble and uncertain and it served little to throw back the night that gathered around, thick, heavy and dreadful, as if all the Senhouse ghosts waited to see what would happen.

The old thing, the druid, was upstairs.

The moaning grew louder. It was a man's voice.

Outside Eleanor heard it start to rain. They could hear pattering on the windows. The moaning grew in intensity, filled with passion and grief.

"It's my father," she said.

Eleanor crossed the first landing and onto the second flight of stairs. The Colonel struggled to catch her. "Don't let your candle blow out, Eleanor."

He no longer tried to convince her all was well. There was no point in doing that.

Finally, Eleanor stood on the landing outside her father's room. The door was ajar, but there was no light inside. "Father?" Eleanor called, but she did not approach the open door.

"Father!"

"Let me." The Colonel stepped past her. "He's probably asleep. Best thing too."

But the Colonel stopped at the open door, as if momentarily afraid. The darkness thickened inside the room. It moved and whispered. And then Colonel Pocklington-Senhouse thrust his candle forward. As he jerked it in front of him, the flame danced wildly, but, by its light, they saw the room was empty.

"Where did he go?" Eleanor asked. "It's pitch black. We didn't pass him. Where could he have gone?"

The rain hammered on the window of her father's room behind the thick curtains. They heard the rumble of thunder.

"You know, I just think it's this hot weather we've had finally breaking. Dratted thunder storm."

"Where's my father?" The presence she had felt wasn't there. "It's been here. Can't you smell it?"

"What's been here, Eleanor?"

"That stag man. That smoke thing. The druid."

"Come, come, my dear. Your father has probably gone looking to see that we're all right. We must have missed him. It's a big, old house. He could have gone down the top corridor and down by the servants' stairs. Come to think of it, that makes more sense. He'd know there would be servants in the house. Perhaps he went to find them and get candles."

At the end of the corridor she saw a rectangle of grey where a doorway let in natural light from outside.

She said, "He hasn't gone down the servants' stairs."

"That's most likely."

Eleanor pointed at the grey rectangle. They could hardly see, but they felt the wind coming in by an open door.

Senhouse said, "That door leads to the roof."

They ran down the corridor. They climbed the short flight of stairs to the door that led onto the rooftop where the wind snuffed out their candles in an eye-blink and the warm rain soaked them. Eleanor's hair was plastered over her face, and she yanked at it so she could see.

The Colonel said, "The roof is quite extensive and not all of it safe."

Just then, lightning cracked, and for an instant, the roof was illuminated in black and white. It was covered in slippery slates with lead walkways at the top.

Ahead, Eleanor saw a figure clinging to a metal ladder that led up the side of the pele tower. The tower was the oldest and tallest part of the building.

She said, "It's my father. He's climbing the tower."

The lightning cracked again. "Yes," said the Colonel. "But there are two figures. See?"

Eleanor saw the shadow of her father clinging to the ladder, desperately climbing, and below him, a man dressed in skins. This other stood at the base of the tower.

"He's trying to get away from that other chap, the one at the bottom. Who on earth is that?" the Colonel said.

"I know who it is."

"It's insane climbing on the roof in this storm. They could be struck by lightning. Let's hurry. He could easily lose his grip."

The roof leading was slippery with rain, but to the right-hand side of it, the slate roof sloped steeply. If they slid onto that, they would fall off the roof and die.

The Colonel gripped her hand and held her. Together, they gingerly stepped onto the narrow lead walkway across to the pele tower. The storm wind buffeted them, threatening to push them off the roof.

Eleanor held onto Pocklington-Senhouse's hand, but she wanted her father.

The lightning cracked, and the thunder rolled, booming, echoing, impossibly loud, right overhead.

She pointed. "I see the druid. He's there, standing with the horns on its head."

"Goodness. Your father's talking to him What's he saying? He's yelling something."

Eleanor heard her father shout, "I will not. I owe you nothing. I have made my own identity and you will not take it from me."

They were close now. But they had to go so slowly to avoid slipping and falling. The pele tower loomed over them, its bulk darker than the night sky.

The Colonel whispered. "It's grabbing at him. It's got his leg."

Eleanor saw her father kick out at it, and then Gerald Reilly screamed and fell.

The funeral was a small one. Maryport Cemetery lies by the road and across the road is the sea. The service was held in the cemetery chapel with Collingwood, the Colonel and Eleanor in attendance. The vicar read the words of the funeral service from the Book of

Common Prayer. The dig workmen stood in as pallbearers and carried Gerald Reilly's coffin to the trench in the turf where it was to be laid in the Senhouse family section as a concession and an honour.

Using bands, the men lowered the coffin down, as the vicar said the last words.

Collingwood stood by the Colonel. He said, "That gold disk is yours, you know, now."

"I'll be glad of it. The British Museum has already sent me a letter offering to buy it."

"It's quite rare."

"Yes. So they indicated. Only three ever found in England, eh?"

"Indeed," Collingwood said. "Three were found. Then one went missing. That was at St Albans, of course."

As the men conversed in low voices, Eleanor stood, tears on her cheeks. "Goodbye, daddy," she whispered. "Though you never believed it, she's waiting for you."

The Colonel took Eleanor's arm as they walked away from the grave with its flowers, leaving it just a long mound in the earth that would one day be merely brown bones and red soil overlooking the sea.

He said, "Death is not the end. We both know that, Eleanor."

She did not reply directly, then, as they were at the cemetery gates, she said, "My father was always such a restless man. He always seemed to be looking for something. Something he could not find, but, goodness knows, he never gave up looking."

The Colonel said, "What was it he was looking for — fortune, fame?"

Eleanor shook her head. "It was all about proving himself in the eyes of his father, I think. Such a waste. My grandfather has been dead thirty years, but father wouldn't let the old man's ghost go."

"Well, I know all about that, my dear. You can't escape the ties you're born into, and even when you try — all your efforts to escape them merely prove their strength."

Eleanor reached out to take the Colonel's hand, as they walked onto the gravel path of the cemetery. Squeezing her fingers, the older man said, "But perhaps he's found a better peace now, a real peace."

Eleanor looked back over her shoulder. "That's all I would wish for him."

The chauffeur, Davey, awaited them by the road's edge. There was a good view over the field to the Solway Firth.

The Colonel said, "Such a clear day. You can almost see Ireland."

CHAPTER 3
THE FAIR FAMILY

Throughout the world there is not a huntsman who can hunt with this dog, except Mabon the son of Modron. He was taken from his mother when three nights old, and it is not known where he now is, nor whether he is living or dead.

— FROM THE STORY OF CULHWCH AND OLWEN

The rain began at Halfway House. It started to spot the windscreen heavily just after Welshpool, and by the time they got to Garthmyl, it was bucketing down.

They'd come down the M6 toll motorway past Birmingham. Dave had begrudged paying the fee, but Angela said you always paid one way or another, either in money or time lost or some other way.

But now they were in Mid-Wales and there wasn't much traffic but what cars and vans there were threw up a lot of spray. The road through the mountains was narrow and full of bends and when Dave got stuck behind a school bus, he couldn't see to overtake, so he sat there crawling along, drumming his fingers on the steering wheel and cursing.

"Overtake here," Angela said.

He shook his head. "Can't see."

"There's nothing coming."

"I'd rather wait."

She sighed. "We'll be late, Catrin will be so upset."

He grunted. "We've got plenty of time."

She exhaled. "No, we haven't."

He muttered, "Quiet. You'll wake Sam."

"It's safe. Just go."

Still he wouldn't. They lapsed into a tense silence.

Samantha, their infant daughter slumbered in her car chair on the seat behind.

As they drove west stuck behind lumbering lorries, the weather got worse. It was September and hadn't been too bad when they drove across from Shrewsbury, but the clouds massed and the sky grew threatening as they entered Wales. Here the wind blew a hooley and the rain lashed and Dave couldn't see the road and he was a cautious driver, anyway. Truth was, he was a cautious man.

A mile later and traffic slowed to a crawl. It was just past Llangurig.

"Are you sure you can't get past them?" Angela said. She pointed through the rain-streaked window.

Dave said "I can't see a thing". The car heater blew warm air on their knees. The glass misted and Dave wiped at it with a micro-fibre cloth that he kept ready on his lap.

"Poor sod. He's worse off than we are," Angela said.

"Eh?"

She pointed through the streaked side window. "That old bloke hitchhiking. He's fifty if he's a day. He shouldn't be out in this weather."

Dave peered, shrugged, leaned forward over the wheel again. "Oh yeah."

"He's hitching," Angela said. "Who hitches these days?"

Dave snorted. "Hell of a day for it."

The traffic inched onward. The old man was stick thin, draped in a ragged-looking black coat, wearing a black hat, of the kind favoured by Roman Catholic priests in the last century. He had a bundle on his back.

"I feel sorry for him," Angela said.

"Yeah, and I feel sorry for us stuck in this traffic." Dave hunched over the wheel.

"Then overtake."

"I can't."

"Well, if you won't put your foot down—"

"—I can't!"

"At least give that bloke a lift. He'll drown in this."

"A lift? He's drenched. He'll soak the car."

She tilted her head. "Please. I feel really bad for him. For him to be out in this weather, he must be in great need."

Dave sucked his teeth. "In great need? He might be a murderer."

Angela laughed. "As if. He's scrawny, and you're a big strong man. You can protect us."

It was true. Dave had played rugby professionally until last year when he'd given up due to a back injury. He'd never regained his nerve to go back on the pitch. He sighed. "I don't really want to stop. It'll wake Samantha."

Angela said, "It's not like we are speeding down the highway. Besides, no good deed goes unrewarded. Please."

And so, because he loved his wife, Dave wound down the window. The rain drove in and cars coming the other way threw up floods against his face but he yelled into the weather. "Mate? Mate! Want a lift?"

Whether he could hear his words or not, the hitch-hiking stranger understood their meaning and smiled and nodded and gingerly picked his way over the streams of rain on the road, avoiding a forestry lorry and a camper van. He approached the car.

"Get in the back. Careful of the little girl." Dave glanced at Angela who beamed at him and squeezed his arm. He'd done a good thing.

Angela liked him doing good things. That made him feel marginally better and Dave wound up the window.

The black-clad man brought the tang of damp and rain with him, but as he clunked the door after him, its closing clamped shut on the wind and road noise and they sat as the rain drummed on the car's roof.

The man spoke. "Prynhawn da, Twm Lyn ydw I. Mae'n dda 'da fi gwrdd â chi."

The man, looking more like a vagabond than an everyday traveller, extended a bony, wet hand.

"Ah, we're not from here," Angela said. She gave a mock wince. "English for our sins."

"Ah, English, is it?" The man said. "I'm Twm Lyn — clerwr by trade," he paused and seemed to search for a translation. Finally, he said, "A minstrel."

Angela raised her eyebrows. "A minstrel? That's an unusual profession these days."

The man smiled broadly. "I prefer minstrel to bard. Bards are too common in Wales these days. So many of them on the radio and at their poetry competitions and the Eisteddfod. No, I am a travelling minstrel, I go from town to town, sit down on the kerb, take out my harp, and sing for my supper."

"That's the harp in that bag?" Angela said, pointing.

"Yes. Waterproof too."

"Where are you headed?" Dave asked, as if keen to be shot of the man as soon as possible.

"I'm going to Bryn Ellyll."

Dave shook his head. "I don't know where that is."

"Not many do, but I have family there—old cantankerous relatives from way back. Bryn Ellyll sits on a hill near Goginan just off this main road but many miles on."

Angela offered, "We're going all the way to Aberystwyth, to a christening."

"A christening, is it?" Twm Lyn said. He turned his head, "For this beautiful baby?" He beamed at baby Samantha who hadn't even stirred at his wet and windy entrance.

"No," Dave said. "It's for a mate of mine's kid."

Twm Lyn said, "But we're going the same way at least. Thank you for the lift."

"If we ever get there," Dave said, indicating the barely moving traffic.

Half an hour went by and the traffic hadn't moved. Dave turned the radio on but the surrounding hills and poor weather made reception patchy, and what he could hear was in Welsh.

So far they didn't know what had caused the snarl up. They sat without speaking, Dave impatiently searching for a station that would help him understand why this road was so slow. He cycled between Radio Wales, Radio Cymru and Marcher Sound, between chat shows and easy-listening 80s hits to what sounded like sports commentaries which he didn't understand but from the nods and comments, Twm Lyn did.

They were at a stop. "I need to find out what's going on." Dave snatched at the door handle, pulled it and stepped out. The gale blew in and he was instantly soaked by the September rain. He peered through the spray. The traffic coming the other way had stopped too. It was three p.m. They were running at least an hour late now. He walked forward into the rain, and got to the car in front.

They were tourists by the look of it. He wanted to ask them if they knew what the delay was but the driver avoided his gaze and the door locks engaged. Dave sighed, hugged himself against the rain and cold and went forward to the next vehicle. This was an unladen forest lorry heading west over the mountains on a homeward run. The truck window was high above him. He put his foot on the step, reached up and tapped the glass.

The driver peered out, blinking and blinded by the rain he'd allowed in.

Dave yelled. "Just wondering what the hold-up is."

The man gazed down thoughtfully and Dave hoped he spoke English. They all spoke English, didn't they?

Eventually the man said, "Floods. Floods all along. It's the rain, see?"

Dave saw. He thanked the man and returned to the car.

"Well?" Angela asked.

"Road's flooded. Multiple places apparently."

Angela groaned. "Oh no. What are we going to do?"

Twm Lyn leaned forward. He said, "There's a back road you could take. Little known."

Dave shook his head. "That'll be flooded too."

Twm Lyn said, "It's higher than this road. This main road collects the torrents running off the mountain. The road I'm thinking of runs much higher, away from the flooded valley bottoms."

Dave grimaced. "I'm not sure. I think we'd be better sticking to the main road."

Angela said, "But if we sit here, we'll miss the christening. Let's give it a shot. I don't want to disappoint Catrin. She was my best friend at Uni."

Twm Lyn smiled. "Catrin? A Welsh girl, is it? She would know this mountain way. She would know it is safe."

"Safe?" Dave said. "A minor road through the mountains in this weather doesn't sound safe."

Angela started to cry.

"Awww, babe," Dave said, reaching over to her.

"I was so looking forward to it. It means such a lot to get there. I wanted Samantha to meet her new friend." She reached back and stroked the sleeping infant in her car-seat. Tears ran down Angela's pretty cheeks.

Dave sighed heavily. "I know, but Ange, it's dangerous."

Twm Lyn said, "Do not fear, Englishman; I will be your guide."

Dave shook his head. "But we don't know you. We don't know anything about you."

Angela peered up through damp eyelashes. "Be brave, David."

Twm Lyn laughed uproariously. "Ah, young David; your wife thinks you're chicken – cyw iâr! Prove her wrong!"

Dave paused.

Angela blinked away her tears, brushed her eyes and said, "Please, Dave."

Dave tightened his mouth. "Okay, which way is this other road?"

"Go on about a mile to Ty'n y Bedw and then you'll see a narrow turn-off to the right."

"Go on about a mile? I can't go on an inch."

"Overtake these cars."

"And drive on the wrong side of the road?"

Twm grinned. "There's probably nothing coming anyway. Floods, see?"

Dave gripped the steering wheel with both hands. "It's crazy driving on the wrong side of the road."

"Do it, man." Twm chuckled.

Angela said, "I don't want to miss the christening."

"But we've got Samantha in the back."

Angela pointed. "There's nothing come the other way for fifteen minutes at least."

Twm smiled. "We will all be safe. A christening is a very important thing after all." He looked sideways at little Samantha. "Has your fair young daughter been christened by the way?"

"No," Angela said. "I think it's better for her to make her own mind up about it when she's grown. If she wants to be baptised then, that's up to her."

"Very broad-minded," Twm said with a twinkle in his eye. "I commend you for your modern ways."

"Okay," Dave said. "I'm going." He tipped the stalk by the wheel, and the lights flashed bleary through the streaked window, and Dave pulled the car into the oncoming carriageway. He could hardly see anything through the downpour. He leaned forward and peered, shoulders hunching, fingers gripping the wheel tight, edging forward.

Some of the cars they passed honked their horns, but most didn't. Nothing was coming so far.

"Look out for oncoming traffic, Ange." Dave gulped though he had nothing to swallow.

"Thank you, Dave." She leaned over and kissed his cheek as they drove, going slowly, staring into the rain.

From the back seat, Twm Lyn smiled.

The straights were scary enough, staring through the deluge, blinded by the bucketing water, but the corners were a white knuckle ride. They could see nothing. Dave just had to hope a big timber truck wasn't heading the other way.

They rounded the first corner. Dave exhaled. He could see maybe thirty yards ahead now. He was torn between the terror of speeding and the terror of going too slow, but he stamped his foot on the pedal and they jerked forward. He wanted to zoom down the road and past the long line of stuck cars and wagons and reach the turn as fast as possible.

They ploughed into a deep puddle. The water braked the car, it slowed, struggled and coughed. Dave pushed the pedal. "We're a sitting duck here," he said. The car recovered. "I didn't see that," Dave said.

"You can't see anything, to be fair," Twm Lyn grinned.

"You're doing brilliantly, Dave." Angela stroked his shoulder. "I'm proud of you," and despite the anxiety that coursed through him, Dave smiled at his wife's praise and began to be proud of himself and pushed the accelerator down until the car heaved its way out of the water and onto a marginally drier section of the road.

"There," Twm said. "On the right."

Dave threw his head round. "Where?"

Dave squinted to see. Though it was not night, the heavy clouds and constant rain drained the daylight.

"There!" Twm said.

Dave saw a small turn off where a single-tracked road led away through a stand of conifer trees

"It's tiny. Are you sure that takes us very far?"

"Oh, yes. It's a locals-only road. Only local folk know of it."

"Why is nobody else coming this way?" Angela said.

Twm said, "It's an old road. Memory of it is lost among the young."

"But you know it?"

Twm's eyes glinted. "I am old, ancient you might say. And I am very local." He gestured. "I spring from this ground."

Angela whispered. "We have no option but to trust him."

Dave answered, "Yes, we do. We can turn back and refuse to go up this scrappy, narrow trail."

"But then we'll miss the christening," Angela said.

Twm heard them whispering and laughed. "And to miss a christening is a terrible thing — to miss a christening allows all sorts of wickedness in."

Dave narrowed his eyes. "You don't look very devout. Are you a Christian man then?"

Twm Lyn guffawed. "Oh, I wouldn't go that far. I was around here long before the Nazarene was heard of in these parts, though I admit that I was better known back then, and better honoured. Now I must earn my keep as a wanderer and dabbler in minstrelsy, but master of cynghanedd still, and brilliant-tongued at barddas yet.

"Let's hurry along, Dave. Please." Angela squeezed his arm and Dave took the turn onto the road less travelled, his darling babe Samantha, still slumbering in her seat with its jingle bells a-jangle and its fairy mobiles dangling at her delight.

The narrow road snaked on and up and through the forest revealing sudden precipices and terrors of rocks to their left. Rocks that had once rolled sat now quiet under the drizzling rain.

Up and up they went until it was as if they had entered another country once hidden and now revealed in the bare mountain heart of Wales. On all sides rolling hills rippled away for mile after mile until they were lost in weather wide and wondrous. The land basked in a strange twilight under clouds underlit as if by a thousand will o' the wisps.

The car emerged above the clouds, which melted below them like dirty candy-floss. It was not raining here but this land of marsh and bog and sedge swept away on all sides, and dark water pools decorated with bog cotton and bullrushes glinted and gleamed under an odd sun.

"What a strange colour the sun is," Angela said, pointing. "It's almost as if it were made of brass."

Dave look around him as he drove. "These trees are weird too. Very stunted. I've never seen the like of them,"

In the back, young Samantha slept and Twm Lyn's eyes grew brighter.

"From where the sun is, we're heading west," Dave said. "That's what we want."

Twm Lyn sat forward. "That's the road we travel, yes. From the east to the west, under the sky and over the hill, by sunlight and moonlight, by rain and snow, wind-blown and weather-beaten still, we travel."

Silence grew in the car. A strange atmosphere built until finally, Angela said, almost in a whisper, almost as if she was frightened to ask it, "Who are you really?"

The old minstrel cleared his throat. "I am Twm Lyn, or Son, son of Mother, and I was much younger once, but now am reduced to singing for my supper and earning my scraps in ways that were far beneath me in the days of Gwydion and Llŷr."

"I don't know what you're talking about," Dave said.

"At least the rain has stopped," Angela said and shuddered as she gazed around her at the eerie landscape. "But this is a wild place."

Dave edged the car along a road that twisted and turned at times, and was straight and narrow at others. They saw no other vehicles nor any sign of humankind. They saw no houses nor habitations of men.

They saw the sky turn amber and the land transform from the colour of beaten iron and back again to robin's-egg-blue and salmon-scale-silver.

And they fell into a meditation as they drove. And strange lights appeared ahead and to the sides.

"What are those?" Angela said finally, coming to herself, hand to her throat.

"Nothing to be afeard of," said Twm Lyn. But his eyes searched the mist walls too.

And mist gathered thicker, rolling over the moor and in the fog faint shapes were seen moving.

"What are those things in the mist?" Dave said, foot paralysed on the accelerator as if frightened to go so slow that they might stop yet scared to go so fast that he might by chance come off the road. For if the car rolled onto that odd earth, what strange tendrils would grow up to occupy it? What strange beetles would scuttle in and make it their home?

"Nothing to be afeard of," said Twm Lyn again.

And all this time, little Samantha did not wake.

The fog rolled and thickened and grew close like the cold breath of a dying man. The shapes within it shuffled and shifted and shambled and were never still, but instead they peered from within the mist with blinking eyes, bright and curious and carnal, yet their nature was never clear and their faces always veiled by fog.

Light coruscated within the fog, blues and yellows and reds and greens and purple and gold like a rainbow rippling over the boggy ground.

And then someone was in the road in front of them.

Dave hit the brakes hard and the car skidded forward and came to a stop.

Standing there as if expecting a toll, was a man astride a goat that had eyes like the devil's and a beard like the devil's son's beard and the goat's skin was white as milk and its ears red as blood, and the man on its back was dressed as a king in a fine cloth of gold and his face was sharp and his eyes were black and his eyebrows white and his hair ivory-pale as if he came from Winter.

And stranger still, beside him stood tall and pale his queen, with white hair to her waist and eyes like gems, jewel-bright and fiery-blazing with sapphire for the iris, quartz for the sclera and tourmaline for the apple — or as the Welsh have it: the candle — of her eye. And if the king came from Winter, it was as if this queen came from Spring.

"What the hell?" Dave said with the air of a man who knows he is not where he should be.

The car stood still on the road, engine turning. The king and his queen did not move, but instead spoke in Welsh.

Angela said, "They're demanding something."

"A toll," Twm said. "This is their road."

Dave turned. "You knew. This is a trick. You're in league with them. This is some kind of Welsh mountain Celtic shakedown."

Twm pursed his lips and looked mildly troubled. "They're not always here. Mostly I get away with such trespass."

The King spoke again and brought down his blackthorn staff across the bonnet of the car.

"Hey!" Dave said.

"Get out and have a word with them," Angela said. "Explain. We're strangers."

But Dave didn't move.

Eventually, after a long while, Twm said, "I have an appointment. I can't be lingering here."

Angela turned and whispered, "Help us."

Twm Lyn obviously knew this place and these people. Maybe he could help.

Twm Lyn nodded gravely and reached for the door handle and turned it, pushing open the door and stepping out into the damp air.

From within the car, scared to budge, Dave and Angela huddled together and Angela reached back and put her hand on her beloved baby, Samantha, but Samantha stirred not, and neither did she wake.

Twm Lyn stood tall and ragged as an old crow on the roadway that now seemed crusted in gems rather than stone.

And these gems glinted and gleamed, under the mild fog, in the cold lights that flashed in the strange mist.

And the odd figures in the mist became clearer and crowded closer and Angela gasped and held onto Dave's arm for fair as were the king and queen, ugly and misshapen were their subjects: half-men and half-things, almost vegetal, growing from the ground like stumps of trees or weird fungus or leaf-mould primeval and unnatural and sempiternal.

And as the trespassers sat in their car, these mist-bound monster shapes shuffled and huddled and muttered and watched.

"I'm scared," Angela said.

Dave said, "I knew we shouldn't have come this way. I knew we shouldn't have trusted him."

"Too late now. You should get out. You're a big man. Maybe if they see there's two of you and you mean business, they'll let us past."

"Or we can pay," Dave said.

"That depends what the price is."

"I'd pay most things to be out of here."

And the goat-riding king spoke: "Henffych, o Fabon mab Modron. Pa bwrpas a ddaeth â chwi yma, a ninnau heb eich gweled ers cyhyd?"

And the pale-eyed queen with eyes like opals and skin like topaz muttered, "Er yn tramgwyddo ar ein tir ni! Tâl sydd i bob trosedd, cofiwch chwi hyn, Fabon."

"A thalu a wna i, frenhines, a chyfarchion i chi, Gwyn ap Nudd, sy'n frenin y fangre hon, ac sydd yn gyfarwydd i mi ers oes oesoedd."

"What are they saying?" hissed Angela.

"How would I know?" Dave said.

Angela trembled. "I feel so foreign here. This isn't our country."

And they were right. It wasn't.

Dave said, "I'm going to go for it. Just drive off."

"You'd leave him?"

"Yes. He brought us here. He's local. They won't harm him."

Tear's rolled down Angela's cheeks. "What if they follow us?"

"We might get away," Dave said.

"But where does this road lead to?"

"Away from here. That's all that matters."

Angela looked at Samantha in the back. "And she's sleeping through it all."

"It's for the best that she sleeps," Dave said.

He looked out. "He's discussing something. Like they're negotiating a bargain."

And the tall, rag-tag man nodded and clucked and grimaced and held out his hands as if he was trying to strike a deal with the strange king and his hostile queen.

And eventually there was nodding and agreement and Twm Lyn came back to the car. "We can go. The King has given us passage through his country."

"I still think you knew he'd be here," Dave said.

"And he's just letting us go?" Angela asked, her brow furrowing as she studied Twm Lyn's lined face.

Twm shrugged. "My words are milk and honey. They work wonders with such as he."

"What is he, anyway?" Angela said. "And what are those?" she pointed through the window at the crowd of gaping monstrosities.

"Those are the fair family," Twm said, "Y Tylwyth Teg. Though they are not fair and only called such for fear of offending them if their true monstrosity was declared. But let us leave now they have allowed us passage. I have to be at Bryn Ellyll before nightfall and you have a christening to go to. You and young Samantha here, who has not herself been christened." Twm leaned and pulled Samantha's blanket so that it covered her face.

Angela didn't stop him.

"So she sleeps better," he explained.

And Dave sighed in relief and set the car off and drove and the mist clung to them and it seemed that the crowd of misshapen beings always kept pace and they could never be free of them until eventually the road pitched downwards and the strange moorland with its rolling colours and roiling mist was left behind.

They were still in wild country but at least it was wild in a way they recognised. Sheep sheltered behind stone walls, and here and there were lonely farmhouses.

"I'll be stopping here," Twm Lyn said quietly.

"Here?" Angela said, "But it's the middle of nowhere."

"Bryn Ellyll, the home of my relations is not far. This will be sufficiently close, as close as such as you can get in fact. My people await me, and thank you for bringing me so far. I am not as late as I feared."

Angela said, "Thank you for helping us out of that awful situation with those strange people."

Dave said, "What bargain did you strike with them that convinced them to let us through?"

Twm smiled. "A toll was asked," Twm said, "And I had to be here by nightfall, and now we are."

"What toll was asked?" Angela said, but Twm Lyn spoke no more.

When the minstrel was gone, Dave started the car. Angela wound the window down to watch Twm Lyn leave and, as he disappeared into the distance, said, "he's carrying something."

"His harp?" Dave said without looking.

"No, that's on his back. He has something in his arms."

Dave grunted and drove on. "I don't know and I don't care. Good riddance to bad rubbish."

The rain had all blown away as they drove down Penglais hill into Aberystwyth. They parked outside the B&B on South Marine Terrace and in a pool of yellow sodium streetlight Angela turned to her baby in the back seat. "I can't believe she hasn't woken through all of this," she said, pulling away the blanket that Twm Lyn had drawn over Samantha's face. She recoiled with a gasp, her hand to her mouth.

"What is it?" said Dave spinning round.

And they both looked at Samantha. But it was not their smiling serene girl child they saw but a toadstool-like thing of misshapen fungus that leaked mucus into the blanket around it.

It had a mouth like a cut and eyes like a wound and it blinked its slow yellow lids looking at Angela, and with its slash of a mouth it said, "Mam, mam."

CHAPTER 4

THE LITTLE BLACK BOOK

April already. That morning snow fell unexpectedly, covering the daffodils in a delicate white drift, and, for a while, returning us to winter.

That day too, my uncle died, unforeseen. He left me something—an inheritance, though it took a little time to get it, and longer to learn what it was worth.

At first, I had no idea even what it was. It dropped onto my mat, looking like a book, but it wasn't a book, not exactly. It was a journal.

It came wrapped in brown paper, with a covering letter, but before I unfolded the letter, I flipped open the journal.

It was small: hard-backed, thirteen by twenty-one centimetres, dotted design, made by Moleskine and covered in densely-packed writing, written with a black fountain pen. The handwriting was familiar, but I didn't place it immediately.

The solicitor's letter made it all clear. The journal was a gift from my Uncle Adrian.

Adrian was my father's younger brother. We were in touch each Christmas by card, only a line or two, but now it was Spring, and he was dead and he'd left me this. Most curious.

Adrian left his house to a charity but sent me his journal. It came with the cryptic message that there was treasure contained inside. What treasure?

I showed it to Jenny, and we shook the journal upside down, but nothing fell out. She laughed. "Were you expecting a golden ticket?"

"I don't know, but where's the treasure?"

She shrugged. "Inside the book."

I tapped the cover. "It's probably a puzzle. He was mad about puzzles."

And then I sat down to read.

Uncle Adrian was a meticulous man. He compiled lists of things to do and each day recorded the weather, his weight, his waistline, what birds he'd seen in the garden, stock prices, his thoughts on politics and odd bits of poetry.

There were weird marks on the paper's edges: straight lines and diagonal lines, some slanting up and some slanting down. They might be simply decoration.

On the entry for my birthday, after noting he'd seen a charm of greenfinches and that his shares had gone down, there was a note.

"John," he wrote. "I want to leave you fourteen thousand, three hundred and sixty-seven pounds. I know you are struggling at the moment, and this money will be helpful. But remember, money isn't the most important thing."

Jenny stroked my head. "I only met him a few times, but he was a lovely old man."

I said, "Fourteen thousand, three hundred and sixty-seven pounds is a very odd amount to leave anyone."

That night, we were watching a programme about George Washington, the First President of the USA, when it came to me, "It's about twenty thousand dollars."

Jenny said, "So he wanted to leave you twenty thousand US dollars?"

The Moleskin journal was open on my lap. "I bet that's what it was."

Under where my finger was, Uncle Adrian had written:

"PS: Don't forget your grandfather was Irish."

Grandpa James, my father's and Adrian's dad, was from Dublin. But what had that to do with anything?

One night I flicked through the journal again. Along with the lists and observations and recordings, were memories.

"That day," Adrian had written. "Paul and I went to the beach. Every day we went, and every day we swam, no matter how cold, and believe me, the Irish Sea is cold, even in summer. What fun we had! We built sandcastles and dams across rivulets of water that snaked over the sand. We fished in pools and found shrimps and sea anemones and tiny dabs that tickled your feet and fluttered away if you stepped on them.

After the long day, mother came and fetched us, and we had ice-cream, and our skins glowed with the salt and sunshine as we walked our Toby dog. And at night, father read us *Just William* stories until the moths came, fluttering about the gas lamps, and the moon rose, and the curlews called far away. I miss my brother, Paul. He has been gone too long, but soon I will see him again."

I sat there reading his words, and wept for my father and my uncle and their long-ago boyhood, lost now beyond remembrance.

My grandfather was Irish.

What was that to do with anything? They hadn't holidayed in Ireland. Grandpa James settled in Whitehaven, and they holidayed up the coast in Allonby. They took a cottage every year there and spent all summer on the beach.

At precisely three-thirty in the morning, I woke from a dream. "It's Ogham", I said and snapped on the lamp beside my bed.

Jenny struggled from the sheets beside me. "You what?"

"That's what he was going on about the Irish connection. On the page edges, it's the Ogham alphabet."

I grabbed the little black book, then got my phone and Googled the Ogham alphabet. That's what it was. The marks on the page edge spelled something. I reached for a pen and paper.

"You're not doing that now," Jenny said.

"It's worth twenty thousand quid."

"Dollars," she corrected me. "Not as much."

"Still, we need the money."

"Not now. It's the middle of the night."

I groaned but put the Moleskine book back and switched off the light. Jenny was right. She usually was, but I didn't like to tell her that because it encouraged her to be even more righter even more often.

I translated the Ogham the next day. It said, "The treasure is where your father and I found it, long ago in Allonby."

Uncle Adrian was so meticulous that he'd even recorded the address of the house my grandparents took every year: The Bank House.

Jenny couldn't get the time off work, so I went on my own. The train took four hours to get to Carlisle. I took another train to Maryport and a bus to Allonby.

I had a reservation at the Ship Inn and left my bag there. I asked where The Bank House was, and the landlord told me. First I went to walk on the seashore.

The tide was out revealing acres of sand. The wind whipped white tops on the waves that rolled in from Scotland and Ireland and further. They came from beyond the line where the waves and clouds met, perhaps even from America.

Two boys played on the sand, digging sandcastles. They were having a rare old time, and the towers they made were high and strong. A shrimping boat halfway out caught my attention for a while and when I turned back the two boys, brothers perhaps, were gone.

Time to face up to the owner of The Bank House. I would ask her whether she knew anything about treasure. She might call the police, but this was my best lead.

I walked over the cobbles, clearing my throat, rehearsing what I was going to say. Stopping a few feet away, getting mentally ready, pushing my hand through my hair to look a little more respectable, and still expecting outrage or ridicule, I studied the bright blue door with its shiny brass knocker and rapped.

No one came. I looked at the windows. Maybe they weren't in? With a heavy sigh, for it was a long way to come for no avail, I knocked again.

More silence from inside and the sound of gulls mewing overhead and the wind in the grass. A woman pulled back the door an inch and said, "Yes?"

I smiled sheepishly. "Well, it's an odd tale, but today I've come a long way." I had the Moleskine journal in my hand. "And— "

"You're John Molloy?"

I swallowed. "Yes."

"I'm expecting you. Come in."

It seemed Uncle Adrian had written to Mrs Graham, telling her to expect me. This young Mrs Graham was the grand-daughter of the lady who'd had the house in the 1950s.

"Come through, come through. Here it is."

We entered the back kitchen, and there, on a table, was an old-fashioned safe.

"A safe?"

She nodded. "It's been here years. Your family used to keep their valuables in it. I'd forgotten about it until he wrote. We didn't use the old thing. No one knows the combination."

I saw that it had a wheel combination lock with numbers around the edge. I pulled a face.

"He said for you to take it. It belongs to your family, anyway. It's quite sturdy", she said. "You'd need a pickaxe or welding gear to get into it."

"And that would destroy the money."

She raised an eyebrow. "There's money in it?"

"Oh, I don't know. But there's something in it."

She nodded wisely. "There's something in it all right."

The safe was old and heavy, but I managed it in two hands,

waddling back to the Ship. The next day, I had a full English break-fast and called a taxi to take me to the station.

Back home, Jenny stared at the safe. "How are you going to get it open?"

I shook my head. Three days it was on our kitchen table, looking at me.

On the fourth day, I said, "It seems there's more puzzling to do," and I went back to the Moleskine.

Right at the back, I found notes on letter-to-number substitution codes. Adrian had underlined the title in green ink. That had to mean something. I sat sucking my pencil.

Jenny said, "The safe opens with a number?"

"Yes."

"And this substitution code changes letters to numbers?"

"Sure."

"So, what memorable word could you convert into numbers and so open the safe?"

"I don't know."

"Try your dad's name."

I converted 'Paul' to numbers. "Too short."

I tried Adrian, then John, but they were too short as well.

"Also," I said, "Some letters have two numbers, so 'u' for example is 21. What to do about that?"

"Add them together, so U as 21 becomes 3."

"Smart."

But we got no further.

We went to bed.

The little black book was driving me crazy. I read through Adrian's lists and thoughts and memories, but couldn't figure it. The records of the birds were interesting, but the nicest parts were his reminiscences and the fondness he had for his brother, and the times they had in Allonby.

I don't know why I didn't get it straight away. I said to Jenny, "I'm going to try: Allonby."

1-12-12-15-14-2-25. That was too long, so I tried Jenny's method: 1-3-3-4-2-7.

The safe clicked open. With hesitation, I reached in. My fingers touched, not banknotes, not a cheque, but an old black and white photograph. I pulled it out and stared. It showed two little boys in shorts digging a sandcastle on a big beach. On the back, it said:

"Paul And Adrian, Allonby, July 1950."

A week later, we got a cheque from the solicitor for the peculiar amount, equivalent to $20,000, signed by my uncle.

Jenny said, "So the money was never in the safe?"

I rubbed my chin. "I guess not."

We paid off our bills with the money, and I got the photograph framed and hung it on my wall. I stood back and stared at the two brothers who had no idea then what life had in stock for them, but on that sunny day, long ago, on the beach, with their sandcastles, they were content with what they had.

My uncle was a very organised man, every little detail was in his small black Moleskine book. He'd written:

The treasure is where your father and I found it, long ago.

The cash was useful, but the real treasure Adrian found and left for me, wasn't money, it was love.

I looked at Jenny, who'd brought me a cup of tea, and I stared and stared at her, and she said, "What?"

I shook my head. "Nothing. Just you."

CHAPTER 5

THE PIANO

"Rain at Christmas," Amanda said.

The letting agent turned her head. "It's not quite Christmas; maybe we'll get snow yet."

The woman stood at the top of a flight of worn sandstone steps that led to the front door of the old house in Abbey Street.

As we climbed, the cathedral bells pealed out.

"Practising for the Christmas service, I suppose," I said, following them up.

We first viewed the house on a damp dog day in early December. Drizzle and darkness wreathed Carlisle but I hoped there was still time for a winter wonderland.

Amanda turned at the door and grinned at me. She loved the house. The fabric of the building was far older than its Victorian facade. In this part of the city, the house foundations went back centuries, maybe even to the Romans.

"A six-month let, isn't it, Mr Hutching?"

I nodded. It was pricey, but the company were paying. They had a contract on an engineering project for flood defences. I was the lead engineer. Not the choicest job in the company, but I'd volunteered because I was born in Carlisle and not been back since I'd left aged six.

She struggled with the key in the lock.

The letting agent, a red-headed woman in her mid-forties, said, "Full of character," finally getting it open.

As we entered, the house had a presence; a hush inhabited the vestibule like the place was a concert venue waiting for the performance to begin.

In the hallway, Amanda glanced around, head tilted up, eyes wide. It was old — Dickensian almost. A picture hung on the wall.

"Who's that?" Amanda pointed.

"The current owner's grandmother," the agent said.

"She looks miserable."

I grimaced. Amanda always had spoken her mind.

"The grandmother was a piano teacher," the agent said as if that explained the woman's sad expression, then she changed the subject. "You know it comes furnished?"

I nodded. Amanda stepped up to the picture. "On second thoughts, she looks very gracious—very refined."

The agent either didn't hear or preferred not to answer.

Behind the woman's back, I hissed, "I bet the house is haunted."

Amanda laughed.

She had the Christmas Tree up three days after we moved in. I'd had a soggy day on site, and when I arrived home, she gave me a glass of mulled wine and a mince pie. The tree sparkled. I looked at Amanda and she looked so happy. I was glad. She had been so sad since she lost her mother. It was nice to see her smile again.

That night, I heard piano music. I lay in the dark, and Amanda knew I was listening because she said, "Is that from next door?"

"Must be. Or have you left the radio on?"

"No. Anyway, the piano sounds out of tune. Must be the neighbours having fun."

"It's three a.m."

"Party animals?"

"Party animals playing Chopin?"

I laughed then we slept.

Three nights later, I sat bolt upright in the dark and woke Amanda. She put her hand on my arm. "What's the matter?"

"I thought I heard someone downstairs."

"Surely you locked the door."

"I did."

"Then there's no one in the house but us. There can't be."

Piano music started again — a cascade of notes like snowfall, but still with that dissonance.

"Out of tune again," Amanda said.

"Those crazy neighbours," I joked.

Amanda replied, "It's in this house, and you know it."

When I woke before dawn, it was snowing. Amanda had left the curtain open, and the flakes fell, illuminated by the mock-Victorian streetlamp onto the genuinely Victorian cobbled street out front. I could still hear the piano, soft, beautiful, full of longing.

After that, the piano music came every night. But it was sad, mournful.

"I think her heart's breaking," Amanda said.

I was hanging a bauble — a glittering mouse with a sword on the Christmas tree. How the little thing sparkled, next to the golden deer's head. I stood back admiring my work.

Amanda was next to me. "I love that you still get excited by these things."

The tree gleamed. The baubles turned. I pointed. "There's a draft."

"It's an old house."

But it was the spider that gave it away —a giant wolf spider, the kind that comes inside from the cold when the year is turning.

Amanda stepped back, hand to her throat. "What a beast."

The spider scuttled through a tear in the wallpaper. I'd never noticed that rip before, but now when I looked, I saw an edge. I moved behind the tree, avoiding needles and tinsel. I followed the edge of the torn wallpaper with my eyes then my fingers. "There's a door here. It's been papered over."

"Must be a closet."

"Let's open it."

"No, we shouldn't. It's not our house."

"There's a mystery inside, and you know I can't leave mysteries."

But still, she was concerned. "No, Don. They'll keep our deposit or something."

"It's not my deposit, anyway."

And so, reluctantly, she helped me move the tree, and I went to get a knife from the kitchen. It was a door. Someone had papered over it. And it wasn't just a cupboard. It wasn't a huge room, granted, but big enough.

"A piano!" she said.

"A dusty old piano too."

"Didn't the agent say the owner's grandmother was a piano teacher? It's probably hers."

"And she's probably our ghost."

I went and lifted the lid to reveal the keyboard.

Amanda tried the keys. She knew how to play. The notes plunked — some melodic, but most of them off.

"Let's get it tuned!" Amanda's eyes gleamed.

"I thought you said we shouldn't mess around with things?"

"I've changed my mind."

. . .

The owner was fine about it, pleased even. It turned out her father had closed off some rooms to save money after his wife died in the 1970s. He'd moved the piano in there out of the way, and they'd simply forgotten about it.

The piano tuner couldn't come until Christmas Eve. He fitted us in as his last job before going home.

After we wished Merry Christmas to him and his family, Amanda gave me a personal concert, sitting on the piano stool, playing Schumann and Chopin and Satie, all by candlelight and the soft, quiet sparkle of the Christmas tree lights. Outside on the darkening street, the rain turned to snow again.

That night, the playing woke me again.

Amanda lay quiet beside me. She reached out and stroked my arm.

I said, "She doesn't seem to mind we messed with her piano."

Amanda listened. "Note-perfect. I think she's pleased."

The new tenants came for a look around before we left. I was standing there in the hall when they entered.

The man pointed to the portrait and said, "What a lovely picture of that lady."

And his wife said, "What a beautiful smile she has. Is she a relative?"

Amanda shook her head. "No, but we do know her quite well."

CHAPTER 6

THE FOREST POOL

It seems like yesterday, but it was 1987.

I remember having just been shopping. It was a couple of days before Christmas, and, as usual, I'd left most of my gift-buying till the last minute.

I drove into town from Essex — driving because I thought it would be easier than carrying a lot of things on the Tube.

Looking for a parking space, I turned into one of the side streets behind Knightsbridge, along a street of tall white houses with elegant Christmas trees in their windows, and some where the Christmas tree was outside in the front garden, bedecked with expensive coloured lights.

It was exquisite, really, though the nasty part of me was envious of their wealth. I could never see myself having money like that.

I'm just an ordinary bloke. I live a normal life, do a normal job. In fact, the only thing that's odd about me is that sometimes I think there's somebody else living inside my body.

But probably everybody has that now and again.

And there I was in Knightsbridge, envying all the wealth around

92

me. But it was Christmas, so, I banished such thoughts as unseasonal — good will to all men and all that!

The traffic in the narrow streets was appalling, and I sat there, edging along, watching the lighted needle showing the temperature of the engine of my old car edge upwards into the red.

Then a BMW pulled out from the side, just in front of me, and I nipped into the parking space before someone else beat me to it. There was always lots of competition for parking around there.

It was dark, though it was only about four o'clock. I got out of the car, buttoned my coat around me, and clunked the car door shut.

Then I strolled through the streets where the curtains on the windows weren't drawn, and I peered into other people's Christmas preparations, like a theatregoer staring onto a stage where actors were rehearsing The Nutcracker.

All those beautiful houses with their beautiful decorations and beautiful trees — the children with their mothers hanging decorations; and in one, behind the gauze curtain, an old woman gazing at a glass bauble she held, as if it held memories of places and people she once loved.

I had chosen to go to Knightsbridge to get everything at once and get some nice things, and then to deliver gifts to my goddaughter and her parents, old friends who lived in Fulham.

Inside the shops, there were lights, warmth, and dozens of Santa Clauses handing out leaflets, advertising special offers on sherry and socks.

I visited the Christmas grotto even though I didn't have to, just to see the baubles and the crystal globes and turn them over to make the whirling artificial snow cover Austrian mountain scenes.

It took about an hour and a half to get everything. I bought my goddaughter a small, fluffy rabbit; I knew she liked rabbits. She had a pet one called Nathaniel. Then I left the shops and made my way back to the car, burdened with seasonally decorated shopping bags. I stowed them in the car's boot and turned on the engine.

It was only three or so miles from here to my friend's house, but in this traffic, it would take a while.

I indicated to come out from the car-choked back streets onto Brompton Road, my light ticking on the dashboard. And here I was greeted by a glittering river of jammed buses, taxis, and cars.

I made slow progress. The shops were covered in lights, and snow and baubles in the windows, and one particularly posh shop had a row of illuminated Christmas trees on the roofline that waved about in the slight wind.

I drove down the bright arteries of London, changing gears and lanes, accelerating, then coming to a halt behind buses.

Arriving in Fulham, I turned down North End Road and then down Epirus Road, travelling on darker streets where Christmas trees glowed like beacons of goodwill, and pulled in behind a skip full of building rubble, just in front of Robert's house.

I got out and fished out the gift-wrapped rabbit for the daughter, a bottle of port and Stilton gift set for him, and a glass vase for Elaine — small gifts for the couple who have everything.

To my surprise, they weren't in. They must have just popped out. I thought about waiting in the car, but I wanted to get home, so I left the presents in a carrier bag on the doorstep, hoping that nobody would steal them, and I scribbled a note on a blank page of my diary —another blank day the previous June when I had done nothing.

Then I walked back to the car, but just before I got there, I saw a girl with the bonnet of her vehicle up, peering into the engine with the help of a pool of streetlight.

She had no torch, and the streetlight was inadequate, and the lights in the windows of the houses nearby weren't enough for her to see anything much in the engine.

I got to my car and put the key in the lock, but then I felt a pang of conscience and relocked the door and went over to her.

She glanced up when she saw me approach. She didn't look scared. I guess I've never really looked scary.

I couldn't see her properly in the shadows, but she was about five foot four, with long brown hair, which she brushed out of her eyes, and she was wearing a black overcoat.

She gestured. "I can't get it started. I don't think it's the battery."

I told her to get back into the car and try it again, and I stood over the engine as she did so. I couldn't see much, but the engine gave a few clicks and wheezes and then died.

She got out again. "Any ideas?"

I shook my head. "I'm sorry, I'm not much of a mechanic," I said. "If it had been something really easy, but I think maybe it's the alternator. We should really call a garage or something."

She said, "No. I'll just leave it and get my dad to come get it tomorrow. He'll be able to fix it. I can get the tube back home now."

"Can't your father come and pick you up now?"

"No, we live in Loughton, in Essex. It's a bit far. We can come and collect it tomorrow when it's light. It's not a problem."

I paused and said, "I know this might sound a bit forward, but Loughton is on my way home — almost. I can give you a lift.

"Well." She twisted her mouth and looked at the car and then at the sky. The weather was turning colder. She was tempted.

"I assure you, I'm a man of honour," I said. I used to talk like that in those days. I know myself better now.

She laughed and said, "Okay, thanks very much."

She grabbed her handbag from the front seat of her car and then slammed the engine hood down and locked all the doors.

We got into my car and strapped ourselves in. I turned the key, and my engine fired.

She said, "Thank goodness for that!"

She looked back at the pile of parcels and bags on the back seat.

"Christmas shopping," I said. "That's why I'm down here at all today. I wouldn't usually come near the place at this time of year. I've got friends on this street."

"You're lucky you don't have to come here often," she said. "I work round here."

I switched the headlights on, and the dashboard lit up. By its light, I glanced at her. Her hair was blonder than I'd thought in the dark. She was about twenty.

Something about her face was familiar, so I said, "Have you lived in Loughton long?"

"Yes, I've lived there all my life. It's a bit boring, but it's okay. All my friends are there.

"Where did you go to school?"

"Just locally."

"Maybe I'm wrong then. Just that I thought I recognised you." I set the indicator flashing and pulled out onto the road.

It was a bit odd that Robert hadn't been in because I'd told him I would pop round, but maybe something had come up and he had tried to phone me, but I'd already set off.

The car journey out of London was as bad as I had expected it to be.

To pass the time, we talked about our various jobs. She worked for one of those temporary employment places.

Despite the derogatory comment she'd made about working "down here," she seemed actually quite proud that she worked in the Fulham office of Manpower. Even that seemed familiar.

As we drove, the car was warm, and we had trouble trying to keep the windscreen clear from condensation.

I seemed to have quickly put her at her ease. I was glad. I hate making people feel uncomfortable.

She talked a lot about not much, but I didn't mind. Then we got stuck behind a red light, and I put the handbrake on. I turned my head to have a better look at her. There was something so familiar. I was sure I knew her.

She was chattering about her girlfriend's boyfriend or something, and then the lights changed and her face was lit up by the combined red and amber.

Yes, I knew her. But I couldn't remember from where.

I turned back to look at the road and put the car into first and drove away, but not quickly enough to stop the van behind me from giving me a toot of his horn. She continued talking.

And her familiarity worried me. There was something odd happening, and I didn't know what it was. I half listened to her, but there was a feeling like a memory turning round and round in my stomach.

Suddenly I felt cold, though the car windows were still misting up with humidity.

I placed the memory. I recalled reading a story in the local paper about a girl who had gone to work in town one day just before Christmas last year and had never been seen again.

Her car was discovered broken down on a side street near her workplace. I couldn't remember the name of the street, but I was sure it was Fulham, near where I'd found her.

There had been a photograph. I remembered it because she was so pretty.

I just couldn't remember for the life of me in which paper I'd seen it. Probably it was in *the Loughton and District Advertiser*.

But the memory was vague. It wasn't imagination, though imaginings can sometimes seem like memories.

A panic seeped into my brain. So, I'd read a story about a murder in a newspaper. But why was I scared?

It couldn't be her, no matter how weirdly synchronistic the story was. This girl was real. She was flesh and blood. I could even smell her scent. I heard her Essex accent, not common — lower middle class.

She kept on talking, and I remembered she'd told me her name was Andrea.

The murdered girl had been Andrea too. But Andrea what?

Then I asked her what her second name was, breaking her train of conversation. She looked at me, surprised. I suppose I had been rude to interrupt.

"Andrea Padfield," she said.

Padfield. It was Andrea Padfield. I was sure that was the name in the paper, but now I wasn't sure if I'd read it at all.

It all became vague, swimming in my head. Had I read about Andrea Padfield in the paper, or had I dreamed I'd read it?

Anyway, the story was from this time last year. I was sure about that as much as I'm sure about anything.

She probably thought my asking her second name was weird, so I tried to talk normally, but by first abruptly asking her surname, and now my forced jollity must have frightened her because she went quiet.

I honestly hate making women uncomfortable. I felt guilty and made some stupid jokes, making myself as silly and harmless as possible. I was harmless. I'd never harmed anyone.

We arrived just outside Loughton. I had calmed myself down. And, probably because I was behaving more normally, she seemed to be back to normal too.

We were talking perfectly normally. It was all normal. I asked her where she lived, so I could drop her off.

She said, "I actually live just inside Epping Forest, but if you drop me here, I can get a taxi."

There were pretty, bijoux little villages tucked into the Forest. Her family must have some money to live there, though.

Given the weather and the darkness, I didn't like the thought of her waiting for a taxi, or even deciding to walk.

I should obviously take her home, but I worried it might seem threatening if I offered to drive her all the way home, especially through the Forest, and given that she'd already suggested I drop her here.

I said, "Could you phone your father?"

She seemed relieved at my suggestion. "Yes, yes, I could. And there's a phone box near here."

But there was a falseness in her voice. From the way she said it, I thought that there was actually nobody at home. That's why she hadn't called her dad from Fulham.

But if she didn't want to tell me that, that was fine, and I didn't want to press her to admit it.

But it was dark and cold, and I knew I was harmless, though I couldn't say the same for anyone else she might meet on these dark suburban streets.

I imagined her hanging around for a taxi. I couldn't force her to do that, and I wanted to make up for scaring her before.

I sighed. "Look, I can drop you there if you tell me where it is. Epping Forest's only five minutes out of my way."

She paused as if weighing up the cold wait with the possibility that I might be a madman.

She gave me a trusting smile. My attempts to make myself harmless must have worked because she said, "Ok, that would be nice of you. It saves my dad from getting the car out."

She gave me directions to her house. It was near High Beach.

The locality was the epitome of the suburban dream, within Epping Forest, yet conveniently situated for transport links to Town.

We drove into the forest itself. The road narrowed.

There weren't many cars on the road. The trees clustered around you, making you feel like you were way out in the country. It felt oddly remote.

The damp leaves were edged in rain that reflected back the headlights of my car. And the few houses we passed glittered with Christmas lights until we went by them and were in the clustering trees again.

If there were houses here in this part of the forest, they were invisible behind the ancient woods.

She said, "Just here."

There was a small side road ahead, almost invisible. I would have missed it if not for her, but she pointed for me to go down it.

This place looked different in the dark, and, I was older, and memory changes things, even familiar spots, but I actually recognised the area.

My brother and I used to come here as kids to play in the forest.

I remembered there was a horrible old pond in the middle of the trees near here. Someone had dumped a corpse there in the pool once.

Wasn't that in the news story I thought I remembered reading?

I glanced at Andrea. She was looking at me. She was scared. She said, "Why did you turn down here?"

"You said to."

"No, I didn't. You just turned down this narrow lane."

She was wrong. I stammered, "You definitely said. You pointed and said to turn down here."

We'd got to the car park by the pool. There was nobody there. It was pitch black and raining. Why would there be?

My hand was shaking so much that if felt like it wasn't under my control.

This is where my brother and I used to come playing. I knew it well.

Andrea said, "Please turn round and take me back to the main road. I can walk from there."

I parked the car in the car park by that pool in the forest. The rain streaked down the windows.

She tried to get out. She wanted me to take her to the pool.

I have no memory apart from coming to full consciousness kneeling in the mud by the forest pool.

There was a moon above the trees, and the oily water gleamed in its light, illuminating half-drowned branches. There in that unearthly moon-glow, I wondered where Andrea had gone.

The trees leaned over the pool. It was like they were listening, waiting to see what I would do.

I was soaking. The filthy mud was all over my face and clothes where I had been lying in it. I must have actually been in the pool to be so wet.

I glanced at the water, but the water was still, with the reflection of the risen moon undisturbed on the dark water.

I stood. My clothes dripped with stagnant water, and the polluting stink of it suffocated me.

I stumbled away from the pool, my shoes filled with water. I staggered, and then my feet grew steadier on the damp earth.

I must have cut myself on the trailing briars because my hands and clothes were red with blood. So much blood. Hard to believe thorns can cut you so badly.

My car stood in the middle of the narrow track with the doors and the hatchback open. The headlights were still on.

I write this now, at home, years later. I've wanted to write it for a long time, but something wouldn't let me. Now it seems that something doesn't mind.

So it's Christmas again, and I've had the radio on all night to give me the illusion of company and heard Christmas carol after Christmas carol.

Sometimes I think I saw the ghost of Andrea Padfield, who wanted to show me her last resting place. I know that's weird, but that seems to be the only explanation.

In the intervening years, I searched and searched for the newspaper report I'd read that gave me the name Andrea Padfield, her fate, and the grainy picture of that weirdly familiar face.

In the end, I found the right article. But it wasn't dated 1986.

CHAPTER 7

THE CARLISLE CAPPEL

As you travel around Cumberland, or merely look at the Ordnance Survey map, you may chance to note a number of place-names containing the word 'cappel'. For example: Cappel Fell or Capplethwaite.

Perusing a book of place-name studies will tell you that cappel is an old Cumbrian word (from the Celtic) for a workhorse. But there is another meaning too. A cappel can also be a huge black spectral dog that haunts the woods, byways, and even the graveyards of our county.

In Yorkshire, they call them Barguests, and in Norfolk and Lincolnshire, they call them Black Shucks. But here, when they were more frequently seen than they are today, they called them 'cappels'.

I say they were more frequently seen than they are now, but in truth, they were never a common sight. And if you did see one, you'd do well to run away.

This ghost story, or rather monster story, comes from Carlisle, and it is called, unsurprisingly, The Carlisle Cappel.

There was a tradition, not necessarily a Cumbrian tradition, but one going back to Saxon times, that when you started a new graveyard, the first creature buried there would rise again to become the graveyard's guardian. It is said that in those days, believing this legend, our ancestors would slaughter a ferocious dog and bury it there before any humans were laid to rest. In this way, the spirit dog would prowl the graves and keep away the graverobbers, treasure seekers, and anyone else who intended ill to those resting there.

Now, it is also said that in some graveyards where the first burial was a human, it fell to that poor soul to be chained to the earth after death and never set foot outside the walls of the burial ground. This spirit's job was to guard the graves until the graveyard itself fell into disrepair and was lost from usage and memory, and when there was no longer any trace that the dead had been buried there with all formality and ceremony, the enchained spirit could be freed from his age-long task.

But all this is an aside, and our real story — the Story of the Carlisle Cappel — begins in the 19th century, when a man named John Carter moved to the Carlisle area.

John Carter came from London, and he was a blacksmith by trade. The story goes that he got it into his head that there were better opportunities for a blacksmith in Carlisle than in London in those days, or perhaps he hankered for a more traditional and close-knit community that he would have enjoyed in London. But whatever the reason, John Carter moved from The Great Smoke to The Great Border City at the beginning of the winter of 1840–1841.

John Carter had made inquiries and got good information that brought him to the Carlisle area; he would have gone to Newcastle, Durham, or Kendal just as readily, but it came to his attention that there was a requirement for a blacksmith in the village of Aglionby.

The family packed their belongings and caught the train, John Carter, his wife, and their two small daughters.

It was a long and tedious journey, but, sitting in the carriage and looking out of the window at the countryside, which grew wilder and more magnificent the further north they travelled, John clasped his wife's hand and told her to trust him.

It is fair to say that Anne Carter had not wholeheartedly shared her husband's enthusiasm for a move so far from her friends and family into the cold climate and reputed barbarism of Cumberland. But she was a dutiful wife, and he persuaded her that all would be well, and so she smiled and nodded while their daughters dozed in their seats all the long hours that the journey took from Euston Station to Citadel Station in Carlisle.

It was around six in the evening when they finally arrived.

John Carter had arranged for his family to be met by a man with a pony and trap to take his family and their few belongings from the station to Aglionby.

The driver, a man from Currock named George Guardhouse, was waiting in the crisp December air outside the station. It was ten days before Christmas, and the land was locked in ice as the northern winter, colder than any winter John or his wife had experienced before, set them shivering as they left the station, bags in hand.

Grey clouds covered the sky, and the air was damp.

The Carters hoped to be settled into their new home soon, well in time for Christmas. George Guardhouse created a favourable first impression of Carlisle folk, and they looked approvingly at his green and gold painted carriage as he called down, "Are you Mr. Carter, the new blacksmith, as is going to Aglionby?'

Guardhouse wore a heavy black overcoat that was well-kept if not new, and he wore a bowler hat and held the whip in his right hand.

Once he confirmed it was the right family, he stepped down from the carriage to help Mrs. Carter and the girls abroad.

The girls marvelled at Guardhouse's Cumbrian accent and could hardly understand his thin vowels and tapped consonants, and for his part, he struggled to follow their fat southern vowels and their slurred consonants, but by gestures and nods and speaking slowly, they eventually understood each other well enough and were off, George Guardhouse gently cracking his whip in the air as a signal to his horse, Bess, who needed no touch of the whip to obey her master's commands.

The carriage set off east down Warwick Road, Bess trotting with high steps along the Victorian terraces.

John Carter remarked how foggy it was. As they trotted on, the damp air amplified the sound of the horse's hooves as the mist rolled in thick and fast, making it difficult to see the nearby houses.

The Carters were used to yellow London fog, but this country fog was something different: not acrid, certainly, not stinging the eyes, but heavy and damp, redolent of bogland and river banks, of high fells and salt sea marshes.

The fog didn't seem to bother George Guardhouse, and Carter was somewhat alarmed to notice that instead of slowing down for safety in the foggy conditions, Guardhouse had in fact speeded up.

As they left the houses behind and crossed the Laundry Bridge that goes over the River Petteril, Guardhouse was causing Bess to go along at a breakneck pace.

Anne Carter clutched at her husband's arm and whispered, 'Why's he driving so fast? I'd rather be late in this world than early in the next.'

Carter comforted his wife. 'Don't worry, Annie. He knows what he's doing.'

Then he lowered his voice and whispered to himself: 'At least I hope he does.'

But even John Carter grew alarmed as Guardhouse cracked the whip again and urged Bess to go at a gallop, causing the carriage to jump and jerk and the wheels to clatter even faster.

Coming near the turn into Botcherby, they sped so fast that the left hand side of the carriage lifted up, and at this, Anne screamed.

Carter decided he must speak and said, 'For the love of God, man, slow down. We want to get there in one piece.'

Guardhouse cleared his throat. 'Very well, very well,' he said. 'If you say so, Mr. Carter.'

For three minutes, Guardhouse allowed Bess to slacken her pace, and the horse gave off steaming clouds of breath that joined with the fog that was now so thick they could hardly see six feet in front of them.

And then Guardhouse, as if he could no longer bear to go so slowly, clicked his tongue and suddenly urged Bess on. Soon they were going on as fast as they ever had, and here, further out of town, the road was rutted and in places the cobblestones were loose, making it more dangerous to drive so recklessly.

Once again, Carter and his wife became afraid at the speed they were being driven, and the little girls clutched at their mother because they were frightened they would be jerked out of the carriage, so fast it went.

Carter spoke up, his voice now strident, 'I say it again, Mr. Guardhouse, will you please slow down. Your rash speed is putting the fear of the Lord into my wife and children.'

Guardhouse sighed. 'I will if you say so, Mr. Carter. But this fog is unusually thick. It isn't often this thick at this time of day, and when it gets like this, folk round here bolt their doors and don't wander the streets and lanes away from their houses.'

Carter said, 'It's bad weather indeed. But we shall soon be at our new house, and you're welcome to a warm drink once we are and to stay until the fog clears.'

Guardhouse lifted his bowler hat and wiped his seamed forehead with the back of his gloved hand. He was sweating profusely despite the chill in the air. He said, 'That's very decent of you, Mr. Carter. I'll slow down.' He sighed, gave a weak smile, and said, 'I'm sure there's nothing to worry about, despite this unnatural fog.'

But within five minutes, Guardhouse had urged Bess on again, and again they hurtled down the uneven road.

It is hard to say where they were. Certainly they were past Botcherby, but perhaps not so far as the Scotby turn. In any case, it was open country in those days, and if there were houses round about, none could be seen through the coiling walls of fog.

It was the little girl, the youngest, and perhaps because her young ears were sharper, she heard it first.

Her head turned around. Then her sister started, wide-eyed. 'What's that, mother?' she cried.

'I don't hear anything,' Anne Carter said. Perhaps it was true, or perhaps she chose to say that so as not to frighten the girls further.

But George Guardhouse was not so thoughtful. 'Yes, I heard it,' he said, and he cracked the whip. 'We must hurry from here.'

And soon the carriage sped along even faster, at a dangerous rate.

John Carter had heard nothing. 'What did you hear, my loves?'

'A growl, a deep growl, like a big dog,' said the youngest, and her sister nodded furiously in agreement.

Carter turned to the driver. 'What was it, Guardhouse? You know more than you let on, that's obvious.'

'What it is, I won't say,' George Guardhouse replied. 'But the sooner we are at your house, the better. The sooner we have doors locked and bolted between us and this thing, the better. I was a fool to agree to come out this way, what with the weather, but I had promised to meet you, and I'm not a man to break his promises.'

Carter thanked him for his diligence, if not for his driving.

And so they raced on. The carriage jerked and jolted along, going so fast that Carter worried the wheels might come off and spill them into the street.

'Slow down, man! Whatever threat is out there, and I am not yet convinced it is not wholly the product of an overactive imagination, your haste, heedless of all good sense, will make a quicker end to us than any spook in the fog.'

But despite this admonishment, George Guardhouse slowed not a jot.

Even hanging on for dear life in the rattling carriage, against the thundering hooves of the horse, behind the frenzied snorts of the beast, Bess, the girls heard something again, and this time, John Carter himself heard the low growl of a creature and a sound like a great dog running, claws clattering on the cobbles of the turnpike.

Guardhouse cracked the whip and made the horse go faster when it seemed hardly possible that she could, and the horse did not protest for she too was afeared of whatever followed them, and her eyes rolled and she snorted, possessed of the same mortal fear that gripped her driver.

The girls wailed, and Ann Carter sat white as a sheet, squeezing her husband's arm, her eyes closed so she could not see.

'Slow down, I tell you!' John Carter yelled.

But without turning, through clenched teeth, George Guardhouse muttered, 'No, I will not slow. I dare not slow. For if I slow the pace, it will catch us.'

'For Heaven's sake, man — what will catch us? Is this not merely childish superstition?'

Guardhouse said, 'Your daughter heard it, even if you did not. She suspects what it is'

'But what did she hear? You're talking in riddles, man. What manner of thing did she hear?'

'She heard the growl of the Cappel, and so did I.'

And despite his modern thoughts and his schoolboy learning, John Carter shivered and thought to himself: And so did I, though I know not what it may be.

The carriage hurtled at breakneck speed, but now even John Carter became aware of a shape in the mist trailing them. It was hard to make out what it was. It was the height of a pony, but shaggy-headed like a wolf, and its fur was jet black and fuliginous, as if it had come straight from the sooty fires of hell and then, through the fog, and for the first time he saw the baleful, red, burning eyes and knew this was no mortal dog. As he stared, open-mouthed, it roared and leapt.

John Carter started and grunted in his fear, and George Guardhouse yelled, 'The Cappel is upon us!'

He cracked the whip. Bess gave a burst of speed, and the Cappel fell short.

But still the terrifying creature raced along just behind the carriage. Carter saw it clearer now. It was huge and coal-black, with evil, glowing eyes and a lolling yellow tongue, and every now and again, this hell hound reared up on its hind legs and jumped and raked its sharp claws along the neat green and gold paintwork of George Guardhouse's carriage.

Then, with a roar, the Cappel clawed the door of the carriage and almost dragged it open, and the womenfolk shrieked and John Carter barely kept his manly bearing.

His head in his hands, Carter, now yelled, 'Go faster, go faster!'.

And his wife and daughters screamed with fear and pressed their eyes closed with their hands.

From his seat in front, George Guardhouse said, 'Do you see now, sir? Do you see now why I did not want to slow down the carriage?'

John Carter could see all too clearly and finally understood the driver's speed.

With another thunderous leap from the Cappel and the raking of its talons on the carriage, Carter shouted, 'Safety be damned, just get my family away from this damned thing.'

For a long mile, and then another, the carriage thundered along the turnpike through the empty countryside with thick fog on all sides.

Even as fast as they went, they could not lose it. The spectral dog would fall behind, but moments later, to their horror, it caught them up again.

Eventually, they approached the narrow bridge over Pow Maughan. The bridge was then in a poor state—a narrow, rickety thing that was perilous for wheeled traffic at the best of times, and below the bridge on this day of deep winter, the beck was choked with ice and boulders.

Peering ahead, Guardhouse cried, 'I'll have to slow down to get across the bridge.' But as he slowed, the Cappel leapt and caught and dragged at the vehicle, slowing it, but Bess found her strength and pulled the carriage free.

But Bess's burst of speed meant they were approaching the

bridge too fast. Guardhouse hit the brakes, and the Cappel saw a chance and leapt, landing four-footed on the carriage's top.

The Carters were inside the carriage, but the driver sat afront in the open.

On the roof, the Cappel slunk forward, jaws open, yellow teeth and yellow tongue a-slaver, meaning to take off Guardhouse's head, but George Guardhouse cracked the whip, and, Bess, with the last of her strength, dragged the carriage left and overbalanced the huge dog.

The Cappel lost its footing just as they were leaving the Pow Maughan bridge and skittered off the carriage top and over the broken stone parapet, falling into the mess of rock and ice below.

'You've thrown it off!' Carter yelled through the open window, and his family cheered.

'No time for jubilation, Mr. Carter. It's a fell creature and will be back if we don't make haste now,' Guardhouse said, and he leaned forward to pat Bess's lathered flank as she gasped and groaned to catch her breath. 'Come on, lass!' Guardhouse said, 'Nearly there now. You've done so well.'

'She has that,' Ann Carter said.

Guardhouse cracked his whip, and Bess trotted forward again.

'I can hear it, Daddy!' the youngest girl cried, and so could John Carter. The Cappel, not wanting to be cheated of its meal, roared from the riverbed, and they knew it would scrabble its way up the sides and be back on land soon and after them.

So off they set again, with Bess finding her second wind.

Bess went so fast that the Cappel did not catch them. And they came to Aglionby where Guardhouse knew where the house the blacksmith and his family were to occupy was. The fog was lighter here. But still, they took Bess into the stable and locked her in with oats and water. Listening warily for the sound of the Cappel.

John Carter was so grateful to the coach driver from Currock that he offered him what guineas he had on him. At first, Guardhouse would not take the money, but Anne Carter insisted.

'Please, Mr. Carter. Buy yourself a whisky, a silk ribbon for your wife, and a new coat of paint for your carriage, and above all, make sure that horse Bess gets the best oats for a month. It was you and she that saved our lives, and we'll never forget it.'

The driver told the blacksmith and his wife that the Cappel had roamed Carlisle and its surrounding country for generations. And the locals were so frightened of it, that no one would speak openly about it, and those that did were shunned.

Carter settled down as blacksmith of Aglionby, and as an old man, with grown children, grandchildren, and even great-grandchildren babbling on his knee, neither he nor his wife ever went near Pow Maughan bridge again without a shudder, terrified that they should encounter once more the hound from hell.

Now it may be that you do not believe in the story of a great black dog with glowing red eyes that haunts Carlisle and the district, but in 2007, a young man returning home after a night out came across a large black dog with glowing eyes at the bottom of Fusehill Street that regarded him and then padded off across the street.

Then in 2011, someone crossing the car park behind Cecil Street, which is the County Council car park saw a huge black dog. There was no mention this time of the glowing eyes, but they were so frightened they ran off into the housing estate.

A third sighting was in the autumn of 2020 during the COVID lockdown, when the roads were very quiet and not many people were out and about, and this was a young woman coming home after being out visiting in violation of lockdown restrictions. She was walking down Warwick Road and saw what she and I believe to be the Carlisle Cappel, a big black hound with red eyes watching her from, the mouth of an alley.

Even though you probably don't believe a word of these stories, it might just be in your best interests to take special care and look out for huge black dogs when you're walking home late at night.

Make sure you have some doggy treats.

The Cappel is said to be particularly fond of man flavour.

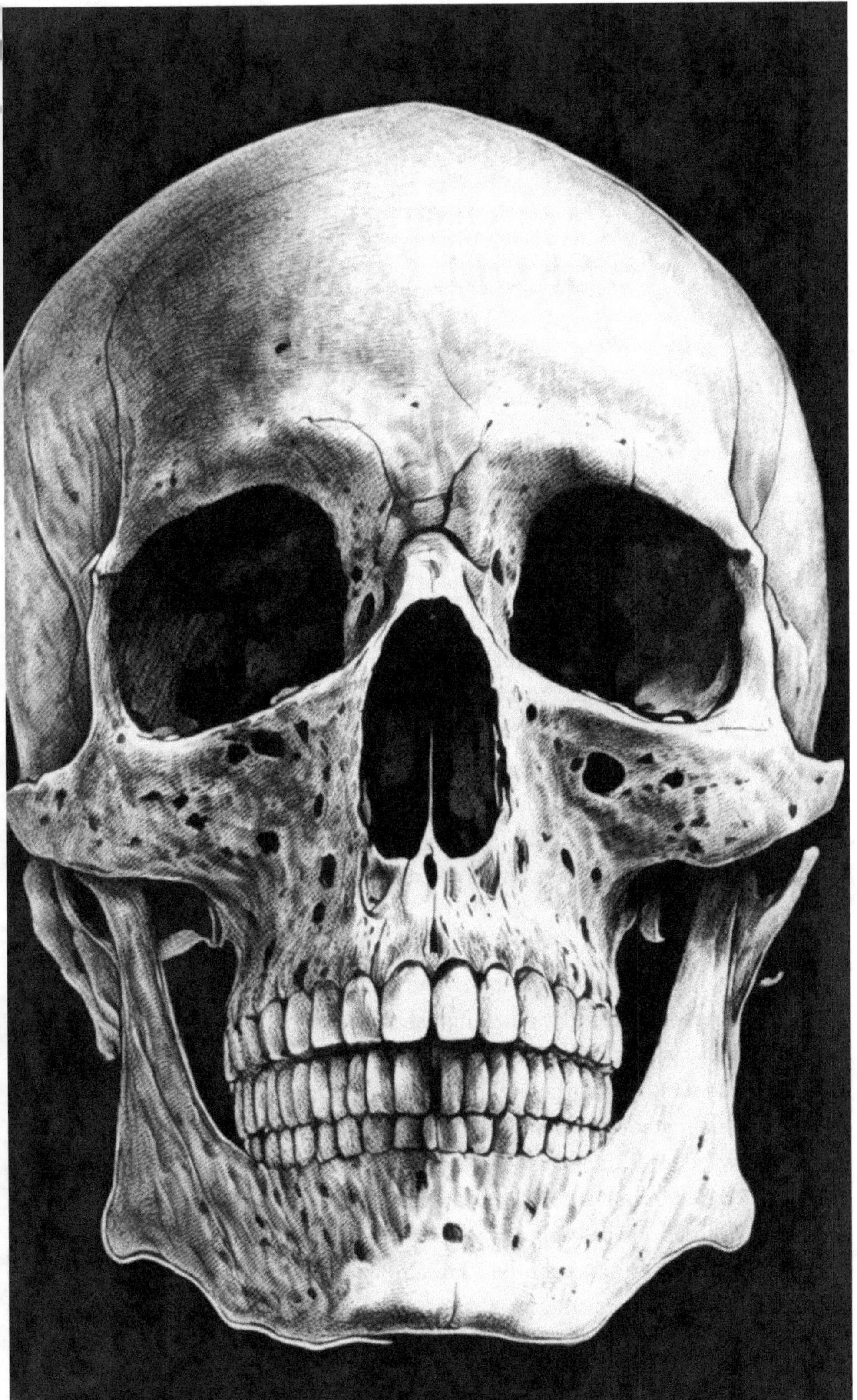

CHAPTER 8

THE SKULL OF ST BEES

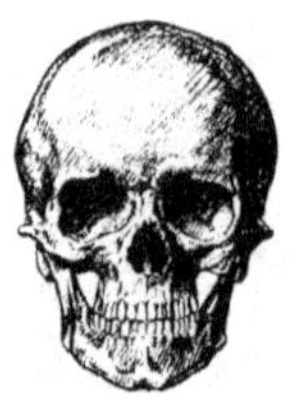

St. Bees is famous for its large sandstone cliff that juts out into the Irish Sea, and this cliff, with its wheeling seabirds and fogs and wild weather; stands with the Solway Firth to the north and the Irish Sea to the south. At the top of the cliff is a light-house that used to warn off ships from the perilous rocks below, and just on the landward side lies an old house called Tarnflatt Hall.

Tarnflatt Hall is the only substantial house there these days, but it was not always so.

There was once another house on Hannah Moor, called, unsur-prisingly, Hannah Hall, but this building fell into ruin at the end of the nineteenth century and languished as a home for sheep and owls until it was demolished just after the Second World War.

It was not that there was anything wrong with the building. It was a substantial dwelling with thick sandstone walls to keep out the wind and a good greenslate roof to keep out the rain. Hannah Hall dated from 1710, and it was always considered an unlucky place.

It could never keep a tenant. People stayed there a short while and moved on, and the hall lay empty for long periods. Over the years, the owners sold it on to a business group of Norfolk farmers who travelled the nation purchasing and renting out properties like this. Except they could never let Hannah Hall out, and it became a liability for them.

I am about to tell you why.

The tale may go back longer, but it first appears in documented evidence in the form of a diary of the Right Reverend Henry Lord and a report in *Ware's Whitehaven Adviser* from 1823. *The Whitehaven Adviser* was late to the story because it all began in the spring of 1821 when Hannah Hall was finally let after a long period of vacancy.

The person who took up this tenancy was a young man in his mid twenties called Joseph Messenger and his wife Mary. Messenger was a yeoman farmer's son from Maryport and was now setting out on his own. They brought with them a housekeeper whose name was Elizabeth Coulthard. We can confirm this information from the census return from 1821.

While the house itself had been empty, the land that belonged to the house had been sublet to neighbouring farmers, but Joseph Messenger took it all in hand. The neighbours were happy to farm the land, but none of them wanted the house. The reasons for this were never disclosed to Joseph Messenger. Although he was a Cumberland man, and from only twenty miles away, twenty miles was a long way in 1821, and he was thought of as an outsider.

The house was in a poor state when they moved in. Messenger invested his money in the stock and hired labourers to help him, but again, these preferred to live nearby rather than at Hannah Hall itself. Messenger laughed this off and called them, to himself and his wife at least, superstitious fools. He considered himself modern-thinking and was an admirer of John Christian Curwen and his model farm at Schoose, just outside Workington.

As he set to farming, his wife Mary and the servant Elizabeth Coulthard set to renovating and refurbishing the hall, obtaining new pieces of furniture, painting, and papering. They began at the bottom of the house and, as the weeks went by, worked their way up until they arrived at the attics.

This attic looked like it hadn't been used for a very long time. And when they began refurbishing this room, they found a small green door in the interior wall that was bolted. And this bolt was rusted and stiff and draped in old cobwebs. Out of curiosity, Mary Messenger reached to draw back the bolt.

The maid said, 'Mrs Messenger, I think you need some grease on that bolt. It looks awkward stiff.'

'Aye, but I've got it, Elizabeth,' and with a tug, she pulled the end of the bolt and drew at it until at last it squeaked and came all of a rush.

Now they could open the door.

'I wonder what they'd keep in a la'al cupboard like that?' Elizabeth said.

'We will soon find out, lass.'

And Mary Messenger tugged at the small green door, which resisted at first due to the lack of use of its hinges, but then opened stiffly to reveal a dark cupboard. It was hard to see into it, for the attic was dark enough of itself, and the closet behind the door was three feet deep into the eaves.

'There's something in here,' said Mary Messenger, "but I can't see what. Go fetch a candle, Elizabeth."

So the maid got a candle, and they looked into that small cupboard and saw there was a niche built into the brick work, and in the brick work was a brown and decayed object that at first defied identification.

Perhaps it defied identification through lack of light, but I think perhaps it defied identification because it was not the sort of thing to find in a cupboard in an attic.

Elizabeth put her hand to her throat and said, "What is that, Mrs. Messenger?"

Mary held the candle up and peered, saying, " I do believe it's a human skull."

"Lord bless us and save us. What a thing to find."

They left the skull where it was. When Joseph Messenger came in from the fields, his wife told him what she'd found, and he went with her. He too was bemused, but he saw that his wife, who was only twenty-two, and the maid, Elizabeth, who was younger still at sixteen, were rattled by the thing, and their nerves were set on edge by the grinning bones that stared at them with empty eye sockets.

"What should we do with it, Joe?" Mary asked.

He looked and scratched his chin and said, "We leave it for now, then I'll get the policeman."

This was mere weeks into their tenancy at Hannah Hall.

The police constable, William Teasdale, was called from the village. He was a local man, and when he visited to see what they'd found, one of the farm labourers and a ploughman called Adam Waugh inveigled his way into the attic with them, where they stood —three men and two women and pondered the brown, age-worn skull in its brick niche.

"It's old," said the policeman, Teasdale. "It's not a new thing. So I don't think there's any question of foul play. I would say it's not the law you need, but the Church."

Though none present had any inkling before this that the attic at Hannah Hall contained a skull, set up in a cupboard in a niche made from bricks apparently created especially for it to rest there, and none of them had any more of an idea why such a thing would be done or by whom, Waugh ventured: "This'll be the cause of it all."

"The cause of what?" the constable asked just before Joseph Messenger could ask the same.

"The noises. The disturbances. The reason no one will rest at Hannah Hall."

"It's black magic, that's what it is," Elizabeth Coulthard said, her voice shaking.

"It's nothing of the sort," Joseph Messenger barked. "If thou canst say nowt sensible, then hod thy wisht, thou foolish lass."

But the constable kept quiet, as if it had crossed his mind that it might indeed be black magic.

And Adam Waugh said, "But you need a clergyman, sure enough, to exorcise this skull and give the house rest."

Joseph Messenger turned on him. "It needs no rest. There is no disturbance here. There is nothing supernatural. There are no noises."

"Even so, I would go to the Theological College and seek their advice," said the constable.

Adam Waugh and the Constable Teasdale were soon gone, and neither entered that house again in all their lives, though their lives were lived out within a mile or two of Hannah Hall, and it would have been a small matter for them to see it again should they have wanted.

Though it was true that up until then, there had been no noises, or disturbances of any kind, it was as if Joseph Messenger's dismissal of such things had conjured them forth.

After that, there were strange noises — sounds as if something was being dragged along the floor upstairs.

From outside in the fields as the evenings darkened, Joseph Messenger would sometimes see a light in the attic, but not such a light as would be cast by candle or lamp. The light had the colour of a corpse candle or a will o' the wisp that you see out on the marshes when the day has failed and night has come to swallow it up. And he shuddered, but he kept his quiet, not wanting to make his wife or the maid afeared. But when they lay in their bed in the deep of the night, halfway between dusk and dawn, when the darkness is almost solid and sits heavy in the room, he had a feeling that there was someone in the house with them.

Someone who moved. Someone who waited. Someone who watched them.

At first he had delayed going to the vicar in case the learned clergyman mocked him as a credulous, agricultural who was ignorant and giving too much heed to the old folks' talk of dobbies and boggarts and suchlike nonsense.

But in the end, he went.

The cause of his going was one night around 2:00 a.m. It was a Sunday going into Monday, and there was a scream that rent the air. Joseph jumped out of bed. Mary beside him lit a candle, and Elizabeth knocked at their door and stood as they opened it, wrapped in a blanket, hair down, eyes filled with tears of sheer terror, and her fingers twisting in the blanket and saying, "A's fleat."

"Where did it come from?"

"Upstairs."

"The attic."

"Aye, that."

"I'll go look."

Mary clutched at his arm and said, "No, there's no need, Joe. Don't go."

"But I must, Mary. I must see there is no intruder in our house."

"It's not a man, Joe. We know what it is."

But he went anyway, and the two women came with him as much to help him with his fear as to stop their own from being left alone without him.

And in the attic, the green door was open.

"Did either of you open this?"

"No, Joe," and "No, Mr Messenger," they said, and "Why would we?"

But the green door was open nonetheless. And the skull was not in its niche. Someone had moved it and set it on the floor, staring at them, its eyeholes shifting and flickering in the light of their candles until it looked as if it was waiting for them.

Joseph Messenger ushered them out and said, "We must get a padlock for this door and never enter."

"A padlock will not do, Joe. We need a priest."

And after that, the skull would move around the house, and they found it when they came in.

At that time, St. Bees had a theological college, which was started in 1816, and the parish priest was also one of the lecturers at the theological college. And he was a man called the right Reverend

Henry Lord. And he was a modern Anglican vicar, and he did not believe much in superstition and devil worship.

He did not believe in witches. He did not believe in spirits, and his view of Christianity was very modern and scientific, but the Right Reverend Henry Lord's curiosity was piqued by the description given to him by Joseph Messenger, and he agreed to come up to Hannah hall to see this skull that lurked in its brick niche in this small room. He fancied himself as something of an amateur antiquarian, and he considered the skull an archaeological curiosity or folkloric oddity.

After they'd inspected the skull, Joseph Messenger urged Reverend Lord to take the skull and give it a Christian burial in St. Bees churchyard, for, he believed that by giving the skull a Christian burial, his house would be at rest and the spirit that haunted it would be banished.

The Right Reverend Henry Lord took the skull and placed it on his mahogany desk in the theological college. Though Messenger had urged him to bury the skull, he had no intention of giving it any kind of ceremony. The skull was too interesting, though his interest in it was merely archaeological. Despite his initial enthusiasm, after consulting his books and coming up with no obvious explanation for the skull, he put it aside and moved onto his sermon. And whatever he had said, he had no intention of behaving like a superstitious local and giving it a Christian burial. He did not consider this a lie, for one tells simple folk what they can understand and what will not disturb their placid minds. That is a kind of truth, a kinder truth, in fact.

He asked his friends and other local antiquarians about it, but they could come to no conclusion other than that it was very old, they couldn't link it to any particular period or any particular personage.

Back at Hannah Hall, even though the skull was removed from the house, the noises and disturbances continued. The Messengers could make no sense of this — the skull was gone. How could the hauntings continue?

And then, one day, Mary Messenger went into their bedroom, and on the dresser, sat the skull.

The Reverend Henry Hall had had the skull in his study, but he did not notice it had disappeared until his day was disturbed by a frantic knock on his study door. It was his servant, Dixon, and behind Dixon, Joseph Messenger, hat in hand, wringing it in despair, fear in his eyes, a tremor in his voice.

'Did you bury it?'

'Bury what?" responded Lord.

"You know fine well what — the skull. We asked you to bury it. To give us peace. But we've not got peace."

The Reverend Lord cleared his throat. "Of course. Of course. Why would I not?"

Messenger sighed. "It's back in the house."

"Back in the house?" Lord's eyebrows rose, and his voice had an edge. He suspected some knave's trick played on him by his colleagues or students, perhaps with the connivance of this peasant farmer. His mind raced. He could get himself out of this. They wouldn't laugh up their sleeves at him — the rogues! It would be the other way round. Indeed, it would.

"Then it's worse. If you hadn't buried it, it would be easier to understand how someone had returned it to Hannah Hall. But as you buried it— where did you place it?"

In a quiet voice, Reverend Lord said, "In the churchyard."

"In the churchyard, of course. Then this is surely the Devil's work, for how else are we to explain such witchery?"

"Don't be so hasty. Let me come again and take it."

"You'd do that? I was hoping, but didn't dare hope as well. But you'll take it? And exorcise it?"

Lord smiled. "I am not an exorcist. The Anglican Church has little time for such Popery. But I will remove it, and I assure you—nay, I promise you, Mr. Messenger. The skull will not return to plague you further."

Lord was sure of it now. He could almost see Farraday and Johnson laughing at him. They were probably outside his study, sniggering up their sleeves. Well, let them. He would find a way to turn the tables and make them look like fools. But for now he would play along with their mummery.

Together, Joseph Messenger and Reverend Lord went back on Messenger's horse cart to Hannah Hall. The two women waited outside the door. "Thank heavens you've come, Reverend. We didn't dare go back inside the house. We've been out here waiting for Joseph's return and hoping you would come along with him."

"There's no need to worry now, dear lady." Lord slipped off the cart's seat and brushed himself down fastidiously, then looked around furtively to see whether his clerical tormentors lurked somewhere around the house to see how their joke was going, but he saw no one.

"Show me the artefact—the skull."

He was shown to the kitchen, where the skull sat on the scarred oak table.

"You put it here?"

"No," said Elizabeth Coulthard. "It wasn't here when we stepped outside. It moves of its own will."

A fine joke. It seemed the thick-witted maid was in on it too. Lord pursed his lips, smiled, and took out his cotton handkerchief. He wrapped it around the skull. It felt light and dry and strangely warm through the cotton.

"I'll take it now."

"What will you do with it?" Joseph Messenger asked. "You tried a disposal by earth?"

"And now by air and water. We will go to the cliff's edge and throw it in the sea."

The women looked alarmed. Joseph Messenger looked uncertain, but they all three followed Reverend Lord out of the house and across the fields to the edge of the cliff.

The cliff stood more than a hundred feet above the foaming tide.

It was made of faulted sandstone, and seabirds whirled and cried. The Isle of Man stood off to the south, seeming ever so close, and Galloway across to the west, further away and hazy.

"Watch!" Revered Hall, drew back his arm and hurled the skull, keeping hold of his handkerchief, and it flew in an arc, buffeted by the breeze, losing height and being blown back against the cliff where it struck a rock, bounced, fell, stuck another, broke into pieces, and the pieces fell like pot fragments into the unquiet foam of the sea.

"There. It is gone. It will not return from that."

But it did.

That evening, Joseph Messenger, drawn by a fearful curiosity, crept up to the attic and drew back the door to see the skull on the bare boards, grinning at him, victorious and demonic.

He gave a shout.

The women came running. They screamed also. Elizabeth Coulthard was inconsolable. "We saw it destroyed. We saw it fall into the sea. We saw it broken. So how can it be back here mocking us?"

"The power of the Devil," Mary Messenger said. "It is the work of the Evil One. We are haunted by this thing and can never be free." She turned to her husband. "Fetch Reverend Hall."

"It's nine o'clock at night."

"We won't any of us sleep in this house until he comes and lifts this curse on us and the house."

Dixon at the Theological College did not want to admit Joseph Messenger, because his master would be at port and cigars with the other reverends, but he saw Joseph Messenger's haunted eyes and his drawn face, and he said, "Very well. I'll pass along a message. If he won't see you, then you'll have to come back tomorrow."

"Tell him it's come back. Even though he destroyed it. It's come back."

Dixon heard the sound of laughter from behind the study door, but knocked anyway.

"Yes?"

The fire roared, and the three clergymen sat around. Lord hadn't got them to admit their joke yet. When he'd hinted at it, they'd looked at him blankly. But he didn't press it. He was known for his subtlety, and the truth would out at some point.

"Yes, Dixon?"

"Joseph Messenger's here, Reverend."

Lord groaned. "What? Again?" He glanced at Farraday and Johnson. "Is this more of your chaffing?"

"Don't know what you mean, old man," said Johnson.

"I have no idea what you're talking about," Farraday echoed his friend.

"Hmm. We shall see. Dixon, did he say why he was here again? I only was there this afternoon."

"He says it's back again, sir."

"What— the skull? It can't be. I saw it smash."

He turned to Farrady and Johnson, who were not laughing. Not even the ghost of a smile haunted their smug faces. This was exactly the kind of prank they would enjoy, but he had to give them their due. They were keeping the joke well.

"It can't be the same skull."

"Should I let him in?"

"Lord, no."

"Then sir, should I send him away?"

"No, I'll come out."

Farraday said, "You can't go up to Hannah Hall again, Henry. It's after dark."

"Very good, Farraday. But I will see this joke through to its end. Then we will see who's smiling. No one gets the better of Henry Lord."

Tight-lipped, Lord listened to Messenger, who appeared terrified. The two women who sat on the cart as they had been too scared to stay at Hannah Hall. Damn them, but they were good actors for such common people without education. One would think they'd been schooled at the Lyceum under Garrick the way they held their abject looks and even trembled as if with terror.

"It can't be the same skull. This is some trick."

"It is the same, sir," said Elizabeth Coulthard. "The very same, without doubt."

"We shall see," Lord said. "I will get on your cart and we shall go up forthwith."

Within fifteen minutes, they were back at Hannah Hall. Lamps had been left lit, but their yellow glow gave an eerie cast to the hall as if it were full of eyes.

The skull was in the attic. Lord had been convinced this was a joke, but now, as he saw it, he felt the first whisper of fear, the first feather of disquiet, the first uncertainty that unsettled his stomach and brought moisture to his palms and brow.

"It's been chosen because it so resembles the first," Lord said.

"It is the same," said Joseph Messenger. "God strike me down if I lie. I would for anything it was not, but it is the very same."

The evil, ancient thing sat, and though it was dead, it lived. It was filled with a malign intensity, a personality, and it haunted them.

"Bring me a hammer and tongs," Lord said.

Joseph Messenger went to the grate downstairs and got fire tongs and sent Mary to the shed where he kept his tools for an iron lump hammer, and together they brought these to Lord, who took them with grim determination.

"I will see an end to this, Messenger. I will not be made a fool of."

As if now afraid to touch the skull with his hands, Lord gripped it in the tongs and took it down to the hearth downstairs. He placed it on the sandstone apron in front of the fire, and bade them bank up the fire with wood and coal until they thought the blaze might set the chimney afire.

Then, when the fire burned yellow and the coals glowed almost white in the air that sucked up the flue, he grasped the skull with the tongs in his left hand and raised the iron lump hammer in his right.

He brought it down with a mighty blow and smashed the skull into three large pieces and many smaller ones, some so small as to be no more than a boney grit. And not satisfied, he raised the hammer again and muttered through clenched teeth. "No one makes a fool of Henry Lord." And he brought the heavy hammer down again mercilessly, breaking the sandstone hearth under the skull as much as he pulverised the skull. And when there were only pieces the size of eggshells, he took the coal shovel and the fire brush and swept them up and threw the bone bits into the heart of the blazing fire. And he watched them burn.

They all watched them burn, and they all saw that the skull was completely destroyed.

"And so, we tried earth, water, and now fire," Mary Messenger said. "Pray that fire puts an end to the cursed thing."

"Amen."

"Enough of this tomfoolery," Lord said. "It is late. Drive me home."

And Joseph Messenger was glad to do so.

That should be the end. True, the noises disappeared. The disturbances were gone, and the sense of a presence in Hannah Hall vanished. Joseph Messenger was seen to smile again. He and his wife were more loving, and they blessed the maid with praise, kind words, and a day off.

And then, after three weeks, a tragedy occurred. The Right Reverend Henry Lord was mounting his horse from the mounting block he always used by the church wall, when the horse shied, spooked by something none of the others could see. Henry Lord was thrown from the horse, and his head struck the stone wall that stood at the churchyard's edge nearby. He was killed instantly.

Henry Lord had been an important man, and many came to bury

him, including the Messengers. They felt they were in his debt for his lifting the curse of the skull from their home.

Henry Lord was buried in St. Bees churchyard.

And two days after his burial, the haunting came back to Hannah Hall. A piercing scream rang out in the night, and knowing from where it came, Joseph Messenger climbed the attic stairs with his lamp in hand. He went into the room and saw nothing. And then he approached the small green door and drew back the bolt.

With a beating heart, he lifted his lamp and saw that the brick niche was no longer empty. Sitting there was a human skull. But this was not the same skull. It was not old and brown. It was fresh and white. But it had the same presence. The same personality The same evil.

The Messengers left Hannah Hall before it was dawn. They went back to Maryport to Joseph's father's farm and stayed there until they took another tenancy near Sebergham two months later. They never went back to Hannah Hall, and the place stood empty. As I said, it was demolished some decades later after falling into dereliction. Whether the second skull was in the house when it was demolished, I don't know.

One odd fact is that in 1981, when archaeologists were working in St. Bees church after the finding of the famous St Bees man, they had to move some of the graves and reinter them later.

One of those graves was that of the old head of the Theological College, the Right Reverend Henry Lord.

A volunteer opened the grave and noticed that the Reverend's skull was missing, though the rest of his skeleton was intact.

The reason behind the missing skull remains unknown.

CHAPTER 9

THE SECRET OF PIEL WYKE

What I'm going to read to you falls into two parts.

The first section is a planned book by John Graham, a journalist who spent many years working for *The Times & Star*, titled "The Secret of Piel Wyke." Unfortunately, the book was never finished because John Graham disappeared before he could publish it.

Being West Cumbrian, everybody knows everybody, and my mother knew his mother, and so the manuscript came to me.

After the part of the book that John Graham wrote, which is preserved as a typescript, there are further handwritten notes and diary entries about the 'Piel Wyke' incident. These represent an extended version of the story that appeared in *The Times & Star* in the autumn of 1976. The story was syndicated to the national newspapers and was quite well-known at the time.

It's odd that it is almost forgotten now.

So here we are: "*The Secret of Piel Wyke*" by John Graham, unpublished:

This is a true story. It happened as I tell it. The newspapers at that time reported the incident as a simple 'disappearance'. Yet,

132

when you read between the lines, it's clear that it was far more than a simple disappearance.

It was the summer of 1976, with its long, hot days, endless sunshine, and a plague of ladybirds. Peter Aston was a GP engineer, from Cockermouth, who'd moved away after he got his HNCs and found work in Birmingham. He'd lived in that city ever since.

His wife, Louise, was a housewife. Peter and Louise had two children: Amanda, their daughter, aged 12, and a son, Raymond, aged 10.

Despite living two hundred miles away, Peter maintained his connection with his home area and, most summers, rented a holiday cottage near Cockermouth, usually within the boundaries of the Lake District National Park.

In 1976, Peter rented a cottage at Wythop Mill for two weeks. He and his wife liked the quietness of the area, and the children enjoyed playing in the extensive woods and by the lake.

The rented cottage nestled under the slopes of the fells and was about a mile from one of Peter's favourite watering holes—the Pheasant Inn.

Peter went there often. He liked the olde-worlde bar of the Pheasant, and he would often go to sink a pint and chat with the locals while Louise took the kids to sail in their rubber dinghy on Bassenthwaite Lake. Sometimes the whole family would gather for a bar meal at the Pheasant or the Wheatsheaf in Embleton. If they were at the Pheasant, they were happy to sit in the bar chatting while the children went out to play in the forestry plantations behind the inn on the slopes of Sale Fell or on the old hill fort called Piel Wyke, lost among the trees.

Things were simpler then, and parents didn't worry about their children playing outside all day. The weather was wonderful; it was light for hours, and it didn't seem that much harm could come to them.

After their drinks, Peter and Louise would stroll back to the cottage. Sometimes the children would come back with them, but if they were happy playing, they were allowed to stay out until supper-time, when they would find their own way home.

Over the weeks they were there, the family fell into a routine. A few cans of McEwans for him while Louise had a gin and tonic as she prepared the evening meal. Peter would read his novel, and about seven p.m., the children would return to the rented cottage, brown with the sun, green with grass-stains, sometimes grazed and blood-ied, but always grinning.

"I wonder what they find to do all day." Louise said one evening, while preparing a chicken fricassee. She was a slim, blonde woman in a brown dress, younger than her husband by five years.

Peter, his dark curly hair now greying at the ends and with a bit of a belly under his tank top, hardly looked up from his cowboy book. "Climb trees, dig holes, and dam the becks." He shrugged. "I suppose they have friends."

Louise said, "I don't see many other kids in the area."

Peter said, "There are other kids on holiday in the area. There's the little caravan field towards Thornthwaite and other rented cottages. Anyway, they seem to find lots to do."

When the children returned, Louise told them to go wash their hands. That done, Amanda and Raymond sat around the formica-topped table, and as their mother served out the fricassee, she said, "What do you find to do all day out there?"

Amanda said, "There's plenty to do, mum. We've got a den, and we make up games."

Peter said, "You'd better be careful in the old forestry. There's stumps and branches hidden in the grass, and you could break your ankle if you don't watch out."

"We don't want any broken ankles or trips to Whitehaven Hospi-tal," Louise said.

While they were eating, she said, "Do you have any friends? I'd hate to think you were lonely."

Peter thought he saw Raymond shoot a glance at Amanda, but

his daughter smiled and said, "We do have some friends. We're not lonely. We've got loads to play at."

Peter, who always had an interest in archaeology, said, "Do you ever go onto the hill between The Pheasant and the lake? That's called Piel Wyke. It's an old Celtic hill fort, but you can't see much. Not that I've been there for years—too many trees now." Peter shook his head. "They shouldn't have allowed the Forestry Commission to plant on that ancient monument."

His wife said, "Nobody cares about old things now, Peter. Kids these days think about the future—whether they'll live on Mars, or play synthesisers in a rock band." She laughed. "They're not interested in a fuddy-duddy old hill fort."

Peter said, "Anyway, who are your friends, kids?"

"Locals," Amanda said.

"What, like farmers' children or foresters'?"

"I don't know what their parents do."

"You should ask. Where do they live?"

"In the woods," Raymond said.

"They live in the woods? Which woods?"

"They must be foresters' kids," Louise said. "They've got some cottages towards Thornthwaite."

"That'll be it," Peter said. "You should ask them, though. I might know their family."

Louise laughed. "You still think you're a local. You've lived in Birmingham for fifteen years. Once you leave Cumberland, that's it. The connection's gone and you're just another incomer when you come back."

Peter looked hurt. "I'm Cumberland born and bred."

She sighed. "Of course you are. Now eat your fricassee before it gets cold."

The next day, Peter suggested they go for a mooch around Keswick. Louise asked the kids if they wanted to come.

"No, thanks." Raymond said. "We're going to our den." He stood, auburn-haired, freckled by the sun, his legs and arms as thin as pipe-cleaners.

Amanda, ever the older, wiser sister, with her oval face and confident hazel eyes, said, "Yes, we're building a rampart."

Peter tried to cajole. "We can go to the model shop. I'll get you that Airfix Spitfire, Raymond."

The lad looked tempted. His eyes lit up and his mouth curved into a smile, but his sister tugged at his jumper. "We've got to build the rampart today, Ray."

Raymond sighed and shook his head. "I can't today, dad. Could we maybe go next week?"

Peter looked disappointed, but said, "Sure, sure. Of course. Your mum and I will go. Are you sure you'll be all right playing out all day?"

Louise said, "I'll put the door key under the plant pot in case you come back before we do."

"We won't come back until teatime."

"I mean, if it rains or something," Louise said.

Peter pointed through the porch window at the porcelain blue sky. It was hot already. "Not a cloud in sight. I don't think it's going to rain."

"But just in case they need to come back — in case anything happens."

"We'll be fine, mum," Amanda said. "Come on, Raymond, let's go to the den."

Peter and Amanda watched their children skip down the garden path, pass through the green-painted wooden gates, and vanish down the lane.

He said, "Oh, the joys of being young, eh, Lou?"

His wife laughed. "Come on, let's go to Keswick. We can have a bar meal at the Dog and Gun."

It was August, with only three weeks left of the school holidays. On a clear day, and it was always clear that summer, it got dark at about 9 p.m.

After dusk, the heat sat on the land and simmered inside the houses, so everyone slept with the covers thrown off and the windows wide open. If there were lights on inside, in fluttered hordes of white moths and spindly-legged Jinny Spinners.

The owls hooted in the trees as Peter and Amanda, long back from Keswick, sat in the front room watching TV. It was still sweltering. They'd enjoyed *The Bionic Woman* and *Morecambe and Wise,* but it was now a *Panorama* about pollution, and they were hardly paying attention.

"They should have been back before dark. I've told them to be back before dark," Peter said.

"Do you think we should go out and look for them?"

He sipped his tea. "There's a torch in the kitchen. Let's give them another ten minutes, and then we'll go."

Time passed. Silence grew. Amanda said, "I'm switching this boring rubbish off." She shook her head. "Where do you think they are?"

Peter frowned. "I'll tan their hides for this. They're not going out tomorrow. They can come with us."

"Come on, let's go and look. You said ten minutes. It's been ten minutes."

He checked his watch. "Seven."

"Doesn't matter. Let's go."

Peter stood.

He fetched the torch, and they stepped out of the cottage, not locking it behind them. Light glimmered in the west towards the coast. The sun was down, but the day lingered, reluctant to leave. The west glowed red, but the east sank blue. It was dark that way where the still trees stood on the silent hills — hordes of them, like an army, unmoving and dense.

Louise said, "Their den is down past The Pheasant, isn't it?"

"Piel Wyke, I thought. The hill fort."

"Let's not wait around, Pete. I'm worried. I think something's happened."

The parents went out of the garden gate, torch in Peter's right hand. He flashed it around in front, its yellow beam falling like an eye on the road on the stone walls and the sleeping bracken.

Then they heard running footsteps — children's footsteps. There was the sound of stifled giggles as the children ran through the darkness, rounding the corner of the road.

"It's them," Amanda said.

The kids appeared in the circle of light from Peter's shifting torch. He yelled, "Where the hell have you been?"

Louise snapped, "Get in this minute! You did *not* have permission to stay out so late."

The children stopped, lit up by the circle of torchlight, shamefaced, round-shouldered, eyes averted. "Are we in trouble?" Raymond muttered.

Peter was furious. "You're ruddy right, you're in trouble. Get home this instant! Straight to bed. What on earth were you thinking, staying out so late?"

"We were with our friends," Raymond said, chin down.

"If their mothers and fathers are decent folk, they'll get a rocket too for staying out after dark."

No one spoke as the children walked home beside their parents.

At the cottage, the porch light illuminated their round faces. Despite the telling off, they seemed full of excitement, thrilled even. But when their angry parents looked at them, they fell silent.

"What's that you have in your hand, Raymond?" Louise said.

The boy clutched the object to him as if his mother had caught him out.

She repeated, "What is it?"

"It's only a head."

His father said, "A head? What are you talking about?"

He replied, "Amanda's got one too."

His father said, "A head? Make sense, lad. Show me."

The boy opened his fist and displayed a round stone the size of a small apple. It glittered in the electric light, a myriad tiny crystals sparkling like mica in granite.

Peter reached out to take the stone, but Raymond moved his hand away.

"Give it to me, Raymond."

Eyes downcast, almost crying, the boy finally handed the stone to his father.

Peter took it and weighed it in his palm. It was heavier than he expected and hot in his hand, and, as he held it, it tingled as if it held an electrical charge.

Peter turned the head over. It had the carved features of a man — a slit mouth, lentil-shaped eyes, and a ridge for a nose. That was it, nothing sophisticated.

"Did you get these from the hill fort?" Louise said. "They look..." She searched for the right word, "... archaeological."

Peter said, "Let me look at yours, Amanda."

The girl showed her father the small stone head. It was like her brother's, but not identical. The face was more sophisticated somehow, its expression crueller.

"Where did you get these?"

"Our friends gave them to us."

"These friends you talk about! I have a good mind to look up their parents and have a word with them for leading you into such naughtiness. You shouldn't be taking ancient artefacts from historical sites."

"I don't know where they got them," Raymond said.

"From Piel Wyke," Amanda whispered.

"So they dug them up and gave them to you?"

Amanda said, "They didn't dig them up. They have lots of them. They just have them. I think they make them."

"What are the names of these friends of yours?"

Amanda said, "I don't know their names. They're just our friends."

Raymond said, "I don't think they have names at all. They don't speak words. They just talk into your head — like a dream."

Louise sighed. "Now you're just talking silly. You're overtired. Get to bed, and I don't want to hear a peep out of you until morning."

Later — it must have been about 2 a.m. because it was pitch black—Peter jerked awake and lay listening. Next to him, Louise breathed gently, in and out, a slight sigh with each out-breath. At first, he thought the noise had been in his dream, and he had dragged it with him to the waking world, but the noise trembled behind the darkness.

Louise woke beside him with a start. "What's that smell?"

Peter smelled it too: ozone — an electric smell like something shorted out, or a coil glowing too magnetic and failing, crackling into fire.

Louise blurted, "Are we safe?"

Peter sat up in bed, listening to that otherworldly fizzing noise, aware of the odour of ozone, as if power were being channelled into their house. The ozone smell buzzed.

Are we safe? she'd said. The first thing she said But she was half asleep, dragging her own dreams back with her.

Of course, they were safe. How could they not be safe? They were in a pretty little holiday rental at Wythop, under the shadow of the friendly fells he'd known since boyhood.

And then he knew. They weren't safe. The fells weren't friendly. Things had lived here before men arrived. These things were old. They had messages. What messages?

What an odd thought. He pressed the little rocker switch at the base of the lamp on his bedside table. The light clicked on yellow and inadequate.

He stared at Louise.

She was staring at him, too. "Your hair's standing on end!"

So was hers.

She laughed. He laughed. But it wasn't funny; it was the strained, over-jovial laughter of people coming round from anaesthetics.

A noise lurched in the house—something heavy, something hard to place. It came from outside their door on the landing.

Louise's voice went quiet. "What was that?"

"Do you think the kids are awake?"

"I don't know." He lay there, listening.

With both hands, Louise smoothed down her hair, but it forced its way back up like she'd touched something electric.

He laughed again. Maybe it *was* funny. He wasn't sure. He felt like he'd breathed in laughing gas. He touched his own hair.

"It's sticking up again," Louise said. She started laughing, canned laughter—like from an American sitcom that wasn't funny, but the laughter came anyway.

What a funny thing. He felt like laughing. He felt ill.

"Check on the kids," she whispered.

Peter swung out his legs and stood beside the bed in his pyjama bottoms. He'd taken the top off because it was too hot.

"What's all this electricity?" she said. "Do you think there's a short circuit?"

Peter worked with current; he knew electricity. Short circuits made no sense. He shook his head.

"Check on the kids," she whispered.

He didn't move.

"What's the matter?" she said.

"I don't know."

"Do you think it's the electricity gone wrong?"

"No, no. This is static."

"How?"

"Well..." He had no answer.

"Go on," she said. "Go out. See the kids."

"I will."

"Go then."

The door had a plain, angled aluminium handle. He reached out. His hand flew back. "It's live!"

She said, "What? How can that be? Static, you said."

He shook his head. "It's not the mains. That would have killed me. It's just static. It must be the weather."

"Go to the kids. I'm scared."

Peter got his pyjama top, wrapped it round his fist, and gingerly grasped the door handle. It buzzed, but he pushed the handle down, opening the door.

The landing filled up with silence. The deep quiet of the country-side pooled and gathered, pouring in from the woods and hills. Moonlight splashed in through the hall window, white and cold.

No buzz now, but it wasn't gone; it was waiting.

The children had a bedroom each at the end of the hall. He went to Amanda first. She was his favourite, though he'd never say so. Pyjama jacket round his hand, he touched the handle of her door. No static. But the door seemed to open by itself. He told himself it was to do with weight and the hinges. It was normal. Of course it was.

He whispered, "Mandy?"

He couldn't hear her breathing.

His heart hammered. "Mandy?" he said again, stepping in, his knee pushing the door wider. "Are you asleep, baby?"

Amanda had her curtains open. How could she sleep with all that moonlight?

But Amanda wasn't asleep. She lay rigid in her bed, her hands on the top of the blanket, pulled up to her nose. "Daddy," she said. "They're here."

He stared. "What?"

"Don't look."

"Who's here? What do you mean, Mandy?"

"Our friends."

"Your friends that you play with in the woods? The ones that gave you those silly little stone heads? They're here?"

She whimpered. "Yes, daddy. Don't look."

"Don't look where? How can they be here? It's the middle of the night. They'll be home with their mummy and daddy. We locked the house doors. How can they be here?"

"Don't look."

"It's just a nightmare, Mandy."

"No, daddy. It isn't. Don't look at them."

"They can't be here, Mandy. How can they be here?"

"Don't look, daddy. Please."

"Don't look where?"

Peter turned.

John Graham, the journalist, wrote this. It was to be part of the book he never finished. Checking his personal notes, we see he interviewed the Astons the next day.

In John Graham's handwritten notes, it says Peter Aston said he remembered turning around. He remembered there was something behind him, but he didn't remember what. It was something jarringly odd, something he didn't want to remember.

When he was next conscious of time, it was 8 a.m. and daylight. He was lying on the landing floor, and everyone else in the house was in a deep sleep. Peter had shaken his wife awake and then his son and daughter. They all remembered *something* being in the house.

Louise told John Graham that someone had been talking to her. She said it had lentil-shaped eyes and a mouth that was "too big for eating". With her hands covering her face, she whispered, "If it wasn't for eating, then its mouth must be for something else."

John Graham asked her what the thing's mouth was for, and Louise broke down. She seemed to retreat into a world of madness.

But Raymond and Amanda told him that was what their friends looked like — with a mouth 'too big for eating', whatever that meant. And the kids explained that they'd never said the friends were children. Their parents had just assumed it. The friends were never children. Never had been children. They weren't people. They had never been people. The children didn't know what they were.

John Graham asked, So who are these friends? Where did they come from?"

Raymond said, "They come from the ground. There's a place in the ground that they come from."

"Those old stones in the wood? Is that where they're from?"

He said, "There's a crack in the world. It goes to another place."

Amanda said, "We used to go into the ground and into their place. It isn't like here. They want us to go back with them."

When her children talked about the other place, even though she was in the other room, and couldn't have heard what they were saying, Louise started to scream. She said she knew where it was. She was shaking. Peter got her some brandy.

John asked her why she'd screamed.

Louise said, "The place in the ground is a terrible place. It's a place where things with faces live among the dead. But these things are not dead. They were never born." She started shaking. She whispered. "I think they come from the stars."

John Graham reports that he left the family in the house and drove to Workington to consult the local archaeology collection in the library. There he found the legend of Piel Wyke. All down the centuries, local people said it was haunted. Apparently, many people had seen creatures with slit eyes and big mouths, and shortly afterwards, all those people disappeared.

An account in 1780 by a woman named Martha Taylor from Bassenthwaite said that there was a fairy fort at Piel Wyke, and the creatures there would snatch anyone who saw them and drag them down into a place in the ground.

The next morning, John Graham went to work at the Times & Star Office on Oxford Street and typed up the interviews with the Astons. He said he had some further questions for the Aston children and drove to the rental cottage, hoping to find them there. He wanted to go to Piel Wyke, anyway, so he thought he'd kill two birds with one stone.

When he got to the cottage, the front door hung wide open. He stepped in and called out for the family, but there was no answer. It looked as if they'd just stepped out. The previous night's dinner plates sat unwashed in the sink, and their coats were gone. It was another boiling hot day, so why would they need their coats?

John Graham went to Piel Wyke and wandered around in the woods, looking for the hole in the rock that the children had gone into. He didn't find it. Weirdly, he says his watch stopped dead — even though it was a new quartz one—and that he found a little stone head lying on the path. He said it was just like the ones the children had been given by their 'friends'.

Graham wrote that he thought that it was put there for him to find. But he doesn't say directly by whom.

After wandering the archaeological remains, such as they are, John went for a pint in the Pheasant back bar, and he asked if anyone there had seen Peter and Louise Aston. No one had. Someone thought they might have gone to Keswick.

After that, John dropped in on the cottage again, hoping to catch them. But he never did.

Two days later, he reported them as missing, and the police got involved.

The police checked with the Astons' employers and school in Birmingham, but they never returned home. Neither were they ever seen around Wythop or Cockermouth again.

They'd simply disappeared.

It was a real Marie Celeste job, and it got the attention of all the national papers, and John Graham had his fifteen minutes of fame, even getting interviewed by John Craven.

But the story died down and was forgotten. It was almost like someone snuffed it out — as if someone didn't want anyone enquiring into it. John became convinced that the story was being suppressed. His notes start to have some odd ideas in them about intruders in his house, and he seems to have gone back time and time again to Piel Wyke, as if searching for something.

And that's it, really. That's the end of the story. John Graham started drinking heavily. He quit his job at the Times & Star, or maybe he was fired. He became a recluse, and then, one day, his house was found unlocked, the door wide open, and the place empty, with a radio still playing. John had gone somewhere. No one ever found out where he went.

One last thing: in the 1780 report, Martha Taylor, the woman from Bassenthwaite, says that the folk in the fort don't want to be found. They don't want you to think about them, but they'll know when you do.

She says: don't go near them, don't let them into your thoughts, and put them from your mind before they hear you thinking.

But it's all nonsense, of course. How could those things even exist — coming into your locked house at night, entering your private dreams, knowing the thoughts you tell no one?

Martha Taylor vanished too.

So, just to be on the safe side: let's try not to think about them. Don't imagine them with their lentil-shaped eyes and mouths too big for eating. Put them out of your mind.

Can you do that?

Things with faces and mouths too big for eating.

No, neither can I.

CHAPTER 10

BELLA SHEEP HEAD RETURNS

Jordan sat in the darkened car, which was parked on a gravel strip on the road's edge. He stared through the windscreen at the bushes. "I'd finished work, and I didn't want to go home, so I just kept driving."

Ryan shrugged. "Yeah, well, you're just on your own, aren't you?'

Jordan didn't look at him, he just kept on with his story. "Aye, so I'm belting down the straight bit past the Dump. You know where I mean? And I swear I didn't see it. But even if I'd seen it, there's not much I could have done because I was really bombing, like. But I wouldn't do it on purpose, you know me."

"Yeah, I know you — sure, sure. So what was it?"

Jordan laughs, but not like it's funny. "It was a bloody lamb."

Ryan shakes his head. "A lamb? At this time of year? Had it got loose from a field?"

"No, it was somebody's pet lamb, but I didn't know that at the time. Bloody hell, what a bang! I knew I'd hit summat. It was dark-ish. I had my headlights on. I mean, not completely dark, but on the way. It gets dark this time of year, about half past five."

"I know. It's terrible, depressing." Ryan lit his cigarette and offered Jordan the packet. Jordan waved it away.

The dashboard lights cast a glow on their faces. They'd had the radio on, but Jordan turned it off when he started his story, like it was important that he be heard.

Ryan lit his cigarette from the car lighter. Then he said, "Anyway, what about this lamb?"

"Bust me headlight. Bloody blood all over the bonnet and bumper."

"Bloody blood, ha!"

"Don't be soft, man. It was awful. That bang, and I knew I'd hit summat, but I couldn't really see, and you know, I thought I'd mebbe hit a person."

"But you hadn't. I mean, it was a lamb. It's not great, but it's not like hitting a person."

"Yeah, I know that, but I didn't then. I was in bits, man. I slammed the brakes on, screeched to a halt, and pulled it up on the pavement. Just where the road crests and you come into Broughton Moor — before the houses, you know? There was a lass there."

"Aye, I know where you mean. So what was left of the lamb?"

"Nowt much. I seen the front of my car first, and I'd dragged this poor laal thing along. I mean, it was dead. It was just like a blood-stained rag."

"It wouldn't have felt owt."

"Mebbe. I don't know."

"It was quick. So what about this lass?"

"Jeez. Well, the next thing I heard was this wailing. She was screaming and yelling."

"The lass? What's it got to do with her?"

"The lass. The lass the lamb belonged to."

"It was her lamb?"

"Yes. Her pet lamb."

"A pet lamb? Well, what did she think she was doing, letting it out on the road on a dark night?"

"I don't know. I mean, it was her fault."

"It was. It's totally her fault. Silly cow."

"She freaked me out though with the screaming, and she just come out of the dark. It was proper dark by then."

Jordan paused. "I will have a cigarette."

Ryan took one from the packet, lit it, and handed it to him. He noticed Jordan's hand was shaking. His face glowed orange in the dashboard lights. They had CFM on, but on mute.

"Then what happened?"

"I was standing there beside the car. Nothing passed us like. The road was empty. And she comes up, and I shit you not. She's smeared in blood."

"Blood? The lamb's blood?"

"Not just the lamb's blood."

"So whose blood then?"

"Her own."

Ryan frowned and shook his head. He could hardly see his friend in the half-light. "What — did you hit her too?"

Jordan took a drag and exhaled. "That's what I thought. First, I thought I'd hit her, and I thought I'd go to jail. I'd lose my job — licence anyway, and then I'd lose my job."

"But you never hit her though?"

"No, but she was all covered in blood."

"What? How come?"

"There was a bit of the lamb on the road. She'd picked it up and smeared herself with it. And she had a knife. She'd cut open her own arms in a frenzy and mixed the blood with the lamb's. And then she'd rubbed the blood on her face, and he was screaming at me: 'Did you kill my lamb? Did you kill my lamb?' Over and over."

"Bloody hell. She had a knife? And all because of a lamb?"

"I felt terrible. Honest, Ry, I did."

"Yeah, sure, but it was only a lamb. It wasn't a kid."

"No, but it was her pet lamb. She told me that. Screamed it at me.

She kept asking me if I'd killed her lamb, like she didn't know. And there she was smeared in blood."

"She's a fruit loop, man. They should lock her up. Anyway, who was it?"

"Don't know. I've never seen her before. Just a young lass, ey."

"Bo Peep."

"What?"

"Bo Peep. She had a lamb."

"Shut up! You're tapped, Ryan. It wasn't effing Bo Peep."

"Who was she then?"

"I said I don't know. I've never seen her before."

"She off the Moor?"

"No. I'd know her. Not Great Broughton nor Laal Broughton neither."

"Mebbe fra' Cockermouth?"

"If she was from Cockermouth, what was she doing walking along that road by the Dump on that dark road with a lamb and a carving knife?"

Ryan shook his head. "Dunno, marra. Just yan of them things."

"It was a weird thing. She must have had a phone, but she never called the police. She just screamed at me, then vanished."

"Vanished. What do you mean?"

"One minute she was there and the next she wasn't."

"You what?"

"I'm telling you. It was freaky."

For those who don't know Broughton Moor, "The Dump" is an extensive area of now overgrown land that has been rewilded, as I suppose they'd call it now. It was a coal mine — Buckland Colliery — that was opened in 1873 and closed in 1932. In 1939, the British Government took over the site for the storage of ammunition. They held it until 1973, when it was leased to the US Navy. They used it as a storage site for NATO armaments until New Year's Eve 1992, when it was decommissioned. It's been disused since then. And empty.

The site is still fenced off and heavily contaminated. At least that's what they say to keep people out.

Rumours have it that they stored nuclear weapons in the old mine tunnels. Rumours upon rumours say that the nuclear weapons leaked and that the tunnels are radioactive. But those are only rumours. We wouldn't want to get involved in any conspiracy theories.

Two days later.

"What a bloody awful dream I had last night," Ryan said. They were parked up in the same place. Again, it was dark. He took the cigarette the first time Jordan offered it to him. "It was a proper nightmare," he said.

"What did you dream about?"

"That bloody lass was all smeared in blood, screaming. And I could see her better than when she was on the street. Her eyes were pure black."

"Black? In the dream?"

"Yeah, in the dream. And she was crawling on the floor, trying to get to where I was."

"In your house?"

"Yeah. In the dream it was in my house."

"The house going okay, by the way?"

"Yeah. I mean, it's too big. I'm not there much, just to sleep. I go to me mam and dad's for tea most nights."

"Still, at least you got it."

"Yeah, but my nana had to die for me to get it, but sure, I got it."

Ryan watched his friend. Jordan stared out into the windscreen, the lights from the turned-down radio turning his face orange. He said, "Gis another fag, eh?"

"Sure, sure. You smoked that one fast."

"I'm rattled."

Ryan shrugged. "So anyway. Do you want to talk about this dream, or not? I don't mind."

"I want to talk about it. See, in the dream, the lass had come out of the tunnels."

"The tunnels under the Dump?"

"Yeah, the old mine tunnels. But that isn't the worst bit."

"Right."

Ryan held the cigarette between his thumb and index finger. The smoke curled up and twisted round and round. It filled the car up, and Jordan wound the window down to let it out. Cold air drained in from outside. It had been raining and felt damp.

Jordan turned to his friend, licking his lips as if trying to moisten them. "You know I said she had black eyes?"

"Yeah."

"She did. But they were in a sheep's head."

"You what?"

"She had a sheep's head on her shoulders."

"Woo. That's weird."

"She's in that house."

"What, mate?"

"She's in that house. My house. When I go back, I feel she's there."

"But she can't be, though."

"No, I know. But she is. She comes in."

A long pause ensued. Ryan screwed up his eyes. He considered his cigarette. He said, "How much did it cost you to get the car fixed? It looks mint now."

"Nowt."

"I thought you said the headlight was bust?"

Jordan shrugged. "I thought it was. But when I looked in the daylight, it was okay. I must have got it wrong."

"But you saw it bust, though?"

"I thought I did." Jordan drew on his cigarette, breathed out, and said, "It was dark, and hitting that lamb freaked me out, and then Bella screaming her head off at me."

"Bella?"

"Bella. Yeah, that's what they call her."

"I thought you didn't know her.'

"She told me."

"When? That night on the road?"

"No. In my dream. Bella Sheep Head. That's her name."

Ryan rubbed his mouth. "Fancy a pint — at the Miner's?"

"Nah, I'm driving."

Ryan said, "Why don't you come round to ours tomorrow? My mam won't mind. It's pizza night. You like pepperoni, don't you? She gets them from Domino's in Workington — two for one. Come on, why don't you? At least you won't be in that big house on your own."

"My nana's house."

"Sure. Me mam'd be glad to see you."

"Aye, maybe. Don't know what I'm doing tomorrow."

"You don't want to be spending too much time on your own in that house."

"Honest, Ry, I'm hardly there. I'm at work all day and then I go to my mam and dad's and I only go back to my nana's house to dream."

"To dream? To sleep, you mean."

"Aye, sure."

"Is it not lonely?"

"Not really."

"Well, that's good."

"I've got my nana to keep me company."

"Oh." Ryan paused. He tilted his head and said softly, "You okay, Jord? You just seem—"

"No, I'm all right."

"Just that, like, you know — your nana's dead."

"Duh! Yeah, I know. I was at the funeral. Of course, I know she's dead. It's just Bella. When she visits, she brings them all back with her."

"What?"

"They're all in the tunnels. They come into the house. They come with her. Anyway, it's getting late. Time for bed. I'll drive you back."

Jordan didn't come to Ryan's house for his tea the next night. He didn't answer his phone. He wasn't seen at work. Ryan left messages, but Jordan left them on read. He'd seen them; he just didn't choose to reply.

Ryan didn't hear from Jordan until lunchtime the next day.

"Hiya, mate. Sorry, I was out. Want to go for a drive tonight? The usual."

Ryan said yes. Jordan picked him up at his house, and they drove around. They went up to Aspatria, and cross-country to Allonby, then back to Maryport taking the top way from Ellenborough to Broughton Moor via Harker Marsh.

Jordan parked up where he always parked. On the pull over spot, off the back road, by the sycamore trees. It had been light when Ryan picked him up. It was dark now. They smoked.

Ryan said, "How was work?"

"I didn't go."

"Why didn't you go?"

"She's told me not to. She said I didn't need to go anymore because I'm going to be opened up."

Ryan shook his head. "What you talking about, marra? Who's 'she'?"

"Bella. I told you — Bella. It's always Bella."

Ryan sighed. "Jordan, I think you should maybe see a doctor. I don't think you're well, mate."

Jordan laughed. "I know I'm not well. But she's going to make me better. Bella is."

"Can I make you an appointment with the doctor? Will you go?"

Jordan shook his head vigorously. "No. There's no point. I'm going to be opened up."

"You said that before. What do you mean — opened up?" Ryan studied Jordan. His face looked strange in the orange light from the instrument lights on the dashboard.

"She can do it with her fingers. Her nails are really sharp. They're like knives. She can do it. She's from the tunnels. I think it's the radiation that changed her."

"Changed her into what?"

Jordan laughed. "Are you stupid? She's got a sheep's head."

"You're scaring me a bit, Jord."

"Well, you should be scared."

"What do you mean, I should be scared?"

"Cause she might open you up too."

Ryan said, "None of this is true, Jord. There was no lamb. There is no Bella Sheep Head. It's just your mind. You're sick, mate. You need a doctor."

Jordan turned and smiled at him. The window was open to let out the cigarette smoke. "That's what you think," Jordan said. "She's out there. She's waiting. She'll be coming soon. She says I have to keep you here in the car with me. My nana's coming too."

Ryan said, "I'm honestly worried about you."

Jordan said, "Listen, I'm sorry, Ry."

"Sorry, what for?"

"It was dark and she didn't know me. I don't think she's used to people, so I thought I could get away with it. I am sorry, but it was either you or me."

Ryan studied his friend, who stared out of the windscreen. "Will you drive me home now, mate?"

"No. You've got to stay here. I mean. I did lie, but she is coming now. She says I've got to stop you if you try to leave."

Quietly, Ryan moved his hand to the door handle.

"I see you. What do you think you're doing, Ry? I told you, you've got to stop here until she comes. You don't want to upset her. She's nasty."

Ryan pulled the handle, shoved the door, and ran. His feet pounded the asphalt road between the tall dykes over-canopied by diseased sycamores and brooding oaks.

A hundred yards later, he turned, gasping, and looked back at the dark shape of the car, to see if Jordan had followed him. Lit by the dashboard lights inside, but faintly, faintly, he saw Jordan's silhouette, smoking, waiting.

He should go back and help him. Maybe call an ambulance. Get a doctor. The guy was crazy, imagining all sorts of stuff. He might even be dangerous.

A noise.

Ryan turned. A dark shape detached itself from the sycamore trees.

"Who's that?" he said.

The thing didn't reply. But it came closer.

"Who's this? What are you doing?"

It grabbed him, and its fingernails cut into his arms. He pulled back from the shadow of the trees, dragging it, but it didn't let go. In the better light, he saw it was an old woman.

"Who the hell are you?"

She pressed her face close to his, and held him with hands as strong as death and as cold as grief. She said, "I'm Jordan's nana."

He twisted, seeing someone else approaching from behind. This one was a young woman with the head of a sheep.

Jordan's nana said, "Bella wants you."

Bella Sheep Head sliced a knife across Ryan's throat, and as he stood bleeding, she said, "Did you kill my lamb?"

CHAPTER II

THE WHITEHAVEN BODYSNATCHER

I rang the buzzer at the front door of the house on Foxhouses Road with my elbow. Perhaps you know the house? It's one of those big old Victorian houses now divided into low-rent flats owned by some buy-to-let speculator who lives in London and has it managed by West Cumbria Properties.

The buzzer fizzed like a fly on a zapper, and at first, she didn't answer. I stood there and waited and thought she wasn't going to, and then I heard her tremulous voice. "Hello?"

I cleared my throat. "Hi, is that Molly?"

Her young-ish female voice said, "Are you from the mental health team?"

"Yeah, that's right. Are you expecting me?"

"I didn't know when it would be. I wasn't expecting you this afternoon."

"We can't be specific about time, you know, because of our work-load. But here I am. Listen, can I come in?"

She hesitated.

I said, "I can't help you if you don't let me in."

Lots of the people in these multi-occupancy houses had problems. They were all poor and dependent on benefits. Lots of them had alcohol or drug problems. Most of them are mentally ill.

So this girl's name was Molly Lewthwaite. She was local. I had done my research. I knew she'd lost touch with her family — some half-remembered dispute over something or other fuelled by drink at a funeral that ended in her mother hitting her and her storming out. There had been two or three abusive boyfriends who drifted in and out of her life. Very sad. Very common.

Molly pressed the button upstairs, and the door clicked unlocked. Again with my elbow, I took the handle, pushed it down, and opened the door. With COVID, you can't be too careful.

I looked around the entry hall, and my nose wrinkled. The shabby lobby smelled of mould, sweat, and piss. Fairly standard. I'd been here before to see other residents.

At the bottom of the stairs, there was a shelf with a plastic plant on it, and heaps of junk mail had fallen onto the floor, and someone had tidied them away with their foot. They were mainly bills and catalogues addressed to people who'd moved on.

Molly's flat was upstairs. I went up the first flight and then the second. That's where she was—flat 21.

I walked along the sticky carpet of the hall and arrived at her door. The door was open, and she was looking out with one eye. She looked to be about five two and very pale, as if she avoided the sun, and she stood like she was timid by nature.

I put on my cheery voice. "Hiya, Molly. Can I come in?"

Molly didn't speak, but she opened the door a foot. She looked unhealthy. Her hair was badly dyed black, and her roots showed brown. She wore a black cardigan whose sleeves had ridden up on their own, and on the forearms I saw a tattoo of a rose, a tattoo of the Joker, and lots of self harm scars. The older cuts were shiny white lines, the new ones angry and red.

"Come in," she whispered.

I stepped inside. The flat was small and untidy. There were cheap pictures on the wall. The kind you see in charity shops. They didn't fit her goth look, as threadbare and faded as that was, and I guessed they'd been there when she moved in and she couldn't work up the motivation to replace them.

Worn curtains were dragged across the window, cutting out what little daylight there was on that grey October day, but there probably wasn't much of a view, anyway.

Dirty mugs sat in a row like Humpty Dumpty and his men on the sideboard. The sideboard mirror was cracked. The room was stiflingly hot. An old gas fire against the wall hissed, looking likely to be leaking carbon monoxide into the room along with its ghastly heat.

The same pervasive stink of neglect as the rest of the building filled the air. But the odour of cheap joss sticks overlay it: Nag Champa, I thought, and I wasn't sure if that was an improvement. Me, I prefer my poverty plain, not covered over with cheap scent. That way, everyone knows how things stand.

"Do you want to sit down?" she said.

I looked around the room. There was a two-seater sofa, again probably from the British Heart Foundation, and third or fourth hand, and two armchairs that didn't match. At least she didn't have cats.

I sat. The room was unbearably warm.

"Will you take your coat off?"

I shook my head. "No, I'm fine. So, Molly. Like I said, I came as soon as I could. How can I help?"

She stared at me.

"Please, go on," I said.

She blurted, "There's a man who comes into this house who steals bodies."

I've heard plenty of things like this in my time. My gaze didn't flicker as I studied her face — the tremor of the lips, the eyes down-turned. I said, "Right. He comes into the house?"

"Yes."

"Into your room?"

"No. Not yet."

"But he steals bodies?"

"Yes."

"Okay, well, just to help me understand: in what way does he steal them?"

She said, "He takes them over. I hear him do it in the night. He opens them up with his sharp fingers and when they're hollow, he puts on their skin."

"He puts on their skin? Okay. But how do you know that?"

"I just know."

"But you can't see him do it." I tilted my head. "Or can you?"

"No, I can't see it. But I hear him do it. The walls are thin. I hear him talking to them. He asks them lots of questions first — lots of questions until he gets to know them and then they relax and they think he's just interested in them, like he cares, and when they're relaxed, he begins."

"He begins? Explain?"

"Like I said, he begins to open them."

"Okay." I tried a different tack. "So you hear them talking? You hear him asking them questions?"

She nodded rapidly, blinking. Her eyes were filmy with moisture, and she rubbed them with the back of her fingers and the tears and mascara smeared her hands, but she trailed them down her cheeks, leaving stains that made her look like a sad panda.

"Do you have a tissue?" I tried to put her at ease. I joked. "I always make people cry. I don't mean to — they just do."

She reached over to the top of a cabinet near her threadbare armchair and plucked out a tissue. I guessed she did a lot of crying.

She took one, then two, and dried her eyes. She squeezed tight hold of the tissues in her fist like they meant something to her.

"Are you okay?" I said. "Just I saw how upset you were. Do you feel you can go on?"

She nodded. Swallowed. It seemed she wanted to go on.

I said, "So, you were saying how you hear him talking? By the way, you don't need to tell me any of this if it upsets you."

She sighed. "No, I'll tell you. I want the help."

"Okay, well, it helps me understand what's going on with you and how I can help. Tell me a bit more."

She didn't meet my eyes. "Yes, he cuts them open with his long dirty nails."

"Dirty nails? But you said you couldn't see him."

"I know his nails are dirty, and long and sharp with dried blood under them. I just know."

"Okay."

"First, he relaxes them. And then, when he's got them quiet, he asks them to turn down the light. "

"Turn down the light? Why does he do that? "

"So they can't see his hands. The hands would give the game away. He only gets out his hands once he's turned down the light. Until this point, he's kept his hands in his pocket. And when he's asked them lots of questions and they feel like he's really interested in them, they just drop their guard and they turn down the light and in the dark he starts to work on them."

"They just let him do it?"

"Yes. But he does it gently at first, in the low light, so they don't even realise what he's doing until they're open and it's too late. He starts with their tummy and unbuttons their shirt and his nails are like knives. And they let him do it."

"But I don't see why they let him."

"Because he gets their confidence. He pretends to be someone who really cares. They're the sort of people who nobody cares about, so they're so hungry for someone's care that they're easy to fool."

"I'm sure someone cares about them."

She shook her head. She was very definite. "No, they're people who are sick. They're alcoholics. Or they're depressed. Or they've got personality disorders. Nobody wants them. Nobody ever wanted them. Everybody's left them alone. Most of the time, their own parents didn't want them, and now they live in these little flats in town where the Council puts them because they're homeless, and they get these little flats and the council stuffs all the waifs and strays together, so they don't bother decent people. And all the people with anxiety problems and mental health get put the with druggies and then the gangsters come and sell them drugs, break into their houses, and steal their stuff."

"But why don't they go to the police if that happens?"

"Because the police don't believe people like them. People like me."

I sat back. "So, you consider yourself one of these people?"

She looked at me like she'd probably looked at all the doctors, police, social workers, teachers, magistrates, probation officers, and debt counsellors all her life. To her, they were all the same — smiley do-gooders who didn't really care.

They'd come into her house to see her mother when she was a kid, and they pretended they cared, but they were really checking on little Molly to make sure her mother wasn't battering her, which she probably was, or her boyfriend was. It's all so predictable and sad, and it can't be stopped.

I knew Molly's type.

I knew all those professionals she'd seen. All the kind teachers who tried to help her at school Then there were the job advisors trying to get her work she could never do and the Citizens Advice people helping her with her debt, the drug and alcohol workers helping her with her addictions, and the community police officers, problem solvers, well-being counsellors, and CBT therapists helping her with her anxiety.

And they all always cocked their heads and listened to her inexhaustible tales of woe, knowing they could do nothing to help her make her life even just bearable. And they spoke softly of compassion, resilience-building, cognitive therapy, and antidepressants, and then sanctioned her benefits and left her to her vicious neighbours and psychopathic boyfriends.

Oh, yes. I knew Molly's world. I knew so many like her.

We had gone quiet. Molly sat. I think she was sobbing under her breath. Just a little sound — like a mouse.

"Just give me a bit more detail," I said. "I still don't understand how you know he's doing this when you can't see him do it."

"I sense it. He does it in the rooms 'round here. Like I said, the walls are thin; the feelings come right through them."

I said, "Okay. Do you ever see this man in the house? In the communal areas, when he's not hurting your neighbours. Maybe you bump into him on the stairs."

"Yes. Sometimes I see him."

"And what's he like? Is he nasty?"

She shook her head. "No, he always smiles and asks how I am. He says, 'I hope you're okay, Molly. You look sad'."

She stopped. "He's got a shirt like yours."

I shrugged. "This shirt? It's a cheap Primark shirt. I bet plenty of people have shirts like this."

"Probably," she said.

"So what does he look like? Can you describe him?"

"He always changes. He always looks like the last one he opened up."

I said, "How does he do that?"

"He puts on their skin and their faces so that no one would know he wasn't them — not even their own mothers. But they don't have mothers, and all their friends are always drunk or off their faces on drugs. So there's nobody going to come to help them."

I said, "Molly, have you ever had experiences like this before?"

"What do you mean?"

"Well, this — it's pretty unusual. Sensing someone doing something like this. I mean, it's pretty serious. If it's true."

Her eyes narrowed. "Of course it's true. I'm not crackers."

I smiled. "We don't use words like that, anymore, Molly."

"So you *do* think I'm crackers?"

"I never said that. But it is serious what you're accusing this man of. We need to be sure. You're basically accusing this man of murder."

"It isn't murder. It's theft. He steals their skins and then he keeps them somewhere."

"Okay, if this is true — why hasn't he done it to you?"

She studied the hands clasped together on her knees, one holding a scrumpled up tissue. "He's just waiting. He's waiting to put me at my ease."

"Like you said, he pretends to care about them."

"Cause nobody really cares about us. We're not stupid. We know folk despise us. They think we're broken biscuits. They think we're a waste of space."

"That's harsh."

"It's true."

I leaned forward. "Molly, I really want to help you."

She said, "Are you sure you don't want to take your coat off?"

"Don't change the subject. I said I wanted to help you."

She looked at me. Her cheeks were wet. She said, "Maybe you do."

"I think life is really hard for you."

"It is."

"I think you've suffered a lot."

She nodded, crying freely now.

I said, "Ever since you were a little girl. And it's not fair. You never asked for a life like this."

"No."

"I don't know what you've done to deserve this suffering."

"I haven't done anything. I've never hurt anyone."

"I know you haven't. None of this is your fault. Really."

She sighed heavily. She seemed to settle a little.

She said, "Maybe you do care. You seem nice. You're not like all the others. You're the first one who's really listened to me."

"I'm glad you feel that."

Then she started. "I should have asked for your ID. Before I let you in."

"Don't worry. I've got ID. Do you want to see it?"

She shook her head. "No, I trust you now."

"I can show you my ID. It's not a problem."

I looked at the wall. "Is that light on a dimmer switch?"

She nodded.

"Do you mind turning the light down a little? It's just a bit bright in here."

"No, it's ok."

"It just makes it more relaxing. If it's a little darker."

"Sure, I will." She put the tissue up to her nose and stood up from her chair. She stepped over to the wall and twisted the dimmer down. Standing there, she said, "What did you say your name was?"

"I didn't, but I'm called Thomas Jardine."

She didn't look disturbed. She seemed resigned. In a quiet voice, she said. "That's what they call him — Thomas Jardine. That's his name."

"Yes. But I don't look like him, do I?'

She relaxed. "No."

"Good. Do you trust me to help you?"

She nodded. "I trust you to help me."

I said, "I'm really pleased, Molly. Anyway, turn the light down a bit more."

It was quite dark now, and for the first time, I took my hands out of my coat pockets.

CHAPTER 12

THE GHOST OF CHRISTMAS PAST

Time is passing, time is passing, Madame. Alas time is not. It is we who are passing.

— PIERRE DE RONSARD

Nearly forty years ago it was Christmas, just like it's Christmas today. But it is different — then there were people and lights and drinking and dancing and flirting, but now I find myself alone. It's Christmas Eve, and the cat is out. Perhaps he has a party to go to. More faithful, the dog curls by the fire where heaped coals burn orange and black, with blue and yellow flames fluttering softly around them. Looking at coals like that reminds me of the tales my grandfather told me to while away the time when I was young. It's sixty years since, and I still miss him.

There was so much time then. There isn't so much left anymore, but that's all right. I'm comfortable with the fire and the dog, Ruby, and await the return of my tabby and white cat, Mungo, from his night on the tiles.

I was an orphan. A banal traffic accident killed my parents on the minor road where it kinks between the trees on the sinuous way from Rottington to Sandwith.

But forty years ago, I was going out with Mair. Mair wasn't Welsh, she was born in Surrey, but her father was from North Pembrokeshire, hence her name.

As noted, I had no parents of my own, but probably because of this, Mair's mother and father adopted me for the three years we were together, and I spent Christmas at theirs each holiday.

This was the first — 1982.

That day, Mair and I had been shopping in Farnham and seen that affluent Surrey town dressed up for the season—coloured lights on strings across the street, a tree big, twinkling with baubles and all-weather fairy-lights, and in front of that, a crib and a Salvation Army band and carol singers shaking tins for donations and swarms of shoppers keen to be finished shopping, still anxious about the presents they'd bought, and stressed about the presents they had yet to buy, but excited too by the air and the chill and the season and the scent of cloves and chestnuts. Just like I was.

As we strolled in the crisp air, I noticed Mair wasn't speaking to me.

Her displeasure was easy to overlook in the merry crowds. That night there would be parties and warmth and sparkle and the girls would wear glittery dresses, and the women dress in brocaded gowns, and the purple-rinsed old ladies in care homes would sport a sprig of holly in their hair and tie tinsel like bangles round their wrists and sip a sherry to remember their long-gone lovers. That's how it was then.

But as I said, Mair wasn't speaking to me. I didn't know why and I couldn't figure it out and, of course, I didn't ask because she would tell me I should know why. And she was beautiful and dark-haired and dark-eyed and brooding and annoyed and I loved her.

But this is not a story about the ghost of my love for Mair. That is long dead.

Reading the situation as we entered the kitchen, Mair's mother offered me a mince pie, and her dad, Tom, being Tom, handed me a glass of red wine. Tom and Anne are long dead too, but this is not a ghost story about them.

This is a ghost story about time and about me.

Remember, forty years ago and Mair is still in a mood, but I don't mind because I've already worked out over the past months we've been together that her moods vanish like the morning mist, and maybe tonight, or perhaps tomorrow, the reason she is upset with me will be forgotten and forgiven. One day it won't be, but that isn't yet.

So, we're sitting around their long oak table in the kitchen by the Aga and Tom has opened another bottle of wine, which is only fair as he drank most of the first one. Anne is sipping black tea and smoking her slim cheroots and talking. She isn't from where we are, but let her tell the tale.

She says, "You know, we moved into this house when my father came back from Ceylon, or Sri Lanka, I should say. The area was much quieter then, of course."

"The house dated from the 1930s and was probably pretty pricey, though I didn't realise that then. It stood with a large garden in woodland on the edge of Yateley Common — a large area of heath and scrub woodland protected under Greenbelt legislation. You just walked onto the heath down an unmade road and when you were there, it was a wilderness as it had been centuries ago before the urbanisation of this part of the Home Counties when local people talked with a country burr rather than an Estuarian drawl."

"And — though I'm not from here — I always loved the area," said Anne. She drew on her cheroot and tapped it on the blue Chinese bowl with a fish design she used as her ashtray.

"People think Surrey is soul-less, but it isn't by a long chalk. It's full of history and myth, same as anywhere, just buried now under middle-class aspiration. The heath here has its legends."

Tom said, "They wouldn't let you build this house where it is today, you know."

Anne turned to him. "Before my father had it built, this was just woodland, and, do you know what, Mark? By the way, would you like another mince pie?"

I would, and Tom took the opportunity to fill my wine glass.

"Another bottle, I should say," He muttered. "Rioja all right?"

Anne said, "As I was saying, there was a legend that this area was under the sway of the fairies."

"Sssh!" Tom said, raising the index finger of his left hand to bar his lips. "Don't mention the Fair Folk. You never know what will happen if you get their attention."

"You just did mention them, Dad," said sulky Mair.

He shrugged and went to fetch more wine.

Anne continued. "So the 'good neighbours', as they call them, linger here. They also call them Pharisees round here — the old local folk do: funny — Pharisees, like in the Bible."

Tom had sat, poured and was half-listening. "Not that kind of pharisee at all. Don't know why they call them it."

"Sssh, Tom. I was saying. So, Mark, I never saw anything here, but my mother did. She swore they came into the house. My father never admitted he saw anything, but he would always go on about things being moved."

Tom said, "That was your mother, dear — charming woman, but quite batty."

Mair snapped, "That's my grandmother you're talking about."

Tom sipped his wine, leaving his lips crimson. "Lovely woman. Of course, being Welsh — we have a remarkable stock of fairy lore, or as we call them, the Tylwyth Teg."

Anne sat forward. "Do you believe in fairies, Mark?"

I grimaced. "Well, no, not really."

Tom said, "He's all about money, that boy — not a sensitive bone in his body."

"Dad!" Mair said. I sat back. She'd stuck up for me. She must be coming round.

"Well, I mean — economics, wasn't it you studied? At where? Preston?"

Anne said, "You're being rude, Tom. You've had too much to drink."

But later, we all went to The Cricketers and drank some more, and I couldn't keep up with them. They were good at drinking, so when it was my round, I bought myself shandy and told no one what it was. We got back to the house on the heath around ten p.m.

Tom had put Radio 4 on the car radio as he drove us home. Yes, people drove after drinking in those days. My father did too. Radio 4 was playing a ghost story for Christmas — one by M R James. I always liked ghost stories, but I was more scared by the thought that Tom would fall asleep at the wheel than at the description of haunted places and weird bedsheets. It was only about a mile, thank God, and the story seemed to keep him awake rather than otherwise, though it had sent both Anne and Mair to doze.

He parked. Mair woke, clicked open the car door. She still was only muttering enough to tell me she was going to bed. I wasn't ready for bed, so I sat up with Tom, who told me his views on Northerners and how they were all right, but not as good as the Welsh.

I suppose that was progress. He asked me again, "What did you study?"

He'd clearly forgotten the chat where he said that I was all about money, but he would remember shortly and probably say it all again.

Tom was an aeronautical engineer and worked at the Royal Aircraft Establishment at Farnborough doing something secret.

I said, "Economics."

"Ah, all about money, eh? Engineering is a proper pursuit for a man. I told you I'm an engineer, yes?"

"Yes." I frowned. Several times, in fact, but it's not polite to bring that up. I pursed my lips. Then he ever so gently fell asleep in his chair.

I sat in the soft blaze of the Christmas Tree. Anne had made it beautiful — hung it with tinsel, sparkled it with lights, put a fairy on the top who was dusted in glitter in some factory in China, but it glistered and glimmered so adroitly that you could forgive the excesses of Capitalism and environmental degradation — sitting there, nicely warm with wine, I could, anyway.

I wondered whether they believed in fairies in China.

It was quiet sitting there. The old grandfather clock that stood in the corner ticked, the filigreed iron fingers pointing out an enamelled circle of eternity as they'd done since the clock was made in 1812.

The ticking of this clock, and the sound of Tom snoring, and the wind buffeting and murmuring and rising and falling kept me company.

Christmas Eve. It was 1982. Did I say that?

And suddenly I felt something. Goosebumps stood up on my arms and I felt the hair rise on my neck. Someone had entered the room.

"Mair?" I wondered if she'd crept down to make up with me.

No answer.

Slowly, I turned my head. The tinsel fluttered on the tree. A draft entered, getting in under the door made restless by the wind outside — a breath of winter from the cold heath and waiting trees.

But there was no one in the room, just the inhalation of the season, betrayed only by the movement of the tinsel, and a touch of cold on my cheek like a frigid kiss.

The word spirit derives from the word for breath—the inspiration of air.

No one was there. No one could be there. No strangers could get into the house, under the door, round the window panes, even down the chimney. The house was secure from all human intruders.

And then I thought of Pharisees. Maybe it was one of them.

"Is there anyone there?" I whispered, though I expected no answer. I said it in fun, just in honour of Christmas Eve, when there might be magic after all, even though now we struggle to find it, not like when we were children, when magic was like jewels in our hands.

No one answered. "I thought not." I said.

And then I heard a voice whisper, "Yes."

And then I slept, like Tom; the two of us gently snoring in our chairs.

I dreamed. In the dream, there was an old man in the room with Tom and I — a little wizened old man — one of the Pharisees. He held an oval mirror in a chipped gilt frame, a mirror whose silver was black in parts and trailed with marks like cobwebs. The Pharisee didn't speak. He grinned. He winked. He pointed at the quicksilver mirror of what was, what might be and what could never ever happen again, and I fell in.

I was a small boy again by the Christmas Tree in the house in Harrington. This would be 1969. It was an artificial tree — all silver because my mother said actual trees shed their needles. And she was there, my long-dead mother. I watched this scene as if it was TV: My mother hanging baubles, giving them to me, so I could string the metallic glass balls on the lower branches of our silver magic-haunted, cheap-tinsel tree. And she said, 'There, Mark. Now get the mouse.' And I went to the cardboard box that I'd completely forgotten about until I saw it, memories flooding back. This was the box where my mother kept the decorations from year to year, and every Christmas we found it under the eaves and took them out one by one and hung them on the tree, and one of my favourites was a mouse with a sword. I don't know where the box is now.

And there I was with my mother like it was still 1969, not 1982 or 2022, and at that moment, at this moment, I knew I exist in all three, who I am splintered in every memory like a reflection in a Christmas bauble.

And she pulled me in and stroked the top of my head and she kissed me and she is dead.

Time itself remembers us.

And then 1969 faded, and I dozed in a seat in a room in 1982 and the pharisee stood with his mirror.

And then the quicksilver vision changed, and another scene assembled itself until it, too, stood ready to be seen.

This one was darker. An old man sat in an armchair in front of a fire. The room was familiar, and I realised it was the room I am sitting in while I write this story in 2022, but it is not 2022 in the vision. The cat, Mungo, is older, grey around his whiskers, and my beloved dog, Ruby, is gone, and the cat and I sit alone on Christmas Eve.

In the vision, I look like Father Christmas, my beard longer and whiter, my face more lined. By my side on the table, a different one to this that sits here while I write this, is a cut-crystal goblet and in it a measure of golden whisky. And somehow I know it will be Japanese whisky — Suntory, which I've never tasted yet, but which the pharisee's vision tells me I will come to love.

Christmas cards stand up on the mantelpiece — one from my daughter Elspeth and one from my son Michael. A string of coloured lights twists around the mirror above the fire like a rainbow. A miniature Christmas tree sits on the window bottom. At least, I haven't forgotten my love of Christmas trees.

I watch as the cat jumps onto the lap of the old man and he strokes its head, and it bows and purrs.

And time remembers the future me, as well as splinters of the past me, boy and young man, and it remembers how I loved Mair and my mother and my children and my cats and dogs.

We are held in the mind of time

So, this is what the ghost story is about. The past, the present and the future are all ghosts. Whenever you think you are, you are always.

These ghosts of who we were, who we are and who we will be, are all real and they are all now.

And when he saw me understand that, the little man, the pharisee, bowed.

Nothing is lost.

And I remember that 1982 Christmas Eve forty years ago in Mair's house, waking and seeing Tom still asleep.

I rise quietly from my chair. I salute the grandfather clock, the faithful servant of time, whose fingers tell me it is just before midnight and soon will be Christmas Day.

I make my way from the front room with the Christmas Tree and the clock and snoring Tom Hughes, heading for my borrowed bedroom.

On the landing, I remember. I hesitate, but then quietly step over to Mair's door. I turn the handle, push it down and there she is, lying in bed, duvet up, mad at me, her black hair spilled over the pillow. She hears, stirs sleepily, and sits up.

I don't love Mair anymore, but I loved her then.

She says, still grumpy, 'What do you want?'

And I kissed her.

CHAPTER 13

THE HAUNTING OF HIGH STREET

"The world is a mystery and we, its shadows, are still more mystery. But there is no one who has not felt the terror of his own strangeness and wished to understand who he is. So we must go down into the dark, down into the depths of ourselves, where we find the face of the unconscious."

—JAMES HILLMAN

Leaving the room, Eleanor paused by the silver-framed photograph and pressed the tips of her fingers against the faded image then laid the fingers thus blessed against her heart.

The photograph in the frame showed a man in his sixties, holding hands with two small boys, both blonde, both grinning with scrunched-up faces, the one on the left slightly older. The man looked serene — happy to be with them.

This was the last photograph she had of him, her father, two years gone.

Memory kept her standing there, but she had a job to do, so

Eleanor locked the front door behind her, took her car key from her coat pocket, pressed the key button and saw the car lights flash.

The white Ford Ka sat outside on the suburban drive of her suburban house in the south of Carlisle — the newly built 'garden village'. She got in and got ready to drive the twenty-five miles down the coast to Maryport.

This new car, this new house, and, in a sense, this new life were thanks to the money left to her by her father. Her life was his legacy, and his wise investments, though his monthly salary had not been a high one, allowed her now to live as she wanted.

Eleanor worked as a parapsychologist now. No longer was she a secretary in the Education Department of Cumbria County Council. She'd been sorry to leave her colleagues, but the mystery of the after-life beckoned, the mystery of where we go when we die.In her more portentous moments, usually after a glass or two of wine, Eleanor considered herself an explorer of the infinite, a seeker after knowl-edge, the would-be opener of the gates of death.

The very gates her father locked behind him when he stepped through and left her behind.

But today, as she cruised down the A596 in the late-winter sun, her mind danced between her nephews, whom she loved to bits and who would be at school in Denton Holme, and Dan Berkley, her colleague, the guy she was due to meet at Maryport, and her dad, and how he had just vanished one day.

Sure, her dad's body had remained, in the bathroom, where he'd left it halfway through his morning shave, but whatever that body was, he was gone.

Then, shifting her thoughts deliberately, she imagined the Masonic Lodge on Maryport's High Street, her destination. She must have driven past it before but never taken notice of the austere building that she knew now from a jpeg emailed to her by her client, Aïsha.

Another ghost hunt, a paranormal investigation. Though she feared, once again, that the ghosts would turn out to be the creaking of old wood, or the low-frequency vibrations of waves or the settling of Victorian bricks.

She hoped in her heart she would discover the dead rising to make themselves known, making plain the secrets of the afterlife.

The weather was fair. The whole thing would be fun. She liked Dan. The client sounded exotic. It was a day out.

Twenty five miles and forty minutes later, a salt breeze off the sea blew through the inch-wide crack in the rolled-down car window and the brightness of the sea-light and the sound of seagulls floating in clouds above the rooflines signified seaside Maryport.

The town's houses huddled shoulder to shoulder, Georgian but dilapidated, built on the eighteenth century grid pattern. Maryport was been founded by the local lord, Humphrey Senhouse, as a memorial to his wife Mary, and it was a port, hence the name.

Eleanor told herself she liked little things that made sense, even while the big things remained mysterious. But it was the big mysteries she was really interested in.

High Street, where the Masonic Lodge was, lay parallel with the sea, southwest-northeast. It ran down from The Settlement and Motte Hill, down into the dip of the Senhouse Street junction before climbing again to the Sea Brows to end at the building that was once 'The Battery', and now The Roman Museum.

High Street's seaward side was the prestigious side and it was here where the sea captains of old built their grand houses. Eleanor imagined the captains sitting, brass telescopes in hand, watching as their ships sailed into harbour, every ship building their fortunes by ferrying coal to Belfast, Dublin and Drogheda.

Eleanor parked the Ford Ka up the top of High Street and put the parking disk on so she wouldn't get a ticket. She would have come back every two hours to change it as long as they stayed here. Not strictly the rules to do that, it said: 'no return within two hours'— but the council were robbers, so stealing from thieves made her Robin Hood, and Robin Hood was a good guy.

As she'd driven by the Masonic Lodge, she'd clocked Dan, already waiting beside his battered, blue transit outside the door.

She strolled down to him.

Dan nodded. "Alright, El?"

"Not bad, Dan. Got the gear?"

"Always." He rapped his knuckles on the side of his van and it returned a tinny echo.

Eleanor glanced around. "Is the client about? She said she'd meet us at ten."

He pointed. "There's a lady in a car down there. White Merc, this year's reg. Must have some money. I hope you're charging her properly."

Eleanor shrugged. "I said I'd give the Lodge a look-over before settling on a price."

Dan made a pffft sound. "You should at least charge a call-out fee so's we get paid even if we don't get the job."

Eleanor shifted her weight to her back foot, and shrugged again. "Don't worry, I'm still paying you, whatever she pays me."

"It's not about me, El. You need to value your time and expertise."

"Whatever." She flicked her brown hair from her ear. "But you are a flatterer. And, of course, you're right. It's not a business if you don't get paid."

"I knows it." He winked. "I knows it," and pulled at the tip of his ginger beard.

A car door clunked and a tall woman extracted herself from a white Mercedes SUV. Eleanor didn't know the model. She wasn't interested in cars.

The woman looked to be about fifty-five, elegant and well-tailored. Eleanor knew you didn't get clothes like that in Primark or at New Look.

The woman wore a blue coat brocaded in gold tendrils, and had lots of rings, gold encrusted with diamond and emerald, and two bangles on her left wrist, none on the right. She wore a bright coloured dress under the blue coat — Joe Brown? It had a design of red roses in haloes of green leaves.

Eleanor thought the woman would feel the cold if she didn't button up that coat. This was Maryport not Monaco. And nice boots too, continental looking.

"Eleanor Harper?" the woman said, and her accent was not local.

Eleanor nodded. "This is Dan Berkeley, my assistant."

Dan rolled his eyes and shook his head. "Assistant?"

He was an electronic engineer by training, with a particular interest in sound, though he'd fix your computer, phone or telly too. He had a Bandcamp account that featured songs he'd made with weird undersea drones of processed guitar. Not Eleanor's thing, but he did well, he said.

The woman extended a hand to Eleanor. "I'm Aïsha."

"Nice name," Dan said.

"Thank you." She smiled at him, but did not shake his hand. She was tasteful. The way she walked, talked, dressed, smiled. It was all tasteful.

"So this is it." Aïsha said.

Eleanor tilted her head.

Even from outside, the old Masonic Lodge exuded a sense of foreboding.

Good.

The building, which as far as Eleanor knew had been boarded up for five years, stood tall and imposing, face to High Street, back watching over the sea. The weathered brick and boarded windows gave the impression of a once grand structure abandoned to the elements.

Eleanor scanned the façade. Overgrown weeds and ivy creeping up the walls added to the picture of neglect.

Above, Seagulls mewed, hanging like skyhooks in the wind. The weather had changed since she'd parked. Now it wasn't ice-cream and buckets and spades, the weather was damp and grey and melancholy.

Eleanor preferred it moody.

Dan said, "Looks the part — very ominous."

Aïsha laughed. "Penny-dreadful indeed. But I need it to be less so."

Dan said, "Supposed to be haunted, is it?"

Aïsha said, "I feel it is. I need what is here to be gone."

"Rats?" Dan said.

"Ghosts."

Dan said, "Explains why you called us instead of pest control. And also, we're cheaper."

Eleanor reached out to touch Aïsha, but stopped, her hand halfway to the other woman. "He doesn't mean to be rude. He's Cumbrian, so he's blunt."

They all laughed, even Dan. He said, "You're not wrong on either count."

Aïsha asked, "You know my plans for the place?"

Eleanor shook her head.

Aïsha said, "I'm a therapist, you see."

"Really?"

"I wondered whether you'd googled me."

"No. Should I have?"

"It doesn't matter. I only say it because my plan is to renovate this building into a holistic retreat centre. That's on my website."

"Oh, nice," Eleanor said.

"Yes. This." She gestured. "I want to turn this faded monument into a holistic retreat centre. Property prices up here are so reasonable, and the setting on the sea brows looking over the sea, and the spiritual resonance of the place!"

"Spiritual resonance? The Masonic Hall?"

"Yes: spiritual resonance, and a spiritual renaissance for this old, wise building."

Dan said, "Don't they just do charity work — the Masons?"

Aïsha shook her head. "Not at all. The Freemasons began life as an esoteric order. They arose from the Illuminati and though, in the main, they lost their spiritual mission, some remained interested in magic. This building," she gestured with her long-fingered hand, "was used by the *Societas Rosicruciana in Anglia*. The SRIA continued to dabble in the occult, and as such, the place should have been perfect for my needs."

Dan said, "You like the occult?"

"I like a place drenched in spirit."

"Good spirits, or evil spirits?"

"The SRIA were not black magicians. They were interested using magic for healing and the good of mankind — like me. But..."

"I sense a hesitation there." Eleanor smiled.

Aïsha looked pained. "Like I say, the SRIA were always light-focused, a holy, healing order, but this place is—"

"—falling down?" Dan said

"Tainted."

"By Ghosts?" Eleanor said.

"Maybe worse. I don't know." Aïsha smiled. "Honestly. But there's something here, and I'd like you to find out what it is and possibly—"

"—get rid of it?" Dan finished her sentence for her, again.

Eleanor said, "That's what they always ask. But, technically, we just research these things."

"But we do have contacts who can get rid of them." Dan blurted. He turned to Eleanor, "Spooky Claire, for example?"

"Can you do it?" Aïsha said. "Cleanse it. I need whatever darkness lurks here gone before I can start my work."

Eleanor said, "We can. But of course there's an extra fee for that."

Dan winked at her.

Aïsha looked embarrassed. "Ah, yes of course. We haven't discussed money, but I thought £500 initially for the inspection."

"£500 for today?" Eleanor said.

"Sounds grand," Dan butted in. "Very fair."

Aïsha smiled. "Good. Then should we go inside? I've got the key."

Aïsha produced a large, old-fashioned, black-metal key from her coat pocket and dangled it. She put it in the lock and turned and grimaced.

She couldn't get it to turn.

Dan said, "It's an old lock. Let me try."

Aïsha stepped back to let him have a go, but the key wouldn't turn for Dan either.

He grunted, and then without asking, put his shoulder to it and the door lurched open, the lock splintering off.

Eleanor cried, "Dan! Oh, I'm so sorry, Aïsha!" Then she turned back to Dan as if he was a naughty child. "Dan!"

He looked sheepish. "Sorry."

Aïsha waved away their apologies. "It was a rotten old door anyway. We'll need a new one. I can get it boarded and made secure. Don't worry. I'm just glad the place didn't keep us out. I sense it wanted to."

"Take it out of our fee," Eleanor said.

Dan grunted.

Aïsha said, "No, it's fine."

Inside, the Lodge smelled musty of damp wood, damp wallpaper, and damp old books. The grey daylight cast a dismal light on the dusty interior through gaps in the boarded windows.

"It's been a heck of place in its time," Eleanor said, looking around. She gazed at the faded frescoes on the wall.

"Those look Egyptian." Dan pointed. "Not original, obviously. Victorian copies, I'd say."

Lower down on the walls, below the damp plaster, the wallpaper had peeled, folding over like a drunk. Underfoot, the floorboards were covered in debris and cobwebs. The furniture in this room was overturned as if the last event here had been a drunken wake, and everything was covered in a thick layer of dust as if that wake had been long ago.

Old cider cans had rolled against the skirting boards and in a hearth backed with Victorian tiles lay the ashes of a fire.

"Someone's been here," Dan said, pointing at the cans.

Eleanor said, "Those could be five years old."

Dan went over and picked up a cider can. "Strongbow. It's still got a price sticker on it saying 50p so it must be old."

The Lodge went further back. There were rooms behind the entrance hall.

As they wandered through, they noticed an unusual number of spiders scuttling about.

In fact, spiders were everywhere, in the corners of the room, on the ceiling, and even on the old piano.

"How come there's so many spiders?" Dan said.

Aïsha shuddered."I don't know, but I don't like spiders."

Eleanor shrank closer to Dan. "I hate them."

Looking at a dangling light bulb, she said, "Any electricity?"

Aïsha smiled. "Surprisingly, yes. The wiring still works, and I've had the power switched on. I was going to get some heaters in to dry the place out, but, I haven't got round to it yet."

She stretched over to the 1930s style metal pin light-switch and flicked it. Instantly, a pathetic 60W bulb, which hung by a frayed cord from a light fitting stuck on the damp-looking ceiling, lit up.

Spiders scuttled over the boards.

"Bloody hell. So many spiders," Dan said. "Do you think it's the damp?"

Eleanor said. "I didn't think spiders liked damp. Stand in front of me, Dan. I don't want them near me."

Dan said, "Sorry to tell you, but they're behind you too."

Aïsha wandered on. "I haven't had a thorough look round everywhere in here," Aïsha said. "I guess I didn't like being here on my own." Then, she stopped and said, "Can you feel it?"

Dan said, "Feel what?"

She gestured for silence. They all went quiet. She said, "The presence. There's something here."

Dan looked bemused.

Eleanor shook her head. "I don't feel anything. Though I admit to being a little freaked out by the spiders."

The spiders scuttled over the floor with undulations of their thin legs. They hung on threads from the pelmets. They crawled over the walls. One had made a web between the wooden struts of a chair. A big one sat in the centre of its tattered gossamer tapestry in the corner of the boarded-up window, tasting the air, raising mandibles, its multi-faceted eyes glittering in the electric light.

"We'll set up our equipment," Eleanor said.

Aïsha said, "What kind of equipment do you have?"

Dan said, "Infra-red cameras, low-light cameras, motion triggers, EMF meters, a Geiger Counter."

"A Geiger Counter? Really?"

"Yes, we've got it all," Eleanor said. "And we still use the Peter Underwood old-school tricks: chalk dust, trip threads, sellotape on door hinges."

"When can you start?"

"Today. Now."

"We've got the gear in my van," Dan said.

"Amazing! And you'll stay here tonight?"

Eleanor nodded. "Maybe not all night, but as long as we need to get an idea one way or the other."

Aïsha said, "To get an idea about whether there are any ghosts?"

"Yes." Eleanor had her sleeping bag and roll-mat on her car, though she probably wouldn't sleep. Night time was their busy time.

"Just you two?"

"Just us two," Eleanor said.

Dan grinned. "And the ghosts."

Aïsha paid Eleanor cash, and, after a short discussion, left, saying she would see them in the morning. She left her mobile number — 'just in case'.

When she'd gone, Dan said. "Do you think it's really haunted?"

Eleanor shrugged. "By spiders. Anyway, she does. We'll just report what we find."

He cocked his head. "Do you hope it's haunted?"

She laughed. "Of course."

Eleanor and Dan spent the next hour placing electronic sensors, EMF detectors and digital audio recorders around the Masonic Lodge, strategically positioning them in areas by doors and entrances that lore said were generally thoroughfares used by spirits.

They set up up infrared cameras and night-vision cameras to capture any ghostly appearances. Then, they made sure that all the equipment was calibrated, and the batteries were fully charged, and the memory cards were empty.

Eleanor felt no evil spirits, only the excitement she always felt at the beginning of an investigation, an excitement that always subsided into disappointment when the results were in.

She looked around the damp old place, willing the ghosts to appear, while they were ready to capture any possible evidence of the paranormal activity.

"That's this floor set up," Dan said. "Went to venture into the basement?"

Eleanor smiled. "You bet."

Dan pulled open the door to reveal the basement stairs. "You know in some cultures spiders can be a symbol of the spiritual."

Eleanor took out a small torch from her coat pocket and pressed the button. As the beam fell on the wooden stairs, it revealed more spiders. These spiders did not flee, nor scuttle away. They hung like rare, intricate flowers in their intricate, ancient webs.

Eleanor said, "God, there's more of them down here. You were saying something about them being spiritual signs."

"I've never seen so many spiders. What do they eat? I can't see any flies," Dan said.

"Maybe they eat us?"

"Lol!"

"You said 'lol'"

"That's what they say, isn't it?"

"They write it; they don't say it. Anyway, you were talking about spiders as spiritual signs?"

"Yeah, different cultures think different things. The Native Americans reckon the spiders weave threads between the living and the dead."

"Interesting."

They were halfway down the stairs now now.

"The Chinese believe they bring good luck and happiness."

"Fascinating. But still yuk."

"Carl Jung, the psychologist said they were symbols of the Great Mother in her darker, more destructive aspect as the Queen of the Damned, linked to death and the afterlife."

"Lovely. Just what I needed to hear."

At the bottom, Eleanor played the torch beam round the basement. It was even damper down here. The basement was a brick room about thirty feet long by fifteen feet wide. It was remarkably junk free, but its corners were ragged old webs. Spiders scurried over the strands, watching them.

Something bulky and dark stood at the end of the room.

"What's that?" Eleanor said, pointing the torch. The shape stood in shadow. She lit it up.

"Looks like a statue," Eleanor said.

"You're right. It does."

She walked up to the thing, trying to make sense of it with her torch beam. It was draped in the obligatory cobwebs. Wanting to see it better, but shuddering as she did so, she brushed the webs away with end of her torch. Spiders ran in armies from the broken strands of web and huddled into the stone crannies now revealed.

The statue stood five feet tall and it was man-shaped, carved from black stone.

"Looks old," Eleanor said.

"Looks Egyptian."

Eleanor nodded. "You're right. It does. Doesn't mean it's authentic. Like the frescoes upstairs"

"It's got hieroglyphs."

Dan leant forward and brushed aside web from the bottom half of the statue. Ancient Egyptian hieroglyphs ran around the bottom face of the statue. It was clear that the statue depicted a man, carved from the waist up, the bottom being squared off and covered with writing.

Eleanor said, "Wonder what all that says?"

"Don't think Google translate can do this," Dan said.

"But I bet it can. Why don't you take a photo and we'll see if we can find a hieroglyph app."

"That's actually good thinking. There's an app for everything." Dan brushed away more web to reveal the statue's head was not that of a man. The head depicted a huge spider and it was perched on the shoulders of a man.

"It's like the spiders have come here to worship it," Eleanor said.

Dan looked at her. "I think you're going a bit too far. Spiders don't worship stuff. "

Eleanor stepped back. "Oh, what's that under the spider legs?"

"The carved spider head's legs?" Then Dan jumped away. "Oh, my god, it's moving."

A torrent of baby spiders poured from the recess behind the carved legs of the statue. Thousands of spiders exploded from their nest among the cobweb. They shot out in every direction, scurrying and crawling across the floor. They ran fast, covering Eleanor's shoes before she could react.

Eleanor jumped and slapped herself as they swarmed over her ankles and up her legs. She screamed, "They're on my pants and coat."

The spiders surged over her like a tiny army, getting into the seams of her clothes, going everywhere. Their spindly legs moved with a frenzied urgency, driven by some unseen force.

There were so many of them: wave after wave of seething arachnids. The clay floor was now covered in a writhing mass of baby spiders, rippling and scuttling as they spread in every direction.

Eleanor ripped off her coat and dropped it on the floor. She beat at her arms and legs. "Get them off me!"

Dan attempted to bat the spiders off Eleanor, but they got on his hands, crawling up his wrists, into his sleeves. He kept knocking them off. Eleanor was panicking.

The tiny siders were also suspended in the air, coming down on threads. They were everywhere. They got onto their faces and crawled among their eyelashes. They got into their mouths

And as the spiders advanced, they seemed to be growing larger and more aggressive. Some of the creatures were pale and fat-bodied their multiple eyes glittering in the dim light, as if they were alive with some dark and terrible purpose.

Dan and Eleanor retreated to the stairs up, still slapping at themselves and hitting the air to get the spiders away from their faces. Halfway up the stairs, the spiders left them alone.

"That was horrible!" Eleanor said.

Dan laughed. "They can't hurt you. But that was nasty. Man, you really freaked out."

Then a buzzing alarm rang from above. "That's the motion detector," Eleanor said.

"From upstairs. Think some kids got in?"

"Or the wind. Let's go look."

The, before he left, Dan said, "Gimme a minute,"and he went and took a photograph of the black Egyptian statue, the flash popping bright in the gloom.

The alarm kept sounding upstairs. When they got to the ground floor, Dan pointed to the small kitchen. "That door."

Cautiously they stepped through the doorway. Eleanor switched on the room light, which was dim but adequate.

There was nobody in the kitchen. "False alarm," she said. "Pity."

Dan said "Wind?"

"There isn't much wind."

"Kids then?"

"I see no kids."

"Spiders?"

"That's not even funny."

Eleanor wiped down one of the wooden seats and sat down. They pulled up tables and she opened up her laptop.

Nothing happened for an hour. Dan checked his screens. Eleanor was on Twitter, where everyone was arguing with each other as usual, screaming and shouting in text about how they were very tolerant but wished their enemies dead.

"Interesting," Dan said abruptly.

"What?"

"Got some infrasound." He pointed at his laptop screen. "See that waveform?"

"Yes. I can't hear anything though."

"That's why they call it infrasound. It's coming from the cellar."

"The cellar? Could it be the sea noise?"

"Could be. Oh, by the way." he said, "I found a close match of our spider headed statue. It's Set, the Egyptian lord of chaos and disorder. They sometimes carved him with a spider head as one of the guardians of the Underworld. Though he isn't as famous as Anubis, the jackal-headed god."

"You know a lot of stuff, Dan."

"I read a lot of websites."

"So Set's our statue downstairs?"

"I think so."

"Did you get anything on the hieroglyphs?"

Dan nodded, his face glowing in the light from his laptop screen. "You know there is a hieroglyphs app?"

"I said there would be. Did it translate it?"

"My picture wasn't clear enough for it to do a full translation, but..."

"But it got part? What did it say?"

"It says that knowledge of the Deathworld is secret and that it belongs to the gods. Mortal are forbidden from learning its secrets and those who deliberately overstep, will be punished."

"Yeah, but what's an Egyptian statue with a warning about the Deathworld doing here in Maryport?"

"Search me." He paused again. "Rosicrucians?" He tilted his head. "Do you think we're trespassing, by the way?"

"What, here in the Lodge? No, we've got permission."

"I don't mean legally, I mean spiritually. Are we intruding — sticking our noses where we aren't wanted."

"Like I said: Aïsha is paying us to be here, so no."

"Again, not what I mean. Are there things that are forbidden to know? That we shouldn't pry into."

"Like the secrets of the Deathworld?"

"Like the door that shouldn't be opened."

Eleanor shrugged. "That's the door that should be opened, as far as I'm concerned. Anyway, this is very spiritual of you. You don't usually bother with the spiritual side of this stuff."

He shrugged. "Must be this place. Or maybe the spider god."

Night had long fallen, and it was a long time since the spider attack so Eleanor gingerly went down to retrieve her coat from cellar.

The statue of Set glowered at her from the back wall. She ignored it, snatched her coat, then ran upstairs and past a dozing Dan and, out through the front door that would no longer lock, to fetch a can of coke from her car.

She had got a parking ticket after all, because she'd forgotten to go back every two hours and change the disk.

She saw a similar yellow and black ticket stuck to the windscreen of Dan's van. He'd be fuming. She knew he hated parking tickets more than just about anything in the world. Best not tell him.

She went back in and wedged the door that wouldn't lock closed behind her with a chair.

Dan was reading his Kindle when she went into the Egyptian fresco room, now their investigation command centre. He was reading something about cryptocurrency — apparently, you could make millions. He was keen on this, though Eleanor had long ago decided she wouldn't bother.

A further hour went by.

She sat quietly, just listening to the building. The odd car drove past outside. Further away, the sound of an ambulance wailed faintly from the main Carlisle to Workington road, then, as the night settled in full and deep, she heard the sea — the slow heavy surge of the Solway Firth.

The waves' endless push and pull mesmerised her, their eternal ebb and flow. Not that they were eternal, but pretty close. The tides began with the creation of the moon and would last until the moon crumbled away, and the earth would pass away too.

Weird thoughts you get when you're awake in the middle of the night.

Then there was a noise.

It had to be expected. An old building like this would settle as day cooled into night. And of course the the wind was getting up, a brisk sea wind.

The noise came again.

She told herself it was wood contracting.

Dan had given up on cryptocurrency and was snoring in his chair, but on his screen, the waves oscillated, rising and falling, out of time with the sea-waves outside. Was that still infrasound?

That noise unnerved her.

It sounded like there was someone in the building with them. She thought of waking Dan. But he would laugh and tell her she was overreacting, like he had about the spiders.

And what if it was a spider — a massive, fat spider with huge, hairy spindly legs. How horrible! She made herself laugh.

Those noises kept on. She would be brave. She was the lead ghost investigator after all. It wouldn't be a spider, and it probably wasn't a ghost. It was never a ghost. But wouldn't it be wonderful if it were?

Then a shuffling sound came from the kitchen. That wasn't contracting wood.

Eleanor stood. And when she had stood, she listened: the kitchen. That's where the motion detector had gone off before, but it wasn't going off now. Had Dan switched it off?

Maybe it wasn't Dan. Maybe they knew how to switch it off — the spirits.

The kitchen door stood ajar. Had they left it ajar?

She stepped forward, past Dan still sleeping.

The door was half open. It was dark in there, the window boarded up. Fingers of light from the streetlamp came through where the board had dried and split, and the light dashed like tiger-stripes against the rear wall, but the luminous yellow lines only made the room itself darker.

Eleanor had wanted to prise open the gates of death and look beyond, and here, inside this dilapidated kitchen, in an old Masonic Lodge, her opportunity had come.

The secret might be within that room.

She stepped forward, left hand holding the phone aloft, throwing a halo of light forward while her right hand reached towards the kitchen door to prod it open.

With three fingers, she touched the door's wood. She pushed. The door creaked as it swung open.

Someone was standing there in the kitchen, back to the far wall, waiting.

How could someone have got in past her? But then, perhaps, he'd been here all along.

She knew who it was, of course.

Even in the gloom, she knew it was her father. Her beloved father had come back to her, but he wasn't smiling. His eyes were empty and his mouth was black.

As she watched, he raised a hand towards her in warning.

"Dad?" She said.

And he vanished.

• • •

She was in tears when Dan woke, jumping forward out of sleep and running to her to place his hand on her shoulder and say, "What?"

"A ghost." Her voice shook. Her hands trembled.

"A ghost? What? In here?" He shook his head. "I see nothing."

She said, It's gone. It was only a second." She didn't explain who she'd seen.

"But, good though? What we're about?"

"I can't stay here," she said.

Dan muttered, "Let me check the recording."

He went to his table, played back the cameras. Then, he stopped at a certain point and whistled, "Well, I'll be damned."

"I can't stay here" she said.

"We've got something, El. Amazing. Look!"

"Please."

The low-light camera had caught a figure, standing in the kitchen corner. The resolution was poor and you couldn't see who it was. But it was proof. Dan thought she should be happy.

"We need to go," she said.

He shrugged. "Okay. Sure. It's getting cold anyway. But wasn't that totally amazing?"

"Amazing. Yes."

Nonchalantly, he started packing away his cameras, telescoping the stands, removing lenses and pushing them into their foam housings. He laughed. "I never believed in them, you know? But bloody hell, we got one on film!"

She'd had time to compose herself. She said, "I'll ring Aïsha in the morning. I need to leave now. What time is it?"

"Three-ish — just after." He looked at her. "You seem pretty shook up."

"I'll ping you your share."

"Sure, don't worry about that." He frowned. "Hey, are you alright, El?"

She forced a smile. "Yeah, I'm okay. Don't tell me — I look like I've just seen a ghost."

. . .

After wishing Dan good night, she drove home. It was still dark and there was nothing on the road.

She drove twelve miles and had left Aspatria, passed the turn for Allonby and was about a mile from Waverton, where the road snakes and turns, and it was there that she felt someone come into the car.

The presence sat behind her.

Her mouth was dry. She couldn't turn to look at it or she'd crash.

Eleanor swallowed, gripped the wheel harder. "Dad?" she said.

There was no answer.

She continued, "Dad? It's ok, dad. I'm just so glad you've come back to show me. I just needed to know there was something, not nothing."

The thing behind her didn't speak. It made no noise, just sat there, and then on the left hand bend, she risked a glimpse.

It wasn't her father.

It was a huge, spider, with glittering multi-faceted eyes, twitching mandibles and six hairy thin legs, crushed into that space behind her, and as she turned, as if her gaze gave it permission, it pushed its way forward.

The Coroner's report was picked up by the next week's Cumberland News. The headline said:

Carlisle woman loses control of car on notorious bend. The vehicle flipped over crushing the occupant. She was dead when rescue crews arrived.

There was no one else in the car.

CHAPTER 14

SPACE CASKET

I sit, hand halfway to my mouth, and notice a hum in the room. A plastic chair padded with foam, covered in vinyl, detailed with designs that are simple to wipe clean, supports me.

I am as if a photograph has come alive, and the figure in it wakes to sentience, in the middle of its life, wondering.

When I pay more attention, I notice it's not the room that hums, but the machinery that it contains. A huge window breaks up the wall and through it I see darkness, and within the darkness, stars — a million stars, a billion, a number beyond thinking: papillon-butterflies of plasma, crisp like someone poked through black paper with diamond pins.

My hand nears my mouth and I find the skin is numb, my lips are dull with the anaesthetic of the amniotic capsule and as I touch my cheek, the flesh feels alien, not mine at all, though it must be mine for if these hands are not mine, then who am I?

I am... and the answer trails, evades memory or, more truly, imagination.

From the idea that I must be someone to be at all, I imagine myself into existence.

202

Then where am I?

I frown, though surely this is an easier question. I imagine (or do I remember?) I am in a spacecraft.

I look around at the thing-in-itself banal and real and actual, phenomenal not noumenal, benches and walls and gleaming machines, but details of this elude me, slipping ever further from grasp like a bar of wet soap from wet fingers.

How memories are chained, one triggering another. I remember a bathroom. This is memory not creation of mind (though memory works like a painter behind the scenes) but I am here, not there, not in memorial, memorising, memorate, memorable, memories.

Real I am.

Knowledge crystallises, feels actual, and the parts fall in place like a child's model. What is going on here?

Yes, I am in a spaceship. That explains the stars, and I am Malcolm Armstrong, and I am an astronaut.

Knowing rushes like a foaming tide and my identity is afloat on it.

I now know everything: who I am, where I am. Everything except what I'm doing here in this room in this spaceship.

I don't remember getting here; either into the room, nor into the ship.

Then I remember the casket and its dripping, iridescent life-fluid.

Then I remember the firing, the fire, the firmament, ascending into space on a great engine.

I last remember — what?

Sleep and cold and dream, so long it was that I dreamt, my mind wandering in shadows, an Odysseus from island to island of images and then the void and emptiness of the world before creation.

The mind, the dream, the void, tangling my thoughts like briars. I need to get up. I need to get moving. Something is wrong.

I remember the fronds and leaves of the woods of Earth. Places out of memory where I am no longer.

Everything remembered is imaginary and is forgotten and leaks out of mind once more.

A pause.

I look around the room. I have the sense I should be frightened, but fear is distant like an alarm ringing in a building three blocks away.

I raise my hands to look at them. I am cold and wet and a trail of ice-water leads to the door, but the door is closed.

From the way the water has drained and the pieces of ice melting in it, I suspect I came in here and the door closed after me.

If that is so, then I don't remember walking. Can I still walk?

I was asleep for a long time, perhaps centuries. All that time I was gone, I was not gone.

I do not sense an absence or a break in my existence. I existed even though I slept through the gloom of interstellar space for decade over decade, always unaware of myself, yet I did not cease.

I was there, though I knew it not.

Shake free, Malcolm, my lad. The alarm of fear rings still, but I don't have enough adrenalin to pay it heed.

They told us our mission would last centuries and the machines would keep us alive until it was time for us to wake and descend and populate the planet selected — Medusa.

But I was awake *now*, and it seemed too early for waking.

I stood, and some rations fell from my hand. I suspected I had been eating. But what I do not recollect.

I remembered now — the eating, but though I saw the rations on the clean floor, square, sweet brown, chocolate-like food, I did not stoop to pick them up.

My mind is slow; it moves like glaciers, huge and broken and breaking.

Food and water and colony planets.

We were to be colonists, but I cannot prioritise. I stood and walked to the window, forgetting why I'd gone until the icy touch of my fingers on the neo-diamond plate that separated me from the void reminded me of Medusa.

(Which part of the sensation belongs to the window, and which to my fingers?)

I looked out for Medusa

I remembered the images; green and blue : another earth, this Medusa, and we were to be the first, but as much as I searched, she was not there.

The craft spun slowly, so if I waited, I would view a full circle of space and in time she would rise.

Minutes turned, but there was no Medusa.

I tipped back my head and said, 'Alexa?'

That one always listened, always anyway, when we'd all been awake. Alexa was an auto-mind, named from some lustrous predecessor of auto-minds, perfect in and of herself, storing all humanity's knowledge in electric nano-spheres.

Humankind's memory was not in humans now , in was in machines.

I called out, but Alexa did not reply. I remembered her velvet tones, composited female for those who preferred such things, male if otherwise, and also androgynous for those who had no interest in either.

I cleared my throat and called again in case she had not heard, but she always heard. Hearing was part of her function.

There is a blank.

I am next standing by my casket.

The formed crystal canopy is open, more neo-diamond coloured amethyst and aquamarine, my umbilicals uncoiled, torn free and leaking glittering life-fluid into the box that held my sleep and now contained my absence.

Fingertips outstretched (I see I have no fingerprints, time has erased my identity), I touch the canopy and feel its chill. Frozen still, it has not been open long enough to thaw completely.

On either side of the room, like the shelves of a family

mausoleum lie the caskets of my crew, translucent with frost, and I know they dream inside like I dreamed.

My name is on the casket side here: Malcolm Armstrong.

That is who I grew up to be.

I remember a childhood and school and friends and flying above Australia, and a dog called Jasper. I remember grief.

I am not concerned if I never become Malcolm Armstrong again. All this time has worn him out.

I scratch my arm. There is a badge of rank on the sleep-suit I still wear. I am the captain. Am I the captain?

I rub my eyes. I am not sleepy and perhaps I shall never sleep again, but I have to plumb the mystery of why I am awake still short of our mission to Medusa.

"Alexa?" I call, yet this time not expecting an answer.

I will seek help from the Bridge. I know where the ship's bridge is and walk towards it on legs weakened from lying down for long years, even with the inline auto-massagers and the electrical fields that stimulate muscle tone.

I pass another open casket. On that is a name: Rebecca Schwartz.

She was the captain, not me; memory and imagination are confused again. Her casket is of ambient temperature and there is no ice meltwater around it. It seems she has been awake longer than I have been.

I must find her. She must know why we have woken so early, with no Medusa in sight. I guess I will find her on the bridge because that is where captains are found.

The tin corridor is long and tubular, with diamond windows showing stars, a great panoply, the heraldic arms of heaven, so many stars.

It is not cold in the corridor and I am thinking about something I can't remember when the voice speaks.

This voice is not Alexa.

I can't see Captain Schwartz, so I do not imagine it's her.

It is a strange voice, unlike any I have ever heard before.

This voice is the sound of pattering on the space-side of the metal tube. But what could be outside in interstellar space?

Then I realise it is not a voice. What kind of voice speaks with the cold pushing of fingers into my brain?

A voice that whispers things that will be heard

I realise I have never known where my thoughts come from. They just appear in my mind. Who knows who is the true author of them?

Then come pictures in my mind. I don't seem to be responsible for them at all. I do not make them. Who does?

That sound again, the one I had mistaken for a voice. But this time it's inside the ship — behind me. I stop. It's so hard to think here. I turn. It's difficult to remember what I should be frightened of.

I notice my heart is beating fast and my palms are sweaty and my mouth is dry so I must be anxious.

Realising that I am anxious, I run along the corridor, and the sound is behind me.

I pass through a door that opened in anticipation of my coming with a slow hiss. This capsule is an entertainment room. I remember that. Though this is not entertaining. The screens are dreaming their own blank-faced void dreams on faces of neo-quartz.

Everyone is switched off.

I become aware of something behind me, and with wondering gaze, turn. Through the windows, I see that something has caught the ship and wrapped round it like a spider bundling up a fly.

Though this is not a spider; this is an Origin.

Another thought from nowhere. What does that word mean: an Origin? It was announced in my head like a proper name. It is a name that belongs to something.

And then an explanation: it means that this is where my thoughts come from and it's wrapped half around the ship and I can see its flabby fingers and a flabby tongue like a succulent plant, all flesh and plump.

The Origin is inside the ship too.

I am anxious again, or perhaps I never stopped being anxious and hadn't noticed.

I run from the entertainment capsule and along another corridor and my feet boom and I hear the pitter-patter of its interstellar fingers outside the metal skin of the spaceship.

And the Origin is behind me too, running like hallucinations in waves and shadows of ruby and emerald.

I scream. I flee. I stumble. I fall.

The door of the Bridge opens and there is Captain Schwartz, seated in her captain's seat, but she is wired up.

Similes fail and metaphors fall adrift like cables that miss their mooring.

Schwartz is not cabled up, though that's the closest I can get to it. It's like a Bronze Age man considering a computer. How could he possibly make sense of what he was seeing?

He would see things certainly, but not know them, and in his struggle to understand them, he would compare them to things that were familiar to him: axes, adzes, golden torcs.

And so do I the same. I call the things that infiltrate: cables, and those that run into her head: wires, and ribbons and tendrils and strings. I see but cannot differentiate which organs they penetrate and suck.

I shake my head. She is not cabled; she is not wired; these green snakes are not briars.

They are drinking her and the closest I can get is siphons: except they did not siphon life from her; they deliver it. They live her.

Schwartz was now identical to the Origin. She came from it.

I hear it moving.

I turn, my hand halfway to my mouth. I see I am cabled. I am plumbed in. I am hard-wired to the murmuring, pattering network.

It is not one thing, I see now, or rather it is one thing, but is in many places as if separate. And now it stands behind me, reaching, this Origin. It is a beetle.

But it is not a creature. It is not a beetle. It is not a person like us. Perhaps it is a phallus.

We should not have come here. This is not our place.

Schwartz's mind opens into mine through the cable that runs into my leg and into my veins and into my central nervous system until it populates and pustulates and palpates and flowers into my brain; making new life, new places, new cities in my mind.

It seems we were not the only colonists.

Schwartz whispers to me, "Two years ago, our Nova Drive failed, and we drifted in space."

I am full of images that are not mine, a shining trapezohedron, a whisper, a mineral. I crystallize out as if from a supersaturated solution.

Schwartz whispers to me, 'This is your captain speaking. Your captain is dead.'

The Origin holds me. The tendril tentatively feels its way down my throat now. The soft tongue is in my ear. My brain is now run riot with an alien fungus. The plastic fragment of a child's toy. A pair of broken shades lying on the tarmac. The long past that had led to now and never, never, never.

We are not the only colonists.

I sit, hand halfway to my mouth. A plastic chair padded with foam covered in vinyl that is easy to wipe clean, supports me seated in a small room that hums.

After ten seconds, I know who I am, but I do not know why I am here, in the spacecraft's galley. I am Melissa Kiraly, colony agronomist. I stand and the sleep slime drips from me. How I hate its iridescence.

I have not been long awake then. But where is Medusa? We should only wake when we are close and preparing for descent to our colony world.

I need to find Captain Schwartz. If she is awake, she will be found on the bridge.

I go there. The door opens. When I stand, the floor is dry around my feet. How long then have I sat here in the galley?

Captain Schwartz will know why we are awake. I will find her.

I hurry along the tubular corridor that leads from the Galley to an Entertainment Capsule. I remember there is another corridor from there to the Bridge.

But when I enter the corridor, I notice that something has attached to me. I don't know what it is — a siphon? A weed? A ribbon? Have I caught my sleeve on a nail and unravelled.

My thoughts are slow, puffing like a sea anemone
The fingers shuffle inside me.
My mouth feels dry, my fingers stiff, and then...

We are not the only colonists.

[My gratitude to all the crew of the spaceship Hawkwind, past, present and future.]

CHAPTER 15

A TRIP TO THE MORGUE

I never minded working nights. We worked one on, so you were alone in the portakabin unit on the north side of the hospital. When the Crisis Team was first started, we used to go to peoples' houses if they called us in the night, but then they cut our staff so there was only one of us on and it was too dangerous to go out in the dark to unknown places with unpredictable people.

Instead, we got the patients to come to us and we'd see them in Accident and Emergency, down the other side of the hospital.

In fact, Police Custody and A&E were the only places we went and safer than going out. Mainly safe, of course.

I've been attacked by patients in both police custody and in the clinic room we used and in a cell once, I had to get rescued by burly coppers who pulled the guy off, and in A&E by a thin, posh doctor who I thought would be soft, but who turned out to be a martial artist.

But I got quick at running out through the cubicle swing doors when I first saw the rage begin to build.

We used to use the kids' room in A&E at first but then they built us a custom-built unit complete with doors on both sides so we couldn't get blocked in by patients.

On nights it was rare I saw someone who wasn't either drunk or drugged. But I digress.

It was the Christmas period. It's always Christmas in my memory of that job but it must have been summer sometimes, or autumn. But that particular night it definitely was around Christmas.

I should say that the hospital was a 1960s build. I think it had been opened by Princess Margaret in 1960, in fact. It was shabby and has since been refurbished.

It's not the new hospital I'm talking about. This all happened in the old hospital.

I didn't mind doing nights, like I said. A crisis team is a demand-led service; some nights were crazy (excuse the pun) and you could be doing assessments one after the other all night and writing them up until the morning shift came in.

Quieter nights were better. There was always plenty of paperwork to catch up on, go through the files to make sure all the actions had been done, do the shift planner for the next day, check the medication cupboards — plenty.

Often when you came on shift, there'd be one waiting for you down in A&E. The easiest ones had been brought in by friends or family and were desperate and wanted help. That's straightforward. Even the psychotic ones were straightforward. I don't mean in terms of suffering, I mean in terms of procedure: we just arranged for them to be admitted to the psych ward.

The tricky ones were some of the people with personality disorders — not all of them, many were just sad and despairing. The most difficult for us were the ones who were sad and despairing and also hated everyone and everything and were raging at the world, and that included us.

Sometimes they'd find our portakabin after we'd left them and come and smash the windows or daub insults on the door. It scared some of the staff being alone in there at night, wondering who was waiting for them when they opened the outer door to go home.

So, that night, a bloke who'd had too much cocaine, a woman who said her GP wouldn't give her the right antidepressants, a youth who thought he had ADHD and ASD and CPTSD because he was following someone on TikTok who had them, and now I'd been called back to A&E to see young lass brought in by her mother who was being bullied at school and who'd self-harmed.

We had an air-lock type affair from our portakabin into the main hospital corridor; I swear it was like being in a space station; you certainly felt removed from the normal world. The wards up our end were closed then, scheduled for demolition and they've gone now, as has our portakabin.

You went through the portakabin, then down a long corridor with locked doors to wards scheduled for demolition: three on the left, and two on the right. The lights here were dim because the way wasn't much used, apart from by us coming from our portakabin.

Then you got to a crossroads with stairs going up or down that was marginally busier and had better light.

Kids ward was left and the Young Disabled Unit right, so there were people in there and nurses doing errands every now and again.

You then walked along another corridor that led to the management offices, which were all in darkness overnight of course. I remember that night, they'd left their Christmas Tree on, twinkling in the gloom. That cheered me up.

There was also a short cut. It saved only about three or four minutes but it was still a short cut. You went down a narrow concrete spiral staircase. I guess it was a maintenance route and not everyone knew about it, but I prided myself on my intimate knowledge of all routes within the hospital.

You could go up to the top floors and ultimately the bell tower. Yes, it had a concrete, brutalist bell-tower. And you could go down to the subterranean levels, to the morgue. Down there was the short cut.

It was spooky down there but also mysterious, but I was more scared of the living than the dead.

The corridor that led between the morgue and the main hospital was full of old beds and commodes and metal crutches all stacked up and things kept just in case they were needed. At one end was the service lift.

The porters would wheel the newly deceased under their tarpaulins on gurneys from the lift to the morgue, out of sight.

So that night, I thought I'd take the short cut.

I descended the concrete spiral, with a pitter-patter of my shoes until I got to the wide gurney road-way. It had some lighting, but not enough to see well in. Nobody was really supposed to be down there at this time of night.

I think it was about 11 pm. I strolled my way to the lift, hit the button and the wide double door elevator came down with the groaning of aged machinery and a hiss as the doors slid slowly open.

I stepped in, punched the button and up I rose to Floor 1.

This was a brighter area. Here you had A&E with the ambulances arriving, but also a cafe that was open that was quite busy during visiting hours. At this time of night, the visitors had mainly gone, but some of the patients who were waiting for discharge would come here because they were bored and they came in their night gowns and smocks and sometimes dragging a drip with them.

Lots of them smoked outside A&E doors, though it was frowned up and officially banned.

"The saddest sight I ever saw was smokers outside the hospital door." That was Editors who sang that.

Like I said, I had to see this young girl who was 14 or 15, I forget, who'd self-harmed. That's a pretty sad sight too.

The A&E nurse cleaned up the superficial wound. It didn't need sutures or glue or steristrips. The girl had cut herself with a pencil-sharpener blade — that was very common.

I did the assessment. That helped them both feel better, I hope. I mainly just listened. I couldn't do anything about the bullying at school but said the right thing, advised her to go and see her GP. I was never sure why we said that or what the GP could do about bullying, but we always said it and then they left.

I went round to A&E Minors because Hayley was on and I quite liked Hayley. She seemed pleased to see me and we did some mild flirting. I think I saw the Sister roll her eyes, but we persisted talking about not much until the phone rang to say they had an incoming code red.

It was an old guy with chest pain. I saw them rush in with him, the paramedics handing over to the A&E nurses.

He looked grim, ashen-faced, sweaty-browed, grey hair plastered over his forehead. He had an oxygen mask on and he was barely conscious.

The Sister turned and said to me, "Don't you have work to do?"

"Have you got any more for me here?"

"Me?" They always say that.

Hayley sighed and said, 'Later, Graham. I need to go into resus.'

I went and got a coffee and saw Hayley return. Her eyes were moist. "We lost him," she said.

"Sorry, to hear that."

But the Sister was there too. "Honestly, Graham, even if you don't have work to do, my staff do, so shoo."

"Bye then," I gave a little hand flap and walked back to the lift.

I should say, that like most hospitals all the patients wear wristbands for identification and the few wandering around here had their green bands with their names and hospital numbers.

If they died, they took the green band off and put a plain red one on and then got wheeled down the underground road to the morgue. I don't know why they had to designate them officially dead, but they did.

Anyway, I got the lift. Once I got back to the portakabin, it would take me an hour plus to do the paperwork for the assessment I'd completed. We had to do letters to GP, risk assessments, then add all the coding in our own computer systems so that our managers could track work flow, et cetera ad infinitum ad absurdum.

I still had half a cup of coffee left when I got to the lift. It was later. Most people had disappeared, but there was one woman patient hanging round by the lift door. I took very little notice of her to be honest. I remember she was dressed in a hospital gown and had neck length dark hair, but I didn't really look at her.

The lift door opened and I stepped in and she stepped in after me. I said, "Floor?"

But she didn't speak, so I shrugged and hit the U button for the under-hospital level. She could press the button to get back to her ward herself.

It was just before 1 a.m. at this time. The lift rumbled down and settled. There was that minute or so before the doors open when I always imagine they're stuck and I'll have to hit the emergency button.

But they opened. I stepped out into the gloomy undercroft of the hospital, the morgue road stretching away into the dark, tiny lights in a row on the top right showing the way. About three of the bulbs were out. I guess down here wasn't a maintenance priority.

The rows of waiting beds either side of the passageway were shadowy and ominous-looking.

The woman got out with me.

I said, "Sorry, this isn't really a patient area. The wards are up on the higher floors. Just get back into the lift and press button 2 or whichever floor you're on. Which ward are you on?" I said trying to be helpful.

She didn't speak. I really didn't need this down here. I said, "Honestly, you can't be down here—" and then I heard it.

It was a groan that came from down the barely lit corridor ahead.

A groan?

And then a shuffling.

The hair stood up on the back of my neck. I'm not superstitious and I don't believe in ghosts and ghoulies, but this was down on the morgue level at one o'clock in the morning and the lights didn't work properly.

I stepped back towards the lift. The doors had closed so I jabbed the call button. The lift was still there so the doors wheezed open and revealed the metal box with its bright neon tube light.

I didn't want to be a complete wuss, so I waited at the open door for the woman to step back into the lift.

Ahead came an awful noise, like gas escaping from a cadaver, and I peered and saw a shape looming out of the dark. It came on two legs, lurching forward. As it stepped closer, about ten yards, I recognised him. It was the man from resus — the guy who'd had the chest pain.

I frowned. What was he doing down here? He should have been admitted. Then I remembered Hayley's tears. No point admitting him.

And in the inadequate light of that passage I saw he had a band round his left wrist.

I stepped back into the lift.

"Hit the button!" I yelled to the woman who stood there motionless and dumb.

The man staggered closer.

"Hit the button, for God's sake!" I screamed.

She spoke for the first time. "Shouldn't we wait for that man?"

I stammered, "No, no. Don't you see the colour of his wristband. It's red!"

And then she lifted her own wrist and said, "What? Like this one?"

CHAPTER 16

WHAT'S UNDER THE BED?

My son Ciarán doesn't sleep well. He's got such a lively imagination, which is a gift most of the time, but at bed time it's a curse, because he always imagines there are monsters under his bed.

I was sitting downstairs with Emily, just about to pour her a second glass of wine and start watching Guillermo Del Toro's *Cabinet of Curiosities* — the episode about the storage unit, when I heard a shout from upstairs.

"Dad? Mum? Can you come, please?"

I sighed. "Your turn"

Emily said, "I don't think so, buster. I went last night. Get yourself up there."

I shook my head. "But do you really think we should go every time he shouts? Aren't we just encouraging him? He's got to learn to deal with his imagination on his own."

"Come on, Aaron; he's only little."

I stood, sighed and said,. "Okay, okay." Then I turned my head and yelled, "Coming, Ciarán."

I made my weary way up the stairs. Ciarán's bedroom was to the left off the landing. He was sitting up in bed looking nervous, the slowly turning nightlight globe casting blue and green shapes around his room.

I said, "Hey, matey, what are you doing still awake? It's late for little boys."

"Dad," he wailed. "I'm scared."

"What are you scared of, baby boy? There's nothing to be scared of. This is your own bedroom and mummy and daddy are downstairs."

"I'm scared, dad."

"Come on, son, what of?"

He pointed. "Of under the bed."

I sighed again. "We go through this every night, Ci. Every night you get me to check under the bed, or your mum, and every night there's nothing there."

"But there's something under my bed tonight."

"You always say that. What do you think's under your bed — a monster?"

"Just something.'

"Oh, come on, my boy."

"Please, dad. Please check."

"There's no such things as monsters, Ciarán!"

"Just look."

"Okay, I will. One more time." I went down on one knee and from there, smiled at him. "Okay, I'm going to look, but I not going to find any monster."

"You will, dad."

And so I lifted the valence of the bed and peered under the cloth and there I saw a little boy. It was my Ciarán peering back at me with terrified eyes, crouched under the bed.

I didn't understand what was going on. I lifted my head and saw the Ciarán on the bed and looked down and saw the Ciarán under the bed.

The Ciarán under the bed tugged at my sleeve.

He whispered, "I told you there was a monster."

CHAPTER 17

THE VOICE OF THE MYSTERONS

I rolled over and threw out my hand to find the other side of the bed empty then I remembered it was Tuesday.

Kate worked every week day as a teacher with little ones at the local school.

Me, Andrew, I didn't work on a Tuesday — O Blessed Day!

I rubbed my eyes. Kate had got up quietly, not woken me, snuck out thoughtfully and gone to work to leave me to snore a few more hours.

But now the sun was up and it was time to stir myself.

I had lots of chores on Tuesdays though those at the house would wait until I'd been out round the village and got what I needed: the post office for a book of second-class stamps, the butchers for pork chops and some Cumberland sausage, the greengrocers for veg for a ratatouille, and then a cheeky flat white at Aroma and a read of the daily paper, before back home to unpack, hoover, tidy and maybe watch Sapphire and Steel on the blu-ray before Kate came home to eat the meal I would cook her from what I bought.

It would be a perfect Tuesday.

Shower and all that but no shave as it was my day off, and then I turned the TV on to catch the morning news as I wandered about.

I was in the shower when I first heard the voice. It said:

"This is the voice of the Mysterons. We know that you can hear us, Earthmen."

But, it wasn't from the TV. It was in my head.

I jumped out of the shower, dripping and smacked my palms over my ears:

This is the Voice of the Mysterons.

    This is the Voice of the Mysterons.

Deep and sonorous, slow and threatening, just like I remembered it from that childhood TV programme.

It was inside in my head.

I thought maybe I'd tuned into some radio station. I'd heard how the metal stems of peoples' glasses could do that and they picked up shortwave or something. But I wasn't wearing glasses. I'd been in the shower — naked.

I stood there, turning the water off in my panic, shaking, dripping, my thumbs squeezing into my ears to block out sounds from the world so I would know if those words had come from inside or outside.

All fell quiet. The words were gone, but the memory wasn't.

Memories of words like the wash of broken waves. The Voice of the Mysterons?

I remembered that.

A long long time ago, it came from the puppet sci-fi series: Captain Scarlet and The Mysterons. Why had that just sparked in my head? What was the trigger — a random thought?

Was I schizophrenic? I'd never had any experience like this before.

The voice was gone and the memory faded so I stepped back into the shower and continued to get clean. It was just an aberration.

Eventually I calmed down and dried and dressed and got my coffee.

Calm, but still wary, looking round the house like some robot voice machine was hiding in the wiring, waiting to pounce.

It didn't.

Then on the TV, there was a big news flash, all bold letters and red banners scrolling across the screen:

BREAKING! BREAKING!

There were pictures that I couldn't initially decipher, until the urgent voice of the newscaster and the rolling images of destruction coalesced:

MARS BASE DESTROYED!

Wow! Mars Base Destroyed? That triumph of space-bro capitalism — private sector initiatives taking us to the planets. The guy who owned the MetaVerse had stumped up to make his dream of a human Mars colony come true. Who knew why? There must be something in it for him or the other Elites, but it was hard for us worms to figure out, perhaps it was ego, perhaps philanthropy.

Maybe sometimes the Elites did care about human betterment. Maybe.

Mars base had been small, I think a crew of twenty, but it was humanity's first significant step into space.

Destroyed, though. What had happened?

No one really knew, but the News doesn't satisfy itself with merely being the News, it has to be the Speculation as well, so maybe it was the Russians or the Chinese or Islamist Terrorists or Just Stop Oil! Or home-grown terrorism, except there wasn't any home-grown terrorism on Mars because Mars wasn't home.

Awful for those who died. What a waste of lives and money, but like most of the little people, I concern myself with my little things and am content with that so, I drained my cup, got my coat and shopping bags and I was in the porch.

Standing there, I had a weird feeling. I felt I'd left something important behind. I went back into the living room to see if I'd left the TV was on, but I hadn't.

So shaky, Andrew, mate. I told myself: get an effing grip. Fresh air would help, so I stepped out of my front door, locking it behind me.

My neighbour from three down hurried by, I said, 'How do?' but he kept on walking not meeting my gaze, and then the woman on the mobility scooter. I saw her every Tuesday and she always spoke, but not today. I greeted her but she turned her head, desperate to avoid me.

What the hell was the matter with people? They surely couldn't all be so upset about Mars Base?

I shrugged. People. People who need people are the luckiest people in the world, so the song says. But are they, though?

There was something odd about the light that morning. I tilted my head back to see a blanket of cloud so dense you'd have thought it was knitted. It kept everything dim and grey, like there was a lid on the world.

The atmosphere was heavy too, unsettling. I got to the post office. I had a circuit for my Tuesdays and they began here. Maureen would be in, or John. The place doubled as a post office and a convenience store full of beer and disinfectant and milk and bread and then stamps. There was always someone in there stamping up parcels to fuel their online sell-from-home business.

It was a right royal pain to be fair if you got stuck behind them, but fortunately the place was empty this morning.

Maureen stood behind the glass pane, glassy-eyed, loose-jawed, eyes not fixed on anything and when she spoke it was like her mouth and her eyes weren't joined up.

I was concerned. "Are you all right, Maureen?"

Maureen didn't reply. She wasn't her usual cheery self. What the heck was it with everyone?

Then she began to nod like she was a marionette and her head was on a spring, but the strings that controlled her were too fine to be visible.

I stepped back and frowned. "What's up? I just want a book of second-class stamps."

She kept nodding, then she whispered in a voice that sounded cloned, "Come behind the counter."

"What?" I stared at her and laughed. I laughed but I didn't get the joke, though I realised it must be a joke because otherwise this was too weird.

"John in?" I said finally.

John was down to earth. Maybe Maureen was ill? John would sort it.

"Come behind," she whispered again in that weird slightly wrong voice.

They had a stock-room behind the counter. That's where they kept the parcels they were sending out or accepting for customers. The door was usually locked shut, but today I saw it had swung open.

"Come," she said.

"I don't think I'm allowed, Maureen."

I forced my humour because if I didn't, I would be scared. People in post-offices didn't behave like this, like nodding-headed puppets with blue glass for eyes and mouths made of painted wood. That's what she looked like.

Behind her, the door hung open and on the floor, when I looked, I saw a leg in black tights and a pair of red shoes dislodged and lying behind the angle of the door.

I didn't accept her offer to go into the store room with her. I turned and ran and outside the post office I dithered, waiting for Maureen to come out, but she stayed in her shop, thank God, and my breathing calmed.

I pushed my hand back through my hair. I still needed those stamps. Then I thought: the person lying behind the door in the stock room was Maureen. And if that was Maureen in there, who the hell was the Maureen who had been talking to me?

My mouth was dry. I tried to get hold of my nerves. The butcher was next, and there's nothing more down to earth than a butcher. They chop up dead animals — that's grounded.

I made a mental note to ask Tom at the butcher's if he knew whether anything was up with Maureen at the post office.

It was my mind playing tricks on me, thinking she was lying behind the door and that her place had been taken by a puppet. Just like my mind had played tricks had when I'd heard that stupid Mysterons voice in the shower.

I decided to walk over to the GP surgery after I'd got the meat to see if they had any appointments.

I'd had no trouble with strange thought since my twenties when I was smoking a lot of weed, but maybe I was relapsing.

Anyway, there I was at the butchers. And even here, I hesitated at the door. There was nobody coming in or out. That was odd; it was usually very busy. All of this anxiety stuff was just in your head; you had to overcome it or it would beat you down, so I entered the shop and the little bell tinkled, proper old fashioned.

That's why I liked it. This village was a blast from the past. It was comforting: Chalfont St. Peter.

Tom was not standing behind the counter. The sides of lamb hung there and half a pig and there were trays of sausages and black pudding and kidneys and heaps of minced meat and a meat cleaver lying there, but no Tom.

The cold room lay behind the counters, a big heavy door stood just ajar and from inside that frigid room came the most awful sound of sucking, as if something was mouthing the meat off a carcass.

And then behind me there was a thump. I turned and jumped. I stared through the sparkling-clean windows — Tom was a stickler for cleanliness.

There were things falling from the sky. They landed with thuds like sacks of potatoes hitting on the ground. Some landed in folks' gardens, some on the pavements, some on the street and I thought they'd get run over and cause accidents, then I realised there were no cars.

There should be cars, surely?

The slurping, sucking sound from inside the cold room stopped. Whatever was in there doing that now knew I was in the shop.

Outside those heaps kept falling from the sky, thumping and thudding every ten seconds or so, but behind me, from the belly of the butcher's shop I heard something stumble out.

I hurried to the door, not so fast as to looked panicky, and opened it and then closed the door deliberately and precisely, and I put my shoulder against the door to stop what was inside the butcher's shop getting out and then I thought: what if I can't stop it? What if I'm not strong enough? What if it really wants to come out?

And outside those things kept falling. They appeared in mid-air, about two hundred foot up and fell heavily to earth, landing with a smack and lying in heaps.

They were covered in — I don't know — cloth, material?

But as I watched, they started to move and shudder under the cloth covering. They were heaps, squirming and moving as if they were recovering from their fall, and I thought: why do they have to fall? Why can't they appear on the ground instead of in mid-air, and it was then, as the heaps shuddered and began to rise that I realised I had to make sure Kate was safe.

I ran to the primary school where she worked. It wasn't far. There were a few stationary cars in the car park but no people. The sound that surrounds every school at playtime wasn't there. It can't have been break. They must be at their little lessons learning about animals and reading fairy stories from picture books.

That was comforting. Like I say: our little world was perfect.

I hurried to the front door of the school. Usually, you had to press a buzzer and the secretaries in the office to the left side of the front door let you in. But today there were no secretaries. The radio was playing, and on it someone was speculating about Mars Base being an act of hubris and of us poking our noses into things we didn't understand, but there was no one around in the school.

I shoved open the school's front door.

I knew where Kate's classroom was, and I ran to it. The door was closed, but it had a frosted glass panel in it and through that I saw the desks, blurred and vague.

There were rows of little desks for the kids and there at the front, a full sized desk for the teacher, for my Kate.

I licked my lips that had become painfully dry and turned the handle. "Kate?" I whispered.

She was the only one in the room sitting slumped in her chair.

I said, "Kate, babe? Where are the children, Katie?"

Kate lifted her marionette head and turned it towards me. She always had hair like a lion, a great towhead of blonde hair, and she was wearing a red cardigan and a black skirt and shiny black shoes and under the cardigan she had on a cowslip yellow blouse and she turned her wooden head to me and her brown eyes were like the glass from a beer bottle and her mouth was shiny like red paint on wood like Pinocchio's and I said, louder, "Kate? Where are the children?"

And she stood slowly up, tottering, as if unused to her feet, and she said, her mouth clacking like it was made of ply-board. "Come behind."

There was the classroom storeroom cupboard behind her and the door was open and I saw a figure lying on the floor, not moving.

But this Kate's arms moved like they were on strings, pulled by an unseen puppeteer, and the way they lifted and danced wasn't right, and I ran and she followed me as I left the school.

Kate had been the only one who gave me comfort. If she had become like this, then I was on my own in this village. I had to get home. I had the idea of locking me in my house until help came.

I sprinted, sobbing, my breath catching, trying to keep out of that other Kate's reach, and, all round the heaps that had fallen from the mid-air were rising and moving slowly, shuffling like heaps of clay and they were becoming replicas of the people of the town, half-created, unfinished, and no one who knew what a real person was like would be fooled by these things. But perhaps whoever made them had never seen a real person, only copies.

Behind, not closer, but still seeming certain she would catch me, Kate tottered.

I don't know, but the thing that was now the only Kate lurched and lolloped after me down the pavement and I got to my house and I could hardly get the key out of my pocket because my hand shook so badly it took minutes to get it into the lock and behind me that Kate came closer, oddly unbalanced, blonde hair hanging down, head aslant, mouth clacking, head bobbing like it was on a spring.

And I got into the house, shoving the door, heaving it shut behind me, waiting with my full weight against it to stop her coming in.

It seemed I had left the TV on. I could hear it from the lounge blaring on about Mars Base saying:

This Is the Voice of The Mysterons: We Know You Can Hear Us, Earthmen.

And I remembered the strange idea I'd had as I left the house that morning — the idea that I'd left something in the house.

As I moved from the front door, the front door handle turned behind me. I twistedto see it opening.

I ran through into the lounge. The TV wasn't on, but the sound was.

There was a cupboard where we kept the hoover and ironing board. The door of the cupboard was a bit open. There was something lying there behind the door.

Kate came in behind me. I saw that something was holding her up, fine wires running from her hands and elbows to disappear into mid-air.

The wires were very fine, you wouldn't see them if you didn't look for them.

She was close now.

Kate grinned at me with her brown glass eyes and her painted wooden lips, and her mouth moved like one of those football-clackers. "Come behind," she said.

She was looking at the cupboard.

CHAPTER 18

THE SEXTON & THE DEMOISELLE

A wisp of snow noticed as it touches the cheek and then nothing more, as if the sky had changed its mind and decided to hold off through respect for the scene enacted below.

This is the scene: the rector stands in alb, stole and chasuble, reading from the Book of Common Prayer:

MAN that is born of a woman hath but a short time to live, and is full of misery. He cometh up, and is cut down, like a flower; he fleeth as it were a shadow, and never continueth in one stay.

Hand up to impose silence on the congregation and then,

I AM the resurrection and the life, saith the Lord: he that believeth in me, though he were dead, yet shall he live: and whosoever liveth and believeth in me shall never die.

So she is gone, fair Madeleine; she whom he had gazed on from afar and never dared to seek out, never speak his words of love, never touch, never sighed to her his heartfelt devotion.

But that is untrue. There had been sighs — not sighs of conjoined passion; he had never dared to do more than dream of that, but many a lonely sigh had broken from the breast of Almaric Deeks, Sexton at St Cuthbert's, Kirklinton, as he dreamed of Madeleine and longed for her and wished her his wife.

Her father stands there — a landowner, known to be stern, but now his pale face bearing the redness of tears stifled and cleared away; though her mother does not hide hers, and sisters and brothers, all seven of them, being consoled by family and the rector himself with kind words in an undertone promising resurrection of those who die pure of heart.

Her father says, "She was pure, aye, never a purer lass was born and remained so until her dying day."

And another stands there, with them but not exactly the same though surely similar. He is Andrew Eliot, a yeoman farmer's son to whom the deceased was promised in marriage. A young man, ten years younger than the sexton, Almaric Deeks, but one who will inherit stock and buildings and name.

Almaric did not doubt that Eliot loved Madeleine who lay now in a box, six feet deep in a hole that Almaric himself graved out.

But though he did not doubt the yeoman's love, what love could compare with Almaric's own for lovely Madeleine, with her face pale as lilies, and black hair that gleamed in sunlight, and her mouth that in life was livid and red, but in death pale and blue?

Almaric had loved the girl as no other could, all through her disregard for him, all through her turning aside when he came near her as if she knew his secret heart. What finer, purer passion than Almaric's could there be — yet she had returned his unspoken, unshown devotion with plain and pointed disdain.

All he'd wanted was to love her. All he'd wanted was to speak to her, and all he'd desired was for her to love him back, though he knew that could never be, not with her status as the daughter of the richest farmer for miles around and his as a penniless, landless, digger of graves, a mere servant to the monuments of St Cuthbert's.

Not only that, but he was no Cumberland man, having been

blown to the Scottish border by some chance from his native Essex — a place called Langenhoe — fifteen years before and, though they tolerated him, they had never invited him into their bosom, and how their Northern voices and his Eastern ones, with their hard consonants and his soft ones, mixed like oil and milk — that is imperfectly, and with many misunderstandings.

But still they came to him for cures and charms and fortunes. They called him a Cunning Man. He lived outside the village and they sneaked there after dark, ashamed of their superstition but greedy for his words and his divination and his charms of love and revenge.

Back home, in Langenhoe, in the flat lands by the German Sea, they'd said his mother was a witch and her godly neighbours set fire to the hovel Almaric and she lived together in.

His mother perished in that fire and the good bodies of the hamlet showed no regret but warned him that unless he fled the parish, he too would burn.

So, Almaric Deeks had come as far away as he could to a place where no one knew him, and where he could start again.

He took with him his mother's knowledge of plants, and potions and tinctures, and with it he earned pennies to supplement his work as the gravedigger of St Cuthbert's and indeed any other church who would pay him to dispose of its dead.

The rector, being an educated man who had been at Cambridge in his time, understood his East Anglian speech, but these farmers and reivers got but half what he said. In his heart, Almaric had hoped Madeleine would have understood his words of love, but she never gave him the opportunity.

He'd first met Madeleine when she'd come with her sister a year before to ask when she would marry. He'd raked the coals and read the embers and told her she never would.

Madeleine stood with a snort. "What do you know — a warlick like yourself, a stranger from no place with no kin and no land nor money? I'll marry sure enough, and I know it because I already have his eye."

And in the candlelight, because his hovel was gloomy despite the daylight outside, he thought she was the most beautiful girl he'd seen, more beautiful because of the pout of her red lips and the pride in her white cheeks and the anger behind her sea grey eyes.

Her sister, Amanda, said, pointing, "What are all these dried flowers and grasses you keep hanging from the beam here?"

Almaric Deeks said, "That is mugwort, and that vervain. That jar is haws and the other rosehips."

"And what is the use of them?" said Madeleine, her pride battling with, and subdued for a while, by her curiosity.

"They are for sleep, and healing and dreams."

"And these red and white pieces? Are these the mushrooms of the fair folk that grow under pines and beeches? What use are they?"

Almaric did not answer, and Madeleine answered for him, "They are poison, sister. He is a poisoner."

And the sister tilted her head, curious, appalled and yet delighted. "Are you a poisoner, Goodman Deeks? Is it true what my sister says?"

Deeks shook his head. "I have never poisoned anyone."

Madeleine snorted. "Not yet, anyway."

He had seen her after she'd been promised to Eliot, not three days ago, on New Year, and he'd offered her his congratulations. He thought that was the only time she'd ever smiled at him, she was so delighted with her match.

He offered a red apple as a wedding gift. He'd picked them in Autumn from the tree by his hut and stored them safe since then.

She took it and bit it and said, "You see, you were wrong."

He shrugged. "Was I wrong, Madeleine?"

She took another bite of the apple, and her mouth was perfect, he thought, and her her flashing eyes and her lustrous dark hair. "Yes — wrong. You said I would never marry and I am to be married to Andrew Eliot whose father is the richest farmer in Hethersgill."

Deeks stood silent.

She taunted him. "What say you to that, Goodman Deeks? Do

you acknowledge that I will be married despite your false words and failed seeing?"

And then he shook his head and said, "You will not marry, Madeline. Never."

She shook her head. "Ah, but I will. I will prove you wrong and come and tell you so."

After the funeral, they all left, the yeoman and his grieving family and the snow began and then the unfulfilled suitor, after a half-glance at the hole, followed them. Perhaps he would find love with the second daughter, the less pretty sister, the second-best to his late beloved. It was business after all.

Almaric watched them depart. For him, no one else but Madeleine would do. She was gone and so it would be just as well for him to follow her and lay in this grave himself.

He stood for a long while and the snow landed on the shoulders of his rough coat and on the rough hands that held the spade with which he would complete his work.

The Rector came and said, "Well, Deeks, that's it done. Fill it in then get away; Tis bitter cold this afternoon and a graveyard is no place to be."

"Yes, sir," Deeks said, but did not move.

The rector was about to leave then tilted his head. "They do say you were sweet on her."

Deeks shrugged. "'They', sir? Who are they?"

"The local gossips. And I see from your face and your tears that it was so. But she was not for you, you know that? They hoped for better for her. You see that, don't you?"

"And did they get it, sir?"

The Rector frowned. "The Lord's ways are opaque to us, though one day, we may know, at his grace. But, in any case, don't linger. Go home to your cottage when you're done, any other work will wait until tomorrow, or better weather — whichever comes first."

And so the Rector left and Almaric Deeks stood alone with his spade and the yew trees and the crows gathering to roost. The snow fell hurriedly now and the graves and tussocks of earth were dusted with white.

Almaric watched as the snow fell thick on the box that held his darling. And still he stood, while the short day withered to grey shadow and the rooks grew quiet and settled in the tops of the yew trees, and the snow kept falling, but then before the light was gone altogether, he stuck his spade in the heap of spoil and threw the first of it onto the box where it clattered with pebbles and wet clay on damp wood.

Almaric's eyes filled with tears and he shook his head as if in reproof of himself.

And then he stepped down into the grave itself and took his spade, got its edge under the coffin lid and twisted and heaved and and broke open the box. Then he took his rough workman's hands and in the cold and wet with the snow falling on his shoulders and drifting into his eyes, he lifted the lid and looked upon her, his dead beloved Madeleine for the last time.

So she lay, pale and dead in her shroud, her hands clasped together, her eyes closed and looking like she was no more than sleeping, though her paleness showed it was the sleep of death, not a sleep that would wake to the sunrise.

He whispered, "I spoke true when I said you wouldn't marry, Madeline. I loved you. But if you wouldn't be mine, then you would be no one's. "

The light was now almost gone and she lying there was nothing but the memory of a love, whiter than the dark wood and the darker earth that surrounded her. He stooped and kissed her cold dead lips, and he replaced the coffin lid and climbed from the grave and finished the burying.

And when he was finally done, he turned and left the churchyard by the path under the bare oak tree that stands alone. And when he got to the gate, he stopped and turned for someone had come down the path following him and was standing there behind him.

There was no light left in the day but she was brighter the dark around her and brighter than any mortal had right to be. It came to him that she had stolen the daylight and enfolded it unto herself.

But she stood, shrouded, her dark hair hanging down like black rags, her mouth that had been red, now pale blue, her cheeks that had been white, now dirt grey.

"Madeleine!" He whispered. "How can it be that you stand here?"

And, in a panic he wondered if he hadn't really killed her and that he'd buried her alive, for such things were not unknown.

Perhaps his poison had merely held her asleep and feigning death until now she awoke. Now he could pose as her rescuer and because he was the one that saved her from being buried alive, she might love him at last!

But, as you may guess, that was not how it would be at all.

Madeleine spoke, "I stand here, Almaric Deeks. As you always wanted me. I have come to you in fulfilment of your deepest wish."

Joy swept over him, but it was a joy mixed with horror. He had not buried her alive, she was dead in her box, and dead standing there before him.

She came to him, and he stood to greet her, and she reached out her arms, and he took them, and she pulled him to her, and he felt the chill of her body and the cold touch of her fingers on his flesh.

"Let me kiss, you, Almaric," she said.

With only the slightest hesitation, he leaned down to kiss her pale lips but just before she let him, she said, "You said I would never marry, Almaric, and I told you that you were wrong."

He said, "But you will never marry, Madeleine, for you are dead."

She smiled. "My marriage vow is in my kiss, and in my kiss is my cold revenge."

· · ·

Almaric Deeks was found under fallen snow, frozen and dead, by a boy from the cottage opposite the church. An alarm was raised and the Rector was called and the gossips gathered. They saw Almaric had completed his work and filled in Madeleine's grave.

The Rector sighed. "He must have died of cold. I told him he should go straight home after he'd done his work, but for some reason he lingered. He must have lingered in meditation of the girl whom he loved, though he never admitted it, and though we might say the cold killed, him, perhaps, more truly, it was his love that did it."

CHAPTER 19
DEATH IN LIFE

Reader, attend! whether thy soul
Soars fancy's flights beyond the pole,
Or darkling grubs this earthly hole,
In low pursuit:
Know, prudent, cautious, self-control
Is wisdom's root.

—ROBERT BURNS

The wind howled through the narrow streets of Edinburgh's Old Town, and William Grant sat alone in the dimly lit room at the top of the house, stooping over his anatomy books and surrounded by flickering candles that cast eerie shadows across the musty walls.

The air was heavy with the smell of soot and damp, and the oak pew he sat on creaked and groaned, old and uncomfortable, as he shifted in his seat, trying to focus on his studies.

He had borrowed a facsimile copy of William Harvey's *De Motu Cordis*, copied from an original by students keen to distribute knowledge of anatomy. William pored over the Latin and studied the diagrams of the human heart.

Not for the first time, he wondered at that miracle that animated matter. Creatures— dogs, horses, fish, insects, and of course humankind itself, grew from the earth, moved and lived but then died as if something broke or was switched off, and then, from the time of death the body, instead of healing itself as it had in life, rotted in the ground.

William wondered what was it that departs the body at the point of death, and can death be prevented?

And, as he mused, he imagined what an achievement it would be for someone to discover the secret of death. And he imagined that it might be him — William Grant.

He was an ambitious student, and anatomy was not his only interest.

Still not returning to his work, his eyes wandered to a copy of the *Edinburgh Evening Courant* that lay on the sideboard.

If he had been thinking about what happens to us after death, the article answered that question plainly enough: we go to lie in the cold clay of Greyfriars Kirkyard, where if we are unlucky and unguarded, someone might dig us up again, and sell us to a doctor who would cut us up in pursuit of the answer to those very questions of life and death.

This *Courant* story was about the bodysnatchers. Apparently, the demand for corpses for dissection by surgeons was so great that the snatchers were digging in older graves where the cadavers were not so fresh.

The bodysnatchers had been at work in Greyfriars Kirkyard, which lay just beside the house where William sat on Candlemaker Row. They had been so industrious in the Kirkyard that the Kirk authorities had set guards.

However, the pay was meagre and the conditions uncomfortable so that the job only attracted old men who fell asleep over their whisky, or callow lads who sneaked off to be with their sweethearts rather than watch the headstones and the recessed tombs with their *momento mori* and crossbone carvings.

There were also tales of a darker thing that made the cold kirkyard its home. According to the fishwives and cart-boys, a ghoul lived there, a stinking thing that lurked in shadows, coming out at night to devour corpses and put the blame on bodysnatchers.

William Grant thought that this thing that lived on even while dead, and reputedly it could speak, and it must know the secrets of death.

William paused to sharpen his quill with a small blade that he took from his pocket, then dipped the quill in ink, and made further notes from the anatomy book on a sheet of foolscap.

The wind rose, rattling the windows, the chill grew sharper, sending him shivering. William pulled his woollen coat tight around him. He glanced to the window. It was getting late, and he wondered where his parents could be.

But as they were out...

William had another book, an old book. He'd been loaned it by a professor at the University who shared his morbid and less public interests. He went over and pulled open the drawer, lifting the papers that hid what he was looking for.

It was a copy of *Liber Juratus Honorii*, a book of demonology that would have him arrested and punished if the authorities found it.

The *Liber Juratus Honorii* was an old, leather-bound book with strange symbols embossed on the cover. The title was written in faded letters.

William flipped through the pages until he found what he was looking for — a section on the summoning of demons. Here was an incantation that summoned and pacified those that chew in the night, the dwellers among bones and decay, the Arabian ghouls.

He did not think that Scottish ghouls would be so different that the spell would not work.

William's heart raced with excitement and fear as he mouthed the incantation, imagining the knowledge such a creature could reveal to him. And, after all, all he wanted was knowledge. What was so terribly wrong with that?

And then he grew frightened — even though he hadn't carried out the ritual described, hadn't even vibrated the demonic names as directed, only muttered them under his breath — was this enough to summon the ghoul?

He shuddered, closed the grimoire and put it back in the drawer.

The wind howled through the narrow streets of Edinburgh's Old Town, and Callum Grant sat alone in his penthouse apartment, his face lit by his MacBook screen with the only other light coming from a tank of tropical fish. Fink played Sunday Night Blues Club from a Sonos wireless speaker on the windowsill.

The room felt damp, probably inevitably given its age, and the furniture, modern and uncomfortable, groaned as Callum shifted in his chair, trying to focus on his studies.

Long fingers on the Mac keyboard, he tapped out his notes on heart sounds: lub, dub, lub dub dub.

And paused.

Callum shuddered like someone had just walked over his grave and looked around. There was a funny feeling in this house tonight. It was probably the high wind outside.

Callum sighed, lowered his head to his studies. The unsettled feeling might also about his forthcoming OSCE examinations, even though they weren't until next month.

He had some brain anatomy to learn too: the parietal lobe, the occipital lobe, where sight was conjured from darkness, the frontal lobe where decisions were made, the left hemisphere that harboured speech and movement.

But he thought: the brain is a lump of tissue. It processes speech, but who is it that speaks? It is all very well to examine the mechanics of how we see, but *who* is it that sees?

That secret has never been found in all the dissections of all the cadavers in history. What animates us is the ghost in the machine.

Callum heard the wind beat against the windows, saw the soft glow of the fish tank, smelled the trace of his mother's perfume that lingered even though she had gone out hours ago with his father.

The apartment was on the top floor with a view of the city skyline. The wind rattled the windows, making him shiver, while, in the stormy heavens outside, the Scottish winter showed no signs of relenting.

Callum went over to the sofa, picked up his hoodie to block out the biting cold and he checked the time on his phone. It was the wee hours of the morning, and he wondered where his parents were.

Such a weird old house.

His dad had done his genealogy research and apparently the Grant family had owned this very house nearly two hundred years before. Dad had said when he bought it that it was like coming home.

He also said there had been a shocking murder in this house a couple of centuries ago. But Callum didn't believe in ghosts and reckoned it was probably just one of dad's stories that he liked to tell after a wee dram.

William Grant lifted his head to a noise outside. There was something going on on the street outside on Candlemaker Row. William heard men cursing and, curiosity piqued, stepped to the window.

Looking out, he saw two men manhandling a cumbersome object wrapped in cloth which they had hefted up from a handcart with much puffing and blowing.

It was hard to see much detail from his high window, but they looked rough-and-ready sorts, the type you wouldn't want to meet on the empty street long after midnight.

William was a pupil at the Royal College of Surgeons in High School Yards, and he guessed the trade of the men below — gruesome, but necessary for the furtherance of human knowledge.

When his curiosity forced him to look again, Candlemaker Row was empty.

The grandfather clock ticked in the corner. Where were his parents? It was unusual for their social shenanigans to go on so late.

William's father was a merchant who specialised in tea from China, and sugar and spices from the Indies. The basement of their tall house was filled with tea-chests from the clipper boats that landed at Leith. His father had wanted him to follow him into the tea trade, but William's heart was set on surgery, and his father relented, muttering that trade could also turn a profit.

A bang rang out from below.

It sounded like the front door opening five floors further down. Surely those men and their burden had not come into his house?

Then he heard the bang again, repeatedly, coinciding with the rising of the wind.

The front door must have come open. It would be the high wind that had unlatched it. Though surely his father would have locked it on his way out?

The banging didn't stop as the wind slammed the unsecured door against its frame in mindless repetition. He sighed. The door would break if he did not go down and close it.

The front door lay at the bottom of twisting stone steps that in the middle space of the house and wound down five floors to the entrance hall. Down there, too, was the door to the basement.

He hoped it was the wind that opened the door, but couldn't drive out the suspicion that the door had been opened by the two men and their grisly package.

Even if they had come in (though why?) they must be gone by

now. Though something had left the door off its latch so the wind could snatch at it and play its games of rat-tat-tat-tat.

The door kept slamming.

William went to fetch a candle.

Callum rubbed his eyes and closed the MacBook. All work and no play make Callum a dull boy, he thought, but he so needed to study. It was 2:45 a.m, and he'd been working far too long. The facts and figures weren't going in anymore — time for a break.

His father and mother were out socialising. They generally stayed out later than he did, still, it was pretty unusual for them to be this late without phoning him. Maybe they thought he would have gone to bed and so didn't want to disturb him.

His parents were a very cool, laid-back couple, and he was their serious only son.

His dad was a builder who specialised in restoring the fine Georgian houses of Edinburgh's New Town and who was so good that he could name his price to the clients who clamoured for his skills.

His mother ran a swanky interior design shop in Stockbridge but they lived here in this restored tenement on Candlemaker Row with its back to Greyfriars Kirkyard.

Callum felt sleepy. Bed time. He hoped his parents wouldn't wake him when they came home.

Then he heard a door banging down the bowels of the house.

Callum had the penthouse flat to himself, and his parents stayed in the floors below. The basement was where his dad kept arty salvage — marble horses' heads, fine bathtubs, replica Greek and Roman statuary and lots of boxes containing he knew not what, some of which they had inherited with the house that his dad had never got round to sorting through.

That banging sounded like a door was opening and closing. It must be that the wind had got up and, somehow, the door had come open.

Down there at the bottom of the stone stairs lay the entrance hall. In the entrance hall there were two doors, the front door and the old door that led to the basement.

Callum didn't like the idea of the front door being open, but he also didn't relish the thought of walking all the way down those stone steps. It was a long way down and, at this time of night, as spooky as hell. Not that he believed in ghosts, of course.

But the door kept banging. He sighed. He'd better go down and fasten the front door up before the wind broke it — or some drunk came in.

William took a candle that stood on a brass dish from the desk where he'd been studying. He stepped out of his attic room to the top of the stairwell where the stone steps ran dizzyingly down.

He could leave the door for his parents to close when they came back, but who knew when that would be? It was not impossible that some vagabond might come in.

William peered down into the dark. He was a young surgeon, rational and ambitious. He was not afraid of ghosties and ghoulies, no matter how dark and lonely these stairs in the depths of the night.

He would have to go below and close the door and so he started down.

The stones beneath William's stockinged feet were cold and damp as he descended the stairs, the flickering candle casting a glow that shifted and danced as the draught threatened to blow it out.

The wind whistled mournfully up the stairwell, and the noise below kept on banging and banging.

As William reached the floor above the entrance hall, he stopped. There was someone there. He cupped his hand over the candle flame and stepped back out of sight.

Two men, their speech coarse and heavy with the brogue of the lower city, seemed to be engaged in a heated debate.

"'Tis not possible, man!" cried the first, his voice laced with an undercurrent of fear. "Did ye not see the state o' that corpse? 'Twas dead as the stones we stand on, and had been for these three months past!"

"Aye, but tell me this," the second man retorted, a quiver in his voice. "Did ye not feel it move as we carried it? Like a livin' thing beneath our fingers?"

The first scoffed. His laughter was tinged with unease. "I thought it was ye, ye great oaf, shiftin' the weight 'round!"

"It wasnae me. Mind this: a thing that should not move, moved."

The second man hesitated, his words halting, as if pulled from a dark recess of his mind that he would rather not delve into. "There was somethin'... unnatural about it when we pulled it out of its stone box in its fancy sepulchre — like the grave didn't want to let it go."

The first man shook his head as if to dispel his companion's superstitious notions. "Away wi' ye! We've done our job and delivered the goods. Let us leave this cursed place and be done with it, and pray we will no be back soon."

"We'll leave, but ye ken weel we'll be back as soon as we run out o' cash, for the maister o' the house is always looking for fresh that he can sell on, and he with his fine reputation is no a man that wants tae dae the digging hissel."

With that, the two men hurried from the building, their footfalls echoing down the darkened street.

The door slammed, and shut behind them, the sound reverberating through the stairwell. William stood, his heart pounding and his thoughts racing.

He went and locked the front door and so now he could retreat to his attic room.

But he guessed what they had brought, a great inquisitiveness seized him. He would just take a peek at what they had laid in his father's storeroom

. . .

Leaving behind his MacBook Air and his Sonos speaker, Callum descended the stairs, the stone steps cold beneath his stockinged feet. The darkness thickened around him as he went.

Ten steps down and the light from the upper attic door was no longer enough for him to see.

He remembered the light switch was back at the top, and the thought of trudging back up to turn on the light was unappealing, so he reached into his pocket to pull out the familiar shape of his phone.

Callum's fingers pressed the screen, and cold LED light sprang to life. He pointed the beam before him, and the shadows withdrew from the harsh glare to lurk in the corners of the stairwell.

He sighed. He really didn't want to go down there, but, the door was still banging, no matter how it had come open. With a groan of resignation, Callum continued his descent.

Now there was another sound — not the banging of the door, but talking.

That was weird. It sounded like there was someone down there, but the voices were distant and heavy, like they were being broadcast across an ocean.

He stood, torn between curiosity and mounting dread, while the voices whispered on.

Inevitably, Callum remembered the story of the vicious murder all those years ago. Maybe his dad hadn't been completely bullshitting. And he remembered the tale that this old house was haunted.

He heard the muttered words.

"...dead for three months, it was. And still it moved..."

Callum strained to hear more. Callum eavesdropped on a conversation not meant for mortal ears. It was plain they were talking about something dreadful.

A man said, "...what have we brought in? What manner of cursed thing have we unleashed?"

Callum couldn't see anything, and, as he rounded the last bend of the stairwell, the banging door had stopped and the voices gone quiet. Pointing his phone into the entrance hall, he found it empty.

But there, the door to the basement loomed in the shadows.

He'd never liked that door, but tonight he was drawn to it. He was party to some strange happening, and he felt somehow that the secret to this mystery was there behind that door.

Callum stretched to touch the door handle, the chill of the metal seeping into his finger-ends.

Standing in the entrance hall, William Grant stretched out his hand to the basement door. The candle, held aloft in his left hand, cast a ghastly glow upon the rough wooden surface.

It was in there — the thing they'd brought.

William grasped the cold iron handle with his right hand, feeling the weight of the door yielding to his push, opening, revealing the yawning room within.

The darkness of the basement swallowed the feeble light of the candle. But by its dancing flame, the shadows that clung to the walls grew and twisted as if alive, and the air was thick with foreboding.

William told himself a body is still a body, and a body is dead. His curiosity was gnawing at him. He just had to see it, so he stepped into the basement and went slowly down the short flight of steps.

Callum knew that this basement room was where his father kept all his most valuable salvage that his mother would then sell in her upscale shop.

What on earth was drawing him into this room? He opened the door and took the six steps down into the basement. The room was large and full of shadows.

Callum swept the light of his phone from side to side. Here were marble horses, suits of armour, large and expensive bath tubs, Thai Buddhas, all made mysterious by the gloom. And there, behind this more recent detritus, were boxes. Shining his light on them, he saw they were old.

Had no one ever looked in them? Some were piled up and draped with old curtains, like some creature had made its lair there in the corner.

It was then that he heard a whisper, low and insidious, that emanated from the piled up boxes, particularly from the corner to the left.

Then the shadows shifted, and something moved out of the darkness.

William lifted his candle so he could see into the basement and the wavering light danced upon the scattered tea chests that filled the room.

But there was more than tea in these boxes. The scent of decay hung heavy here in the air, clawing at the back of his throat. He knew that smell.

He suddenly understood what his father had meant when he said that the trade of surgery could turn a profit. It seemed his father sold cadavers as well as China tea, supplying the College of Surgeons with their grim requirements.

And there, between the boxes, something lay on the floor, wrapped in a shroud and glistening with wet clay.

This was the one the bodysnatchers had just delivered. It lay there, waiting for preparation and packing. Presumably his father would see to that on his return.

But then, the shroud writhed and twisted, as if something within it were struggling to be free.

William jumped back.

The sound of whispering filled the air, a voice that seemed to seep into his ears and his mind.

Something pulled itself from its wrappings, and William screamed but there was no one in the house to hear him, and the thick stone walls kept his scream tight within.

The thing struggled free, and then, with a suddenness that left him reeling, the creature leapt forth from its shroud, lunging at him, bearing him over, smothering him, its cold, dead weight knocking him to the floor and keeping him there.

The stinking creature lay on top of him staring down, mouth open, fangs bared.

William shook with fear. He thought it would kill him, and then it blinked.

William had dropped his candle in the assault, and it lay nearby on the stone floor, on its side but still burning, and by this light, William saw the thing's yellow eyes.

It spoke in an old and rasping voice, "You summoned me here, wretch. By ancient magic I am bound to answer one question, to give one gift. But I will give you only one."

William found the courage to say, "I did not summon you, you unholy thing."

The ghoul gave a low, snickering sound that William realised was it laughing. "Ah, but you did. You spoke the conjuring from the Book of Honorius. Do you think such magic words meant nothing?"

"But I whispered them! I did not say them out loud."

"The ears of he who is master of all such sorcery hear words whether they are whispered or shouted. It is the intent that he hears. So what is your intent?"

William knew what he wanted, but he hesitated to frame the words.

The ghoul snarled. "Be quick, for I must feed."

With dry mouth, William muttered, "All I want... All I want is to know the secret that you must know — the secret of life in death."

And the ghoul laughed. "You wish that as a gift? It is bitter thing that you will come to regret."

"But I still want to understand."

"You should know there is a price to be paid."

"Anything. I will pay any price of the gift of living forever."

"The price is a price of death. And when you pay it, you will never die of natural causes, and you can only be killed the hand of your kin."

And then, William heard the front door creak open, and the muffled voices of his parents reached him, their laughter and tipsy banter a stark contrast to the terror that gripped him.

They were oblivious to his plight, their thoughts consumed by the gaiety of the party they had just left behind.

He heard them climb the stairs. Some minutes later he heard them calling his name. The shouts of his parents seemed to come from a great distance, their voices tinged with concern and confusion.

"William, where are you?" his mother's voice floated down, muffled by the walls between them.

"Where can that boy be?" his father chimed in, the lightness in his voice belying the concern that lay beneath.

"As I said: there is a price to be paid," hissed the ghoul.

William took the knife from his pocket, the one he had used to sharpen his quill. The blade was short, only four inches long. But even a blade this short can kill when wielded by someone who has knowledge of human anatomy.

Callum stood in the basement, shining his torch into the corner where someone stood.

He called out, "Who the hell are you? How did you get in here?"

And a voice replied, "I have lived here a long time, waiting for the right person, waiting for someone like I was."

The phone light revealed a young man, about his own age, but dressed in the fashion of centuries past. He was pale, as if he never saw the sun.

"I'm nothing like you. You look... strange."

The man laughed. "I am William Grant, a man of your blood. I know you, I have watched you in this house, and like you, I wanted to know what creates life in a man so that we can learn to defeat death."

"I don't know what you're talking about."

"I have watched and waited until tonight, which is the anniversary of the bargain I made."

Callum said, "You say you know the secret of life? And does that mean how to evade death"

"I do, and it does."

Callum shook his head. "This is so strange. I don't know if I believe you."

"But you have wondered at this mystery, like I have."

Callum nodded. "Of course. It is a secret that all men want to know."

William said, "Especially people like us: doctors, physicians, surgeons."

"I still don't know if I believe you. But if you do have this secret, what do I need to do to obtain this knowledge?"

William held out his hand. "Take my knife."

"What? Are you crazy?"

William whispered, "You told me that you want to know the secrets of life and death."

Callum said, "I do."

"Take my knife."

Just then, Callum heard the front door open. His parents had finally returned from their night at the party, their voices light and tipsy as they entered the old house.

"Callum, where are you?" his mother called out, her voice lilting and carefree.

"Where can that boy be?" his father added, a note of amusement in his voice as they continued to climb the stairs, unaware of their son in the basement.

And Callum remembered the story of the murder. "Was it you who killed your parents all those years ago in this house? Was that the price you paid to escape death? You have to kill a family member?"

William did not answer.

Callum said, "So, I get it. You want me to kill my parents."

But William shook his head. "No," he said. "I want you to kill me."

ABOUT THE AUTHOR

Tony Walker is a British author and narrator, specializing in the ghost and horror story genre. He was born and raised in Cumberland, where he developed an early interest in local folklore and legends. After completing his studies in Celtic literature, he embarked on a career as a writer and storyteller.

Walker's stories are known for their vivid descriptions, subtle characterizations, and chilling atmospheres. His writing style ranges from traditional Gothic to modern psychological horror, and he often draws inspiration from the landscape and history of his native Cumberland. Many of his tales feature supernatural elements and explore the boundaries between the living and the dead.

In addition to writing, Walker is also the host of The Classic Ghost Stories Podcast, where he narrates some of the most iconic ghost stories from around the world. He is known for his clear, compelling voice and his ability to bring each story to life with his dramatic readings.

Further Ghost Stories is Walker's latest collection of original ghost and horror stories. Set in various locations but primarily in Cumberland, the book showcases his versatility as a writer and his mastery of the genre. With its mix of classic and contemporary storytelling techniques, Further Ghost Stories is sure to thrill readers and leave them with a haunting sense of unease.

ALSO BY TONY WALKER

9 781739 559601